P9-CQT-345

The Man of the House

Isabella Macdonald Alden

The Man of the House

Copyright © 1993 by Creation House
All rights reserved
Printed in the United States of America
Library of Congress Catalog Card Number: 92-74601
International Standard Book Number: 0-88419-269-5

Creation House
Strang Communications Company
600 Rinehart Road
Lake Mary, FL 32746

Originally published in 1883

This book or parts thereof may not be
reproduced in any form without prior
written permission of the publisher.

Unless otherwise noted, all Scripture quotations
are from the King James Version of the Bible.

CONTENTS

ABOUT THE AUTHOR

sabella Macdonald Alden, under the pen name "Pansy," exerted a great influence upon the American people of her day through her writings. She also helped her niece Grace Livingston Hill get started in her career as a best-selling inspirational romance novelist.

As Grace tells it in the foreword to *Memories of Yesterdays*, her aunt gave her a thousand sheets of typing paper with a sweet little note wishing her success and asking her to "turn those thousand sheets of paper into as many dollars.

"I can remember how appalling the task seemed and how I laughed aloud at the utter impossibility of its ever coming true with *any* thousand sheets of paper. But it was my first real encouragement, the first hint that anybody thought I ever could write. And I feel that my first inspiration came from reading her books and my mother's stories, in both of which as a child I fairly steeped myself."

On another occasion, shortly before Grace's twelfth birthday in 1877, Isabella had been listening to Grace tell a story about two warmhearted children. As she listened, she typed out the story and later had it printed and bound by her own publisher into a little hardback book with woodcut illustrations. She surprised her niece with the gift on her birthday. That was Grace's first book.

Isabella Macdonald was born November 3, 1841, in Rochester, New York, the youngest of five daughters. Her father, Isaac Macdonald, was educated and was deeply interested in everything religious. Her mother, Myra Spafford Macdonald, was the daughter of Horatio Gates Spafford (1778-1832), author and inventor. Isabella's uncle, Horatio Gates Spafford Jr., penned the popular hymn "It Is Well With My Soul" after learning that his wife had survived a shipwreck; his four daughters were tragically lost at sea.

Isabella was taught at home on a regular daily basis by her father. As her guide and friend, he encouraged her to keep a journal when she was young and to develop a natural affection for writing. Under his direction she acquired the ease and aptness of expression for which her writings became known. When she was only ten, the local weekly newspaper published her composition titled "Our Old Clock," a story that was inspired by an accident to the old family clock.

That first published work was signed "Pansy." Isabella acquired that name partly because pansies were her favorite flower and partly because of a childhood episode. She tried to help her mother get ready for a tea party by picking all the pansies from the garden to decorate the tea table. She carefully removed all the stems, not knowing the flowers were to be tied into separate bouquets and placed at each lady's place.

Years later, while teaching at Oneida Seminary, from which she had earlier graduated, Isabella wrote her first novel, *Helen Lester,* in competition for a prize. She won fifty dollars for submitting the manuscript that explained the plan of salvation so clearly and pleasantly that very young readers would be drawn into the Christian fold and could easily follow its teachings.

Isabella wrote or edited more than two hundred published works, including short stories, Sunday school lessons and more than a hundred novels. She had only one manuscript rejected. At one time her books sold a hundred thousand copies annually with translations in Swedish, French, Japanese, Armenian and other languages.

She usually wrote for a young audience, hoping to motivate youth to follow Christianity and the Golden Rule. The themes of her books focused on the value of church attendance; the dangers lurking in popular forms of recreation; the duty of total abstinence from alcohol; the need for self-sacrifice; and, in general, the requirements, tests and rewards of being a Christian.

Reading was strictly supervised for young people in that day, and Sunday schools provided many families with reading material. Thus, Isabella's fiction received wide circulation because of its wholesome content.

Furthermore, readers liked her books. Her gift for telling stories and her cleverness in dreaming up situations, plus just a little romance, held the interest of readers young and old. Isabella was known for developing characters who possessed an unwavering commitment to follow the Master. She portrayed characters and events that anyone might encounter in a small American town during the last quarter of the nineteenth century.

A writer in *Earth Horizon* (1932) acknowledged that "whoever on his ancestral book shelves can discover a stray copy of one of the Pansy books will know more, on reading it, of culture in the American eighties [1880s] than can otherwise be described."

Isabella believed wholeheartedly in the Sunday school movement. She edited a primary quarterly and wrote primary Sunday school lessons for twenty years. From 1874 to 1896 she edited *The Pansy*, a Sunday magazine for children, which included contributions from her family and others. An outgrowth of the magazine was the Pansy societies which were made up of young subscribers and aimed at rooting out "besetting sins" and teaching "right conduct."

For many years she taught in the Chautauqua assemblies and, with her husband, was a graduate of what was called the Pansy Class, the 1887 class of the Chautauqua Literary and Scientific Circle—the first book club in America. The Chautauqua assemblies were an institution that flourished in the late nineteenth and early twentieth centuries. They combined popular education with entertainment in the form of lectures, concerts and plays and were often presented outside or in a tent.

Throughout her career Isabella took an active interest in all forms of religious endeavors, but her greatest contributions came in her writings. She wanted to teach by precept and parable the lessons her husband taught from the pulpit, in Bible class and in the homes of his parishioners. Her writing was always her means of teaching religious and moral truths as she understood them, and her method was to tell a story.

Her husband, Gustavus Rossenberg Alden, was a lineal descendant of John Alden, one of the first settlers in America. He graduated from Auburn Theological Seminary and was ordained soon after his marriage to Isabella in 1866. He served as a pastor in churches in New York, Indiana, Ohio, Pennsylvania, Florida and Washington, D.C. The Aldens moved from place to place for health reasons and to be near their son, Raymond, during his years of schooling and teaching.

Amidst her many and varied responsibilities as a minister's wife, a mother and a prolific author, Isabella found time to play a significant role in her son's career as a university professor, an author and a scholar in Shakespearean literature.

Her final years were marked by a series of trials. In 1924, after fifty-seven years of marriage, Isabella's husband died. In that same year her last remaining sister, Marcia Macdonald Livingston, Grace's mother, died. A month later her only son, Raymond, died.

About two years later she fell and broke her hip. Although in much pain and discomfort she continued writing until the end. Her final letters were filled with thoughts of going "Home": "Isn't it blessed to realize that one by one we shall all gather Home at last to go no more out forever! The hours between me and my call to come Home grow daily less...."

Isabella Macdonald Alden died August 5, 1930, at the age of eighty-nine in Palo Alto, California, where she and her husband had moved in 1901.

The following year *Memories of Yesterdays*, her

last book, edited by her niece, was published. In the foreword Grace describes her aunt:

"I thought her the most beautiful, wise and wonderful person in my world, outside of my home. I treasured her smiles, copied her ways and listened breathlessly to all she had to say....

"I measured other people by her principles and opinions and always felt that her word was final. I am afraid I even corrected my beloved parents sometimes when they failed to state some principle or opinion as she had done."

As Grace was growing up and learning to read, she devoured her aunt's stories "chapter by chapter. Even sometimes page by page as they came hot from the typewriter; occasionally stealing in for an instant when she left the study, to snatch the latest page and see what had happened next; or to accost her as her morning's work was done, with 'Oh, have you finished another chapter?'

"And often the whole family would crowd around, leaving their work when the word went around that the last chapter of something was finished and going to be read aloud. And how we listened, breathless, as she read and made her characters live before us."

May her characters come to life for you as you read this newest release in the Alden Collection.

Deborah D. Cole

THE CHARACTERS

Reuben Watson Stone
Beth — Reuben's sister
Mrs. Stone — Reuben's mother
Miss Priscilla Hunter — a neighbor
Mother Perkins — a neighbor
Edward Harrison — Spunk's master
Mrs. Harrison — Edward's mother
Mr. Evan Barrows — a businessman
Andrew Porter — a local boy
Wesley Dale — a boy at the box factory
Clarke Miller — a boy at the box factory
Grace Barrows — Mr. Barrows's daughter
Mrs. Barrows — Mr. Barrows's wife
Miss Parker — Reuben's Sunday school teacher
Arthur Holmes — a boy at the party

CHAPTER I

His Home

t was a little room, dingy and dreary, without a single bright thing in it.

The sun peeped into the room for about five minutes, just before night fell. The rest of the time it lingered on the other side of the house, where there were windows for it to gaze into nearly all day.

Who lived in the house and stayed in this sunless room? Why, Reuben Stone, his mother and his sister, Beth. Beth's full name was Elizabeth, but no one ever spoke it for she was such a diminutive creature. As for Reuben, since he was the man of the house, he was more apt to be out on the street from morning till night, trying to pick up odd jobs.

School? No, he didn't go to school. His jackets were out at the elbows, his pants were out at the knees, and his shoes were out at the toes. In very cold weather he had nothing extra to wear around him except an old red shawl of his mother's. He didn't like to wear that because the boys shouted after him and called him "Dutchy." So in bitter cold weather he usually did his errands in the evening when the boys wouldn't notice the shawl.

Beth didn't attend school either, for much the same reasons that kept Reuben at home. Besides, there were other needs that seemed more pressing than school. Her mother sat all day in one low chair by the one window and sewed as fast as she could on boys' shirts for one of the wholesale stores in the city. Beth could overhand some of the seams, hem the edges and take enough stitches in the course of the day to help her mother. As soon as their housework was done—and you would have been astonished to see what little time it took to finish the housework—Beth would draw her chair as close to her mother's as she could get it, and those two would sew.

On this particular day it was getting dark in the room. The sun had looked in and bid them good night, as if in too much of a hurry to stay even as long as usual, and the shadow of the barn next to them was creeping further and further over the house. The fire was dying down, too. In fact, they always shut the dampers about the time the sun was expected, so as to save all the coal they could.

Beth shivered and pulled her chair away from the window. "Mother," she said, "shall I open the damper and let the fire roar for just a minute? It's awful cold in here. My hands are blue."

Mrs. Stone glanced up from her seam with a sigh. "Yes," she said, "of course, it won't do to get cold. The next thing would be a doctor's bill. But we must be as careful as we can, for Reuben said this morning he didn't believe the coal would last until Saturday."

Beth opened the damper and poked the dull coals a little, then she stooped down before the stove, warming her hands. "I wish we could have something warm for supper tonight," she said. "Mother, do you remember it is Reuben's birthday?"

"Yes, I do," the mother said, tightening her lips in a thin line. "I thought last week that we would have something warm for his birthday. I meant to have roast potatoes and a little bit of cake. But I couldn't get those shirts done, and so that plan had to be given up."

Beth let out a little sigh. "I wish we weren't so awful poor!" she moaned drearily. "Just think! We can't even have baked potatoes for a treat! Isn't that horrid?"

"We have them for dinner quite often, you know," her mother reminded her.

"Oh, yes, I know. But I'd like now and then to have something for supper. Just bread and milk! Sometimes I'm ugly enough to be 'most sorry that Reuben gets a quart of milk a day for taking care of that cow. If he didn't, we'd *have* to have something else."

"I don't believe I'd take the trouble to quarrel with the only luxury we have," Mrs. Stone said gravely.

Beth sighed again, cleared off the little table and put three plates and three cups on it.

"If you could have a cup of tea once in a while, I don't believe I'd mind about the rest so much," she said, after bustling about in silence for a few minutes.

"Oh, well, I do once in a while. We had tea on Thanksgiving Day and again on Christmas. What are you talking about?"

Beth tried to laugh, but the mention of Christmas made her remember that the first day of the year was very near.

"Just think!" she exclaimed. "Tomorrow will be New Year's Eve! I don't believe there is another family in this town who isn't planning to go somewhere or have company or do something nice on New Year's. Mother, I can't help it. I think it is just *awful* to be so poor!"

Mrs. Stone had no answer to this. Sometimes it seemed hard to her not to know what her children would have next to eat or whether they would have anything. But she had lived long enough to know that it would do no good to fret about it.

Beth moved about the room in silence after that, until the little table was set with its loaf of bread and pail of milk. Then she found new cause for trouble.

"Mother, what do you suppose can keep Reuben so long? It is ever so much later than he generally comes."

CHAPTER II

REUBEN'S QUARTER

t had been what Reuben called one of his "unlucky" days. The errand boys, newsboys and all other boys with regular positions had been on hand. No one seemed to want anything carried anywhere, though the streets were full of people with their arms full of bundles.

The sun was starting to set, the time when he usually arrived home to get orders about the errands for the night, and he had but five cents in his pocket. He knew just how much or rather how little flour, coal and potatoes were in the house, and he knew that his mother had no money. He had hoped to have a grand day for business and bring home at least twenty cents. Here it was, even worse than usual.

Reuben Stone was twelve years old and rather a small boy for his age. He rubbed his worn-out jacket sleeve across his eyes and decided this was a hard world in which to live. Generally, he kept cheerful enough to whistle most of the time, but tonight he kept his lips shut tight and trudged along with his head down.

"Halloo!" shouted a man from across the street.

Reuben looked up. A man with a horse and sleigh standing in front of Morton's grocery was beckoning to him. He clipped over the snowy road in haste.

"Do you know enough to hold a horse, my boy?" the gentleman asked him. He was a young gentleman with a pleasant face and was trying to hold a wicked-looking horse.

"I rather think I do, sir," Reuben said cheerily.

"Well, then, attend to this one. He is hungry and cold and determined to go home before I am ready."

Reuben took hold of the bridle, and the young man entered the store. What a hurry that horse was in, to be sure! He stepped forward a little and, finding himself held severely, tried going backward. Then he reared up on his hind feet. Next he plunged forward as though he were going to jump over Reuben and the carriage in front of him and vanish. Reuben tugged at the bridle and danced backward and forward according to the motions of the horse but held on firmly, all the while giving the horse good bits of advice.

"Come now. Might as well stand still and look about you and take comfort. You will get home just as soon if you don't prance around in this way like an idiot. Oh, you can't go! You may jerk as hard as you like, and I shan't let go — not if I know myself. But you are a spunky fellow now, as ever I saw. My! Ain't it getting cold, though! I don't wonder you dance — good way to keep warm. I guess that master of yours is going to buy out the grocery and set up in business. Here he comes — good for him. *I'm* glad, and I guess you are."

"Well," said the young man, "I made quite a stay of it, didn't I? And you and Spunk had lively times, I'll venture. Isn't that a good name for this troublesome fellow? Here's a quarter, my boy. It'll pay you well for your trouble. Go ahead, Spunk."

A quarter of a dollar for holding a horse for a few minutes! Reuben considered that good pay. In fact he believed himself to be rich. It certainly wasn't that often that he earned twenty-five cents in fifteen or twenty minutes' time. His eyes sparkled, and he rubbed his blue hands together in glee as he slipped the coin into his deepest pocket.

"If I were sure Mother would like it," he said, talking to the curbstone, "I'd have a regular treat tonight. I'd get a quarter of a pound of tea and some sugar and maybe a bit of butter. That would make Beth open her eyes. But I don't know as I'd better, seeing we are 'most out of coal, and, well, everything else, and that plaguey rent has got to be paid again so soon. When I'm a man there is one thing I won't do. I won't pay a cent of rent to anybody. People shall pay me rent then. Won't that be jolly? Well, come on, you and I'd better run home. We're rich, we are! We've done well today and needn't work anymore."

Whom do you suppose he was talking to then? Nothing of less importance than his two feet! Almost as soon as he was born, certainly as soon as he could begin to talk, Reuben had let people know that he wanted a pony. To this day there was nothing in life that he longed so much for. When he was a little fellow, just running along, he played that his feet were a pair of ponies; that he was the owner and driver; and that they trotted with him wherever he ordered them. This notion stayed with him all through his twelve years of life. He didn't talk much about the ponies in front of people nowadays, unless occasionally to Mother and Beth. But the idea pleased him all the same; it somehow made him feel less lonely and the distance he had to travel seem shorter. So he was in the habit of talking to them a great deal and ordering them about in a very horsemanlike manner.

"Come — we are half a mile from home and behind time, so we must step up briskly. Let's take another look at the quarter to be sure it is safe, and then we'll be off. If there should be a hole in that pocket — !"

He dived his hand down, felt carefully among the strings and bits of treasures, brought up the piece of money and stepped under the glare of a street lamp that had just been lighted.

Staring hard at the money, he rubbed his eyes. "What under the sun, moon and stars does this mean?"

He looked again, turning it round and round and over and over. Drawing a long breath, he spoke slowly, "As sure as my name is Reuben Watson Stone, that fellow made a mistake. This is a ten-dollar gold piece!"

CHAPTER III

A Race With Spunk

Reuben stared at that ten-dollar gold piece for as much as two minutes, uncertain what to do. Not that he had the slightest temptation to keep it, provided he could find the owner. Of course he did think, How jolly this would be to spend — all for us! But then he had no more idea of spending it than he had of trying to fly.

Reuben wasn't one of those boys who are honest simply because they have no temptation to steal. He would as soon have thought of going into the grocery store and taking money from the drawer as he would have thought of pocketing that gold piece without trying to find its owner. "We are honest, if we *are* poor," he had heard his mother say many a time, and he knew that he was honest. So, though he stood in doubt, that doubt was all about how to find the owner.

"I might as well try to find a needle in a haystack!" he muttered as he turned the shining thing over. He knew almost nothing about haystacks, and I don't think he ever hunted for a needle in his life. But he had heard his mother use that expression when she was searching hopelessly for something.

"That Spunk went like the wind. Where does he live, and how far is it? That's the question. He went up North Street—I know that much. Well, there is nothing to do but try to race after him. So let's go. Too bad! You want to go home, don't you? So do I, but there is no help for us. Race along now, and see if we haven't got spunk enough to overtake that spunky pony. It may be he has had to stop half a dozen times."

Away they went, Reuben and his two feet, speeding up North Street. Reuben's eyes turned to the right and left as he ran, hoping to see the brown horse standing in front of another store or house. There was nothing to be seen of him. Reuben slackened his speed after a little while and began to have a hopeless feeling that he was racing away from home for nothing. There were so many corners at which the brown horse might have turned. If he had sped on his way, he was far beyond reach, resting in some barn perhaps this very minute.

"We may as well go home, first as last," sighed Reuben, coming at last to a standstill. "What a stupid thing it was not to find out where that brown horse lived! He looked smart enough to tell me, if I had asked him. How I wish I could find him. I hate to have a ten-dollar gold piece that doesn't belong in the house and not know where to take it. I doubt I'll ever find him, and it will be about a dozen years before Mother will let me spend it.

"Halloo! There he is this minute, just turning away from Dunlap's. Hold on there, mister. I say! Can't you wait?" and he was off in pursuit.

But the brown horse was ahead and meant to keep so. Though Reuben did his best, he was quickly lost in a snarl of other horses, wagons and streetcars. And he stood in front of Dunlap's store, rubbing his cold hands together, no wiser than he was before. A sudden thought came to him, and he dashed into the store to inquire the name of the man with the brown horse, describing him as well as he could.

"Don't know him," said the busy clerk. "Stranger, I guess. How many pounds did you say?" This question was for the man he was waiting on.

Reuben turned and left. Now he might surely go home with a clear conscience. He had done his best and failed.

If he *is* a stranger, he told himself, it's not likely I'll ever find him, and Mother might as well use the money. If I could only make her think so, I'd go and pay that rent a whole quarter at a time. I'd like to know what the agent would think of that! I've a great mind to go pay him and get his old receipt and say nothing to Mother about it. Then I'd give it to her New Year's morning for a present. I wonder if there would be anything so very bad about that! I've half a mind to do it. I could tell her about it afterward. But I guess I won't. She doesn't like to be told about things afterward; she likes beforehand better.

"Well, now, feet, are you afraid you will freeze while I stand here planning? I don't know but you will, and your master, too. Well, come on. Let's go home.

"Halloo! Say, mister! Stop a minute!" He shouted at the top of his lungs, for the brown horse had turned around and was speeding past him in the other direction.

For a wonder, the young man heard the shout amid the din of other noises and with some trouble checked Spunk's impatient feet.

"You made a mistake, sir," said Reuben, pressing close to the sleigh and speaking with difficulty. Spunk was determined to step on him or toss him in the air or bite him at least. "This is a shiner you gave me, instead of a quarter."

"A what?"

"A shiner, sir, a ten-dollar gold piece."

"Is it possible I was so careless as that?" he asked, reaching forth his hand.

Reuben dropped the shining thing into it.

"Well, I declare. What a careless fellow I am getting to be! Good for you, my boy. If it had fallen into some hands, I should never have seen it again. Spunk, what *is* the matter with you tonight? You are worse than usual! Do go then, if you are in such a hurry."

And Spunk went, leaving Reuben standing, staring after him. He stood perfectly still for a minute or more, gazing after the flying horse. Then once more he spoke to his feet. "Well, there is one thing I would like to know, and that is, who is going to pay us for standing out there in the snow and holding that horse for fifteen whole minutes?"

Nobody answered him, and he turned and walked gravely and slowly toward home.

CHAPTER IV

ANOTHER DISAPPOINTMENT

eth flattened her nose against the windowpane and watched for Reuben until it grew so dark that she could not tell one person from another. Then she wandered around the room, occasionally opening the door and peering out, letting in a great rush of cold air and saying every few minutes, "Mother, what *do* you suppose has become of Reuben?"

Mother had little to say but was almost as glad as Beth was when at last they heard his step.

"Why, where in the world — ?" began Beth.

But her mother interrupted her. "Why, Reuben, my boy, how cold and tired you look! Where *have* you been?"

"I've been to the end of the world, or the end of the city, or 'most to the end of North Street anyhow," he ended as he sat down wearily in a chair and put his feet on the stove hearth. "Those fellows are tired, you better believe," he said, looking kindly down on them. Then, with Beth fluttering around him and Mrs. Stone putting the last stitches in the shirt she was trying to finish before supper, he told his story.

"Well! I never — no, never in all my life!" said Beth with great indignation when he stopped for breath. "So you had all that tramp and didn't get a cent!"

"Not a cent," Reuben said dolefully. He was too tired to be cheerful.

"Never mind," said the patient mother. "I daresay he was so astonished that he forgot it."

"Forgot it!" repeated Beth. "More like he wanted to save his money. I think he is just the meanest man I ever heard of. I hope I'll meet him and his old horse someday, and I'll stop him and tell him so."

"He looked like a nice man," said Reuben, who couldn't quite make up his mind to keep still and let Spunk's master be abused. "And I don't believe it was because he was mean, or else he wouldn't have given me a quarter in the first place. I never knew a boy to get more than a dime for holding a horse, and 'most always it is only five cents. That reminds me — I got five cents for taking care of Mr. Anson's horse awhile this morning." He shoved his hand into his pockets, brought out the lonesome five-cent piece and with an odd little smile handed it to his mother.

"It is every cent that 'the man of the house' has earned today," he added sadly.

"S'posing he had spent *that* for a cigar, instead of bringing it to his mother!" soothed Mrs. Stone. "I know boys who never bring their mothers even five cents."

"Humph!" said Beth. Whether it was at the thought of the cigar or Spunk's master or what, she didn't say.

Then they sat down to supper. "There's one comfort," Beth said. "The food hasn't gotten cold while we were waiting."

At this, Mother and Reuben had to laugh. Little by little they grew more cheerful.

"Well," said Reuben, as soon as his bread and milk were gone, "I must trot out and tend to Dorcas. I'm not often so late. I don't know what she'll say."

Dorcas was the cow that furnished them with a quart of milk a day; she was quartered in the stable that backed up against their one window. Reuben milked her and took care of her faithfully, usually an hour earlier than it was tonight. So he hurried away; but much sooner than a cow can be milked, he hurried back. "Mother, they've sold Dorcas!" he exclaimed as he was opening the door.

"Oh, dear!" cried Mrs. Stone. She had been carrying a big pan of water and set it down on the nearest chair. "When did they do that?"

"Just now — a man took her away less than an hour ago. Mr. Baker said it was a nuisance to keep a cow in the city anyhow, and she didn't give as much milk as she ought to, and boys were always bothering him about being late. Wasn't that mean, Mother? I haven't been late but twice since I took care of her. The long and short of it is, she's gone!"

"Oh, dear!" sighed Mrs. Stone. The loss of that quart of milk a day meant a great deal to her. She didn't see how they would manage without it.

Beth felt almost guilty. Hadn't she that very afternoon almost wished that they hadn't a quart of milk a day? Well, she had her wish for once.

After a few moments Reuben crossed the room to the pan of water. "What do you want to do with this, Mother?" he asked. On being told, he went to the back door and pitched the water out into the darkness. It was natural for him to save his mother's steps. I think he was more careful about that than Beth was.

The work was all done now, and the little family, much more somber than usual, gathered around the little stand. Reuben brought his book and slate and tried to interest himself in an example in arithmetic. His mother encouraged him to continue his lessons in the hope that some day he could attend school, but the world appeared very dark to him tonight. The old year was almost gone, and the coal was almost gone, and Dorcas was quite gone.

"Come, children," Mrs. Stone said, after the ciphering and studying had proceeded for some time in silence. "The fire is low; it's time we were in bed. I'll just step in and see if Mother Perkins is settled for the night, and then we'll call this day finished."

Mother Perkins was an old, feeble woman who lived alone in one room of the house. Sometimes she was unable to leave her bed for days at a time and had to wait for chance callers to bring food to her. Mrs. Stone had taken her under her special care for the last few days and visited her every night to be sure that she was as comfortable as the dreary room would allow.

Reuben and Beth, left to themselves, stared at the dying coals for a few minutes. Then Beth said, "What would you have bought with that quarter, s'posing it had been a quarter and had belonged to you?"

"Well," mused Reuben, "I had more than two

dozen plans. I guess if I'd done half with it that I thought about, it would have been just a wonderful quarter. You see, in the first place, I wanted to get some coal, a whole bushel at once. We are fearfully low on coal. I don't know how I am going to rake and scrape enough together to do till Saturday. Then I wanted to get some real good tea for Mother. She drinks regular hay stuff now. The clerk sneers at it while he wraps it up, and it's cheaper by nearly a dollar on the pound than the real tea. Joe Bradley bought a pound of real tea for a Christmas present for his mother, and he paid ninety cents a pound! What do you think of that?"

"My!" said Beth impressively. She knew how much a pound of her mother's tea cost.

"Well, then there were two or three things I kind of wanted to get for you. I won't tell you what they were, 'cause it's no ways likely I shall get around to them now, till I'm of age." Reuben had always believed that, when he came of age, something wonderful would happen whereby he could do some of the many things for Beth he knew she would like. Just how he was going to get the money for all these things, he had not yet planned to his satisfaction. But when a fellow was of age, he argued, of course he could get money.

"Oh, I don't care," said Beth quickly, "not about myself. I'm sorry about the coal, and I should like first-rate for Mother to have some real tea. I know that what she has once in a while is of no account by the way it smells. I smell the tea when I go to Redwood to take the milk. My, how it smells!"

"You won't smell it anymore," moaned Reuben, shaking his head sorrowfully. "How he could go and sell that cow is more than I can think."

"The folks at Redwood will be sorry, too," said

Beth. "They liked that milk so much. The baby used to be out in the kitchen with his silver cup waiting for me to come, and he would just shout when he saw me."

"It won't make very much difference to them," Reuben said, shaking his head. "Folks that have as much money as they have — it doesn't matter when a man sells his cow. They can just go to another man, pull out their pocketbooks and say, 'Here, I want some milk from you every day. How much does it cost?' Or, if it comes to that, they can up and buy a cow — two of them, if they want to — just as easy as they can turn their hand over. I'll tell you what it is, Beth: When I'm of age, money is one of the things I'm going to have!"

"How are you going to get it?" asked practical Beth.

"Yes, that's the question. That part of it isn't decided yet. But then I've got a good while to think it over." And, with a gleam of fun in his dark eyes, Reuben arose, walked to the mantle and lighted the end of a candle which showed him the way to his "suite of rooms." This was what he always called them when he felt cheerful. He was imitating a woman for whom his mother sewed and who was fond of describing to her seamstress her grand house in the country.

Reuben's "suite of rooms" had evidently at one time been a large, old-fashioned pantry in two compartments with a sliding door between them. The house itself was an old-fashioned one, looking small enough now standing beside many larger ones that had sprung up around it. Still, it had once been thought of as good-sized, and several families lived in it now! But they were all families who could afford but one room apiece, or, at the most, two. As Reuben lighted his candle, Beth, watching the process, was suddenly reminded of a bit of news she had treasured up for Reuben.

"The south room is rented, Reuben."

"Is it?" the boy asked, spinning around with a curious expression on his face. The most pleasant room in the house had two large windows in it. It had been standing vacant now for several weeks because no one ventured that way who could afford to pay for the sunshine that streamed in at those two south windows. You would be surprised to know how much difference that made in the rent. Reuben and Beth did not believe sunshine was free; they had good reasons for believing as they did.

"Who's taken it?"

"A woman, kind of old, and not so very old either. She's got gray hair, and she is tall and straight. Her face looks sort of nice — not exactly pretty, but the kind of face one likes. Anyhow, I like her chair. I just wish you could have seen it! The nicest chair, covered all over with bright, odd-looking stuff — it couldn't have been calico. I never saw any calico like that — and it was so pretty. Reuben, it would be so nice if we could get Mother a chair like that for a Christmas present."

"So it would be to get her a house and a barn and a cow," said Reuben good-humoredly. "And about as easy, for all I see. Well, Beth, I must put myself to bed for the night." And he took his bit of lighted candle and went off to his clothespress.

CHAPTER V

Miss Priscilla Hunter

ood morning," said a pleasant voice. It seemed to be speaking to Reuben Stone, though whose it was or where it came from he couldn't decide. He stood with his hands in his pockets to keep them from freezing and glanced about him curiously. At last he discovered the owner of the voice—a trim, kindly faced woman leaning out from the upper window, gazing down at him.

"Did you think I was a snowbird?" she asked him, then continued without waiting for his answer. "I suspect you are a neighbor of mine, and I thought I would introduce myself. I've just moved in. Don't you live in this house?"

"Yes'm," said Reuben, "I live in the north corner room, second floor."

"Just so, and I live in the south corner room, second floor. We are very close neighbors, you see. I wish you a happy last day of the year."

Reuben laughed, then appeared grave. "I'm not likely to have a very happy one, as I can see." He sighed a little in spite of his determination not to.

"Is that so? Now that's a pity. I always like to have a year end well; it makes such a good beginning for the new one. Suppose you *make* it end nice, whether it wants to or not?"

This made Reuben laugh again. Her voice was so cheery that he could not help being encouraged by it.

The brisk voice continued again. "Suppose you come up here, show me how to unfasten the spring to my window, and tell me what is going to be the matter with your day?"

"I'll tend to the window," Reuben answered, entering briskly and mounting the stairs two at a time. As to what was going to be the matter with his day, he wished he knew.

The window fastening was turned without any trouble, and the window, when Reuben put his strong arms to it, went up without a hitch.

"See what it is to know how!" said his new friend admiringly. "I suppose I fussed at that window for maybe ten minutes before I decided to ask for help. Well, now, what is your objection to this day?"

"Why, I haven't any objection to it," Reuben laughed. "But it doesn't begin as though it liked me very well."

"What do you want of it?"

"I want it to give me some work to do."

"Work to do! Well, now, I never! Why, the world is just as full of work as it can be. I didn't know there was anything so easy to find as that."

"It keeps itself snug away from me then," said Reuben grimly. "I've been looking for some these, well, ever so many days."

"And you haven't found any?"

"No'm. None to speak of."

"Well, that's astonishing! It must be that you are particular. What kind of work do you want?"

"No'm, I'm not the least bit particular. I'd take any kind of work that folks would pay for."

"Oh, you want pay, do you? That's another thing. To be sure, I never knew anybody to work without pay, though they don't always think of the pay at the time."

"I have to think of it," replied Reuben stoutly. "I need it, you see. It isn't as though I worked for fun or to get some spending money for myself. I do it to support the family."

"So you have a family on your hands, have you? How many? A father and mother, I suppose. Any brothers and sisters?"

Reuben looked out of the window and waited a minute before he steadied his voice to say, "There's no father, ma'am. I'm the man of the house, and I have a mother and one sister to support. At least I want to support them, and mean to sometime. Mother has to work hard now, and so does Beth; but I don't mean it to be always so."

"Good for you," said his new acquaintance approvingly.

Meanwhile she had been starting a fire in her little cook stove, and Reuben had lingered because it was such a bright, pleasant room that he hated to go. How cheery it was, to be sure, and not much larger than their own, but very different.

In the first place, a carpet lay on the floor; it was only spread down, for the newcomer had moved in just the day before. But it was a warm-looking carpet and would cover the entire floor nicely. Curtains — white ones, too — were already up at the windows. Reuben didn't know they were only the coarsest of muslin costing just a few cents a yard, and wouldn't have cared, if he had known. Also, there was a lounge in a colorful pattern and a chair, which must have been the one Beth had admired so much. Two or three plants were already seated on the low window, and the morning sun was preparing to shine on them. South windows in this room, two of them — no wonder it was pleasant.

But the pleasantest feature of the room was that trim figure, filling the small, shining teakettle with water. Reuben watched her admiringly and knew now that she was very pretty. He had not discovered it at first. He could not have told now what he liked so much about her; he only knew that he liked her. He sprang forward when the kettle was filled and lifted it quickly and skillfully to its place on the little stove.

"Thank you," said his hostess, observing him with satisfaction. "So you mean to support your mother and Beth? I shouldn't wonder if you would do it. I kind of feel it in my bones that you will. I had a glimpse of Beth yesterday, I guess. She is a nice, pleasant-looking little sister and seems as if she ought to be supported. How are you going to do it?"

"That's the rub," said Reuben, a shadow crossing his face. "There seems to be nothing that a boy can find to do. Odd jobs, you see, don't pay. You spend half your time searching for them, and maybe half the time you don't find them."

"Just so, and then, according to that calculation, the whole of the time is gone. But there's one thing that is more important than discovering what you are going to do; that's deciding what you are *not* going to do."

"I'm going to do *anything*," Reuben declared firmly. "I don't care what it is. Anything under the sun that folks will pay for, and I can do, I'm ready for. For a good while I picked out the kinds of work that I would like and hunted for them, but I gave that up long ago. Now it is anything."

"I'm sorry to hear it," she said, shaking her gray head as she pulled out a clever little round table and spread a white cloth on it.

"I'm very sorry indeed to hear it. I know of work that folks will pay for, but if you were my boy, I'd rather not be supported than to have you do it."

"What, for instance?"

"Stealing and lying and killing folks, and all that sort of thing."

"Oh! Well, of course, I didn't mean that. Folks don't get paid for doing those things."

"Don't they! There's where you're mistaken. They get paid in more ways than one. If you're talking about *money* pay, they get lots of that. I'm not sure but what it appears to pay almost better in that way than any other business."

"But it's against the law to do such things."

"Anybody with common sense would suppose so, of course. But this is a peculiar world, and it has peculiar laws. I'm ashamed to have to admit that you are mistaken. The law winks at the whole thing."

"Winks at stealing and murder?" exclaimed Reuben, beginning to think that he had made the acquaintance of a lunatic. "I don't know what the laws are where you came from, but in New York state such things can't be done without folks suffering for them, if they are caught at it."

"Bless your heart, my boy. I wish that were true.

I've lived in New York state for seventeen years and have seen this business going on all the time. I know men who have stolen houses and horses and cows and furniture and books, and I don't know what not, and murdered more wives and children than I can count, and the law hasn't peeped. Oh, yes, it has, too. It has given every one of the creatures permission to keep on doing it year after year."

"Oh," said Reuben, the look of astonishment disappearing from his face. "I know what you mean now. Yes, liquor-selling is mean enough business, I suppose. In fact, I know it is. I would never do it for myself."

"For yourself? Oh, no, of course not. But how would it be if you had a chance to do errands for a man who sold it? Carry home beer or wine or even stand behind the counter and sell the vile stuff by the glass?"

"Well," mused Reuben, "I've never looked for work in any of those places. But I suppose I'd take work if it were offered me. Might as well, you know. Lots of boys stand ready to do it, and if I didn't take the place, somebody else would. Yes, sir, I'm in for work; I've got to work. You don't catch me refusing it — though I doubt I'll have an offer like that."

"I hope not," said his new friend seriously. "If those are your principles, I sincerely hope no one will lead you into temptation. You use just exactly the argument that might be used about stealing. Lots of folks stand ready to steal, and I daresay a good deal of stealing will be done, whether you do it or not. Why shouldn't you have your share?"

"Oh, well, now," Reuben said, staring at her in amazement. "That's entirely different, you know.

But I know that every man who wants a clerk to sell his brandy and things can get one. So what difference does it make, whether it's me or somebody else?"

"Listen now," said the hazel-eyed woman, laying down her knife beside the loaf from which she was cutting beautiful slices of bread. She faced Reuben, her eyes looking larger than they had before. "Suppose that sister of yours — you love her, don't you?"

"I should rather think I do!" was Reuben's prompt answer.

"Well, now, suppose she had made up her mind to poison herself today, and she was sure to do it, whether you helped her or whether you didn't. Wouldn't it make a speck of difference to you, when you thought about it afterward, whether it was you who mixed the poison for her and held it out to her or whether it was somebody else?"

Over this question Reuben paused thoughtfully for a few seconds. The color rose slowly on his brown cheeks. "Yes, ma'am, it would. I'd rather it would have been anybody else on this earth than me."

"Just so," said the woman with an emphatic nod of her gray head. "Now I'll tell you something. I don't like to tell it very often nor to think about it. I had a father and a brother and a friend who were each poisoned to death with rum. *Murder,* I call it, though a good many people helped in it, and nobody was hung for it. I'm glad you weren't one of the helpers. I hope, with all my soul, that you will never lift your finger to help anyone else's father or brother or friend to take poison."

To this appeal Reuben seemed to have no answer to make. The bread-cutting went on in silence for a few seconds. Changing her tone to a cheery one, his new friend said, "Well, sir, I think it is time you and I introduced ourselves if we are to be neighbors and friends. I'm Miss Priscilla Hunter, a tailoress by trade. I expect to make a great many vests and coats and pants for folks of about your size or a trifle younger. Now if you are the head of the family, what is your name, and what is your business?"

"I'm Reuben Watson Stone, and my business, you see, is to take care of my mother and sister; but I haven't found how to do it yet."

"You'll do it," Miss Hunter nodded emphatically. "I'll risk you. I shouldn't wonder if you would have a pretty good run of business this very day. Had your breakfast?"

"No'm," said Reuben, his cheeks growing hotter. Did she suppose he was going to tell her that they had only half a loaf of bread left and that he had saved it for Mother and Beth and started out intending to earn his own before he ate it. They were in closer quarters than usual just now, but he did not mean to tell anybody if he could help it. So he said, "No'm, I haven't eaten it yet."

"Pretty early, that's a fact," said Miss Hunter. "Since I was moving, I thought I'd get going early. If you are not in too great a hurry, I wonder if you would buy some tacks for me, a few shingle nails and a tack hammer — I broke mine taking the tacks out with the claw end. And I need a spool of black linen thread while you are about it. Let me pay you with a cup of coffee and a slice or two of my best toast."

"I'll buy the things in a jiffy," said Reuben, his mouth watering at the thought of the hot coffee and toast. "But you needn't pay me. I'll do it to be neighborly."

"Business is business," said Miss Hunter briskly. "But, never mind, we'll begin by being neighborly. You sit down and have breakfast with me for my part, and then go do my errands for your part. And then we'll both be neighborly and even. Don't you see?"

"No, ma'am," laughed Reuben. "I have to go right by the stores and can do your errands as well as not. It isn't worth a cup of coffee and a piece of toast to do them."

"No? Well, then, I'll have you get some buttons and match a piece of cloth lining for me at the trimming store on Broadway. Know where that is? All right, I'll be even with you somehow."

All this while, she had been dashing around her kitchen. She laid two plates on the nice round table, set her coffee to bubble — the pint of water in the small, bright teakettle boiled with a swiftness that would have shocked Beth — and toasted her beautiful slices of bread. In a remarkably short space of time Reuben Watson Stone found himself seated at the table with its white tablecloth, taking a lovely breakfast with Miss Priscilla Hunter.

As he ate, he laughed to think how all this would astonish Beth. He concluded that she couldn't be more astonished about it than he was.

During the breakfast, Reuben found himself telling Miss Hunter the most unexpected and unusual things: how Dorcas the cow was sold, and how he wanted to send Beth to school but couldn't — had wanted to go himself but had given up that dream long ago; how he wanted to buy his mother a house one of these days and wanted in the meantime to pay the next month's rent and get a whole bushel of coal — but he would fail even in these if he got no work. "I'd like to buy my coal by the bushel, if I could," said this head of the house, "because people who buy at wholesale get things cheaper, I have heard."

"Just so," said Miss Hunter, taking thoughtful bites of her toast and suddenly uncovering a mysterious little tin dish that she had lifted from the stove. "Look here — what a present I had yesterday from one of my old neighbors who lives in the country! She keeps a hen that lays eggs on purpose for me. As soon as she has laid six of them, my neighbor brings them along." And she plumped a lovely white morsel just out of its creamy shell onto Reuben's plate.

"Oh!" he caught his breath. "This is too much."

"One egg isn't much," Miss Hunter assured him. "I know a boy who used to eat two at every single breakfast."

That fact so startled Reuben that he didn't say another word. But if there had been any way of tucking that egg into his pocket or his hat or somewhere and slipping away with it nice and warm and white to his mother, how he would have liked it!

"So the cow is sold," Miss Hunter said meditatively. "That's bad, I suppose, for the people who owned her, but I must say it makes my way look clearer. I have a friend about a mile away from here who has milk brought to her from a farm in the country every morning. I buy two quarts a day from her; I'm rather fond of milk. But the problem is, now that I've moved, how to get it. She used to have her boy bring it to me on his way to school, but his way won't be down this street. Now if I could find a boy or a girl who would like to tramp after it for me and be paid in milk, a quart a day, don't you see I would be fixed?"

"We could do that," Reuben said eagerly, "Beth and I. She likes to take walks, and Mother likes to have her — only she hasn't any regular place to go, and Mother doesn't like to have her wandering about. But whenever it is nice and pleasant, she can get the milk; and when it storms or is too cold, I could go."

"Just so," Miss Hunter nodded, and a comfortable little smile seemed to settle on her face.

CHAPTER VI

A WILD RIDE

fter the milk question they jumped —Reuben tried to tell it afterward and could not remember how—to the chair Beth liked so much. His mother and sister, when they heard of it later, thought it the oddest thing that he would have talked so to a stranger. And when Reuben thought about it, he did not wonder at their reaction. At the time it seemed the most natural thing in the world for him to tell Miss Hunter how he had stood lighting his candle only the night before. Beth had told him then about the south room being taken and about the chair and how she would like such a chair for Mother.

"That chair," said Miss Hunter, turning her head and looking at it sideways. She poured a second cup of very weak coffee with a lot of milk for Reuben and kept on talking. He, being polite, of course could not say a word. "That chair has a history. You couldn't guess in a month where it came from. What would you think if I should tell you I found it in a cellar?"

"In a cellar!" repeated Reuben, startled, yet laughing. "Beth would say she would like to get into such a cellar as that."

"Well, that isn't the strangest part of it. What do you think of its once being full of potatoes?" Then Reuben listened in wide-eyed wonder to the story of a barrel that with the help of a saw and a few nails and tacks and a partly worn-out dress of Miss Hunter's was transformed into a beautiful chair!

"You wouldn't believe what a comfortable seat it has," said Miss Hunter. "It wasn't such very hard work either. To be sure, I had some trouble in getting it sawed out just right. I wasn't raised to make chairs, but I caught on after a while. Folks can get 'most anything if they try hard enough. I shouldn't wonder if you and Beth would like to make your mother just such a chair some of these days. I'd be very glad to show you how."

Altogether, Reuben Watson Stone went downtown that morning feeling that he had found a friend. The day looked brighter, and his prospect for getting work seemed better. How much the cup of coffee and nicely browned toast and soft-boiled egg had to do with this feeling, Reuben did not know, and I am not sure that I do.

The next thing to be done was to find work. He felt more eager for this than ever, for hadn't he just eaten a good breakfast, and hadn't his mother and Beth managed without even the milk which had pieced out their breakfast for so long?

"It is a wonder that toast and egg didn't choke me!" muttered Reuben. With his hands in his pockets he sped over the powdery white ground. "I'd have given all I'll earn today for the chance to slip it into my pocket and run to Mother. But, there, I couldn't beg. And Mother would have been the last one to have wanted me to. I *must* earn a dinner for my folks!"

There was never a meaner day for finding work! At least that was what Reuben thought. The people seemed bent on doing their own errands, tying their horses instead of wanting them held, and getting their papers by anyone but him.

"I'm glad it is the last day of the year," he growled, shivering as he poised himself on one toe and peered in at the window of a large bakery to discover whether a boy might be needed. Business was plentiful there, but so were boys; they were flying around like tops.

"Mean old year," Reuben grumbled as he moved on. "It is time you were done. When you can't furnish work in a great, big world like this for an honest boy who has a mother and sister to support, you better stand aside and let the new one come in.

"Eighteen hundred and fifty-two is now forever past. I'll be glad when I can say that. Eighteen hundred and fifty-three will fly away as fast. That's the next line. Well, who cares? Let it fly. I'll risk it though. A year is an awful long time. Seems to me as though I must be about fifty; it was so long ago that I was ten! Halloo! What's that? 'Boy wanted to strip tobacco.' Strip tobacco! For my part I wish it was all stripped up and put in the Pacific Ocean. I think tobacco is nearly as bad as whiskey anyhow, and Miss Hunter didn't say a word about it."

Notwithstanding his opinion, he stopped at the store to see if he could get a chance to strip tobacco, but he was too late.

"Engaged a boy not ten minutes ago to fill the last vacancy," the man behind the counter told him.

Reuben left the store with a sad face, wondering whether he might not have been in time if he had not stopped to eat that lovely breakfast with Miss Hunter. "But then I was so hungry that like as not I would have disgraced myself by eating the strips of tobacco," he said as he walked slowly away.

It was not because of laziness that he found little or nothing to do that morning. He traveled miles, stopped a great many men who looked as if they might have some work for him, looked in at a great many places of business and inquired carefully at the points where he had to do errands for Miss Hunter.

All to no avail. Five cents for taking a letter half a mile uptown for a lady — the five cents was to pay his car fare, but he saved it and trudged there through the icy streets. Two cents for carrying a basket for another lady across the road to the streetcar. One cent reward for picking up an old gentleman's handkerchief and rushing after him with it. This was the extent of Reuben's earnings when the short day was growing dusk.

He had not gone home to dinner. He left word in the morning that, unless he had an unusual run of luck, he would make a day of it and take dinner with his friends at the corner of South Street. These friends of his were an old woman and a little girl who sold penny buns, molasses candy and ginger-snaps. Neither snaps nor candy did Reuben buy; he contented himself with one bun because he had had such a good breakfast.

This left him seven cents. He took them out and inspected them. "I'm afraid," he said, shaking his head reproachfully at the dingy coppers, "I'm afraid that you will make a sorry show at paying the rent for a month and laying in a stock of coal for a week and getting a New Year's dinner for Mother and Beth, besides a present or two to remember the day by."

Just then a card swinging from a window attracted his attention. "HANDS WANTED," read the card in large, black letters.

"How many, I wonder?" said Reuben, taking his out of his pockets and scrutinizing them carefully. "I've got two. To be sure, I want them myself, but then I'd be willing to lend them for decent work and good pay. I mean to try." He opened the door.

A solemn, middle-aged man stood near the window buttoning his coat before leaving. He listened to Reuben's eager questions and shook his head. "It is women's and girls' hands that I'm looking for," he said.

"Women and girls!" repeated Reuben in dismay. "How old must the girls be?" He was thinking of Beth. Not that he meant her to go out to earn her living — he hated the thought of that. But then she was as eager to earn money as he was. It would be just as well for her to know she was too young, for of course she was.

"Oh, almost any age that know how to work — fifteen, twelve and somewhere about there. I have hired them as young as eight, but that is almost too young. Ten will do very well, if they are good, faithful girls and want to work and earn money instead of play."

"Is it in a factory?" questioned Reuben in terror. He did not know there was a place in that city where girls as young as Beth were hired to work. What if Mother would think she ought to go? "I hope they don't get but a cent a week," he muttered under his breath.

"Well, not exactly," the man answered. "There are factories, plenty of them, in town, but I was rather looking for women and girls who would like to take work home and do it. Still, I could find them places enough in the shops, if they liked that better."

"It isn't in this city then?" said Reuben, feeling relieved in spite of himself. Of course Beth could not go out of the city to work. But to have work at home with Mother was no more than she was doing now.

"Oh, no," the man said. It was west of the city, forty miles or so, in a nice village. People were not huddled together as they were in the city. For his part he wouldn't live in the city if they would give him a house rent free.

"How much money could girls of ten earn in a day?" asked Reuben, strangely fascinated by the new idea, although he had no more notion of Beth's ever being one of those girls than he had that he would be the president.

"Well, that depends on what kind of girls they are — whether they are quick-witted and industrious and all that. I've had girls working for us who were no older than that, and they earned their seventy-five cents a day, day in and day out."

Then all the blood in Reuben's body rushed up into his face. At least he thought so — he was so astonished. Seventy-five cents a day! It seemed like a fortune to him.

"Doing what?" he gasped.

"Nice work — gloves, kid ones, soft and pretty — putting rows of silk on the back of them. We used to have no trouble in getting hands, but the girls have all got such a notion of running the big machines nowadays that we are plagued to death to get those we can rely on. What interests you so much? Have you got a sister who would like to go down there into the country and earn her living?"

"I've got a sister," said Reuben, drawing his breath in hard, "but I don't want her to earn her living. I mean to earn it for her."

"You do, eh? Well, that's good talk. I hope you'll succeed. Do you live in the city?"

"Yes, sir."

"What does your father do for a living?"

"We haven't any father. I'm the man of the house and have been for three years. Isn't there anything in your town for boys to do?"

The man shook his head. "Boys are plenty," he said gravely, "as plenty as grasshoppers in August. They all want work, too, or pretend they do. There are seven boys to every job in our town. Girls, now, are different. They all want to dress up and be ladies."

Reuben shook his head. "I'd like to earn seventy-five cents a day, first-rate," he lamented. "But I don't know as I'd like to have Beth pinned down to it — not if I can support them without it." And he opened the door and returned to the street.

"Nice-appearing boy," said the man aloud to himself, gazing after Reuben. "But I daresay he'll go to smoking and drinking before he is anything but a boy." And with this hopeful view of Reuben's future, he turned away from the window and left the store.

Reuben trekked up North Street wondering how they were getting along at home, wondering whether he must give it up and go home with only seven cents. Suddenly a horse dashed by him at full speed. The driver lashed him at every bound, apparently determined to make him run away if possible.

"Ha!" said a man who stopped and stared after him. "He's drunk again! If he gets home alive, I'll wonder at it." At the same moment Reuben recognized Spunk.

Without any idea why he did it, or indeed what he was doing, Reuben spun around and raced after the flying horse. I don't think he could have hoped to catch him, but he had a great desire to see more of Spunk. Sure enough, the young driver pulled up before a saloon with such a sudden jerk that he almost upset himself; threw the reins to a boy in waiting; and disappeared inside the saloon before Reuben reached there breathless.

Several men were gathered in a group, remarking about the owner of the lively horse. "If he takes another glass in there, I wouldn't like to have to ensure his neck," said one.

"What a shame it is that he is bent on going to destruction in that fashion," said another. Still a third pointed out that the man could hardly be blamed for doing what his father had done before him.

Reuben, having nothing better to occupy himself with just then, could not help patting Spunk's foamy coat and sympathizing with him on having been so abused. Meanwhile, the discussion continued about the danger his owner was in if he should continue to drive in that reckless fashion.

Just then the young man appeared, the flush on his face and the wild light in his eyes telling only too plainly that he had been drinking still more of the poison.

"Aching for a ride, are you, youngster?" he

shouted, as soon as his eyes rested on Reuben. "Well, jump in, and I'll 'rattle your bones over the stones' in a way that you'll remember, I reckon. I declare I'm a poet! Who knew it?" A wild, drunken laugh rang out on the air.

In a twinkling Reuben's resolution was taken; he knew how to drive. Many a time he had jumped in with some of his market friends and managed their horses while they exchanged their vegetables for groceries. Besides, he had often hopped on the omnibus that ran from the square to the Garden House. The driver, who was a friend of his, would allow him to drive up to the hotel with a flourish. He would ride with this drunken man, who was in serious danger of breaking his neck. He would coax him to give Spunk into his hands, and by that means he would get the young man home in safety and be paid well perhaps for his work. A wild way to earn money, certainly.

If Reuben had stopped to think twice, he would have remembered that his mother would hardly approve. And, further, he was well warned.

"Don't get in, youngster!" shouted one of the men.

"Don't go with him!" yelled another.

But it all happened in a minute — the shouting and jumping and laughing of the drunken man — and then they were off like the wind.

What a ride it was! Reuben will not likely ever forget it. Away, away over the rough, frozen roads. In some places the snow drifted badly; in other places the roads were almost bare. Where were they going? That was the question that at last began to trouble Reuben.

His drunken companion held fast to the reins, shouting wildly, urging the horse to faster speed every minute. He was so crazy with the liquor and the excitement that he had long ago ceased to speak so that Reuben could understand. Still they flew along—the whip applied every minute to poor Spunk's foaming sides, the shouting growing wilder.

They were far out of the city now, past all the fine houses, on a road that was new to Reuben and as lonely as it could be. There before them lay a railroad crossing! They were approaching it with all speed. And then — oh, horror! — came the shrill scream of a locomotive!

Reuben seized, or tried to seize, the reins and shouted in his companion's ear to warn him of the awful danger they were in. He might as well have shouted to the wind!

What does a madman care about danger? On they rushed, he gripping the reins more tightly than before, close to the track! The flagman waved his signal, and the madman laughed and sailed on over the ties, the sleigh groaning on the irons as they flew. The hot breath of the engine was fairly in their mouths, but they were across and alive and still speeding on! This dreadful death was spared them at least for a time. But what was next? How many more railroad crossings might they not reach before this awful ride was over?

Reuben thought of his mother and Beth waiting for him, watching in the gathering darkness, growing every minute more frightened. He knew now that he ought to have thought of Mother before and not have put himself in this peril. He imagined he could see the little table set for three. It was New Year's Eve, and maybe Mother had been paid and had bought some little treat for a celebration. Maybe everything was ready, and they were just waiting for him to come home and enjoy it. And maybe he would never come! Never see Mother and Beth again.

He had remained brave up to this moment, but now he struggled with the tears. He thought about trying to jump out, but the horse was flying so fast. The sleigh was by no means an easy one to get out of, and his crazy companion had clutched him closely with one hand, ever since he dropped his whip in the snow. There seemed to be nothing to do but sit still and let those great tears that froze as fast as they fell drop on his hands.

If he had not been so frightened, he would have known he was suffering with the cold and that another danger threatened him, that of freezing to death. But it never occurred to him.

On they raced, Reuben so absorbed in his fright and grief that he had not realized his drunken companion was becoming less noisy and was leaning his weight more heavily upon him. Suddenly, the reins dropped from the hands of the driver who toppled forward in the bottom of the sleigh, having fallen into a drunken sleep.

What would have filled Reuben's heart with joy a little while before now filled him with a new terror. Spunk, trembling with pain and fright, felt the reins fall loosely and was seized with the horrible fear that he was left to himself. With a fresh snort, he bounded on wilder than ever. He needed no whip now. Without doubt he was running away.

For a few minutes Reuben gave himself up to uncontrolled terror and cried aloud in his agony. But there was no one to hear or heed. At least poor Reuben had never been taught much about the One who can hear, however far away we are from home and friends, and who is able and willing to help us. To be sure, he knew about God: He was the maker of all people and all things, and He took care of the earth as it whirled on its journey day after day, year after year. He knew that someone named Jesus Christ had come to this earth a long time ago and had been nailed to a cross so that people who trusted Him could be cared for and taken to heaven.

All this he would have told you he knew, if you had talked with him. Yet after all he knew it as much as he did that there was a country named China, away on the other side of the globe. Neither China nor Jesus had much to do with him. At least he did not realize that knowledge of the one was any more important to him than knowledge of the other.

Now as his terror increased, something, he did not know what — and long afterward he could not tell whether it was a voice or not that spoke to him — seemed to say, "Why don't you ask God to help you? Nobody else can. You are far out on a strange road. There is no house to be seen. It is quite dark. And this horse is running away."

Whatever it was, whether a voice or a thought put into his heart, it stopped Reuben's wailing cry. He took his hands down from his face. And, while the horse dashed wildly on, he clasped his hands, half-frozen as they were, and said: "O God, save me. Tell me what to do."

CHAPTER VII

SPUNK'S HOME

hen he grasped the reins firmly in his half-frozen hands and gave all his strength to halting that speeding horse. It was no easy task. Spunk hadn't the slightest notion of stopping. He had evidently not thought of being tired. But the road was growing smoother, and somehow Reuben felt less frightened with the drunken man asleep beside him than he had while the muttering was going on.

He sat up straight and tugged hard at the reins. He let himself be whisked over the snowy ground and tried to calculate how far they had traveled. He felt that somehow, whatever the reason, he was not trembling as he had been, and his hope of reaching home alive at some point began to revive.

On they flew! Spunk seemed less frightened now and inclined to enter into the fun of the thing. He was running away just because he had thought of it and had a good chance. There was no danger of *his* freezing. Indeed, cold as the night was, his brown coat was steaming.

At last — Reuben did not know how long after the first letup of his terror, but sometime during that wild ride — it became clear to him that Spunk had given up the idea of escaping everyone entirely and was quieting into a steady, rapid gait.

"I wonder if he would bear turning around?" Reuben said aloud to himself. "This road is wide enough to turn comfortably, and it seems to me it is about time we were traveling toward home. Maybe, though, he would kick up his heels and take off again like the wind if I should attempt it. Well, what if he should? The faster he went, the quicker we would get back to the city, and I suppose we've got to go back there. I wonder where he lives, anyhow? Spunk, what do you say? Will you behave like a lunatic if I turn around?"

Nobody answered. Reuben was in great doubt about what to do. He thought of his prayers. He was not nearly so frightened. He believed in his heart that some of the terror died out, just as he spoke those words to God. Maybe God would tell him what to do. How did He tell people? Reuben wondered. It couldn't be that He spoke to them so that they really heard words!

Reuben had been to church a good many times in his life, and to Sunday school. He had heard a good many prayers, but no answers. Perhaps only the people who are praying in their hearts hear the answers, Reuben said to himself. He immediately had to admit that he didn't believe he had ever prayed in his heart until a little while ago.

"I didn't hear any answer, though," he said aloud. "Hold on! Yes, I did, too! I *felt* an answer. I guess that's just as good."

Without letting go of the reins, he spoke out the words distinctly in the solemn night, feeling only too sure that none but God could hear him. "O God! Tell me just what to do."

Was he answered? Did he *feel* an answer? He asked himself that question. So interested and strangely reflective was he with the thought that God and he were having a talk together that every bit of fear left his heart.

After a few moments more of steady progress, Spunk dropped into quieter ways with every step. Reuben, watching the road, suddenly pulled skillfully off toward the right and intimated plainly to Spunk that he wanted to travel back over the same road he had come.

Spunk made not the slightest objection. On the contrary, he whisked the sleigh around, with such suddenness as almost to take Reuben's breath away, and was off! Not in any wild fashion, though — just a steady, businesslike trot. Now all this had taken a good deal of time, and Reuben knew that many miles must have been covered.

"You went like the wind, old fellow, when you came this way," he told Spunk, "and you're not going back so fast by a good deal, I'm happy to say. I'd rather go slower and be sure of my bones. But it will take us a while to get home, if we ever do, and I believe we will. At least *I* shall. I wish you could tell me where your home is, Spunk."

All the while that he was talking cheerily to the horse, his heart was full of a little gleeful song. He felt certain that the great God Himself had actually bent His ear and heard his — Reuben Stone's — words and directed his steps!

"What else could it be?" said Reuben, talking

aloud. "You see, one minute I didn't have the least kind of notion what it was best to do, whether to go on or try to turn around or *what*. My mind was all in a muddle. And there was nothing around here that a fellow could see to help me make up my mind. Then, all of a sudden, it seemed to me just as clear as day that the thing to do was to turn right around. Something seemed to say to me that Spunk would behave himself and trot back toward home. I did it, and he *is*. Yes, sir, I believe I got some help from somewhere. I should like for anybody to tell me who could have helped me but the One I asked."

Now, if Reuben had lived a little later in life and become acquainted with a man named Robert Ingersoll and had asked him this question, there is no telling what nonsense he might have been given in answer. But having the good fortune to live a thousand miles away from that foolish man, and living instead among people who had common sense, he never thought of imagining that there could be an effect without a cause.

In the course of time—and it seemed a long time to Reuben—the railroad track over which they had flown in such fury was reached; at least its rails could be seen in the distance. And there, sure enough, was the snort of the engine and the roar of the coming train!

The boy's heart beat fast now. What was he to do? It was not possible to cross the track before the cars would be upon them, and what if Spunk insisted upon dashing on faster and faster? It had all to be settled in a second. Of course, the thing to do was to try to stop Spunk. He did not have to hesitate over that.

To his intense relief, Spunk did not object to

stopping. On the contrary, he seemed to think it a wise idea. Whether he was not in his sensible moments afraid of the cars, or whether he was just then too tired and sleepy to think about them, Reuben did not know. But he certainly stood perfectly still, not even winking so far as could be seen, while the fiery-eyed monster thundered by.

Reuben sighed with relief when the last great danger that he knew of on their way had passed. Stooping down, he drew the great furry robes more closely over his sleeping companion.

"I call that sensible of you, Spunk," he spoke admiringly to the horse, as that animal obeyed a gentle hint with the reins and trotted on. "And I call it very kind indeed in the One who is taking care of us."

Reuben spoke the words reverently. It was all new business to him, this night's work. He did not know how to express his gratitude to the great God in the words that most people would have used, but he felt it very deeply. The long, steady pull continued now in silence, and by the widening road and certain other signs, Reuben judged that they must be nearing the outskirts of the city. He slackened his hold on the reins slightly and puzzled over what he should do when he reached North Street.

"Seems as though I've got to plan a little now," he said aloud. "I've been taken care of so far. But now that we're getting to the city, I ought to know something about which way I want to go, but I don't. Suppose I go home. I'm as good as three miles from there likely enough; Mother and Beth are pretty near scared to death about me by this time, I imagine. And they would be quite shocked if I appeared in such company. How would I get him in? I couldn't leave him outside all night; he'd freeze, and it wouldn't do, anyhow. But I couldn't carry him in, and Mother shouldn't help. What would I do with the horse? It's just as much of a muddle as ever, for all I see. *I* can't plan!"

Behold, just at this point, who should assert his right to plan but Spunk himself! He glanced around to see if all was quiet in the rear. Then, reaching a turn in the road, he suddenly whisked around the corner with the briskness of a kitten and quickened his speed almost into a gallop — so glad he seemed over having his own way.

"Well, I never!" said Reuben, rubbing his eyes with his unoccupied hand. "Where are we now? What road is this, I wonder, and why did you whisk us into it in this manner?"

Something in the impatient snort with which Spunk answered all these questions led Reuben, who had watched horses a good deal, to conclude that this spunky little fellow knew more about things than he had allowed. In short, he knew the way home and was heading there as fast as his four legs could take him.

"I never once thought of that!" said Reuben, delighted at the turn matters had taken. "I shouldn't wonder if he would take this fellow right straight home. I hope somebody will be there to lift him out and put him to bed. Well, Spunk, go ahead. Somebody who knows how to do it is taking care of us tonight, and we'll get safely out of the worst scrape we ever had in our lives, I believe. You've got good taste, anyhow, old boy. This is as wide and nice a road as I ever saw, and there are some splendid-looking houses along here. Since you've taken matters into your own hands — or rather feet — I hope you'll pick out a nice one for us to stop at. Seems to me I've had about ride enough for one night."

As if mindful of this last bit of advice, Spunk, with a neigh of satisfaction, whisked into an elm-lined avenue which wound in and out among great trees. In the summer it must have been delightful. He pulled up presently before a flight of steps that led to one of the finest houses Reuben had ever seen — at least this was what he thought about it afterward. He had little time to bestow upon the house just then, for he was so busy wondering what would happen to them next.

Almost before Spunk had fairly halted, the door opened, letting out a flood of light over the snowy world. A woman's form appeared on the piazza, asking in a low, anxious voice, "Edward, is that you?"

Now Reuben was silent for a moment, in doubt about what to say. He did not know whether it was Edward or not, and he had no way of finding out, unless this woman could help him.

She stepped nearer. "Spunk!" she exclaimed anxiously. "Is it Spunk?"

"Yes'm," Reuben responded promptly. Of that much he was certain. "It is Spunk. He insisted on coming here, so I thought I would let him come and see if it was all right."

Then the woman came entirely down the steps into the snow.

"What has happened?" she asked in a voice which, though excited, was low, as if she was often obliged to keep troublesome things to herself. "Who are you? And where is Spunk's master?"

Reuben had a faint idea that Spunk had been his own master for a long time, but he hurried to explain. "I'm Reuben Watson Stone, ma'am. Spunk's master offered me a ride, and Spunk got wild and ran away. His master went to sleep. He's safe, I guess. I kept him tucked up as much as I could, but he's as sound asleep as a nut."

"Asleep!" repeated the lady, and her tone was full of horror and dismay.

Reuben felt sure that she knew, without any other explanation, just what was the matter with him.

"Wait here," she said. "I'll get a lantern." She slipped into the house. She was back again in a few minutes with a lantern which she set down in a sheltered place on the piazza. Then she came close to the sleigh.

"Boy," she said, still speaking softly, "are you strong? Do you suppose that you and I could get him into the house and to his room without any other help? There is no man in the house but Mike, the new servant. I don't like him and don't want to trust him to see Edward sick in this way. He *is* sick, of course, or he would never have gone to sleep when the horse was running." She turned and tried to look sharply into Reuben's face.

"Yes'm," said Reuben simply. "I'm strong. I think we can manage it." He felt as if the strength of a young lion were in his little body just then! He was so sorry for the lady! He wondered if Edward was her son and what *his* mother would do if her son should ever come home in such a fashion.

I never will! Never, *never!* he said to himself with his jaw set firmly.

Then he hopped down like a squirrel and began tugging at the stupid lump which had slipped to the floor of the sleigh. How heavy he was! Yet he was a very slightly built young man. Reuben wondered how he could be so hard to lift. The mother

— if it was his mother — tugged with all her might. Fortunately the bottom of the sleigh was about on a level with the broad piazza. After much puffing and panting, they had the sleeping mass pulled well across the piazza inside the brightly lighted room.

Spunk stood still and watched with as much quiet patience as if he had never thought of dancing or running.

"Now do you think we could get him on this bed?" the lady asked.

She threw open a door which led into paradise — at least it appeared so to the cold, tired boy. He surveyed the picture almost without knowing it: The grand, beautiful room was decorated with rich crimson curtains at the windows dropping in glowing waves to the floor. A massive hand-carved bedstead was made up in spotless white. A large, crimson-covered easy chair matched the bright crimson of the carpet. The color reminded him of the woods aflame with red-gold leaves in autumn. Two mirrors followed him around, making three or four of him in different corners of the room! At least this was the way Reuben's fascinated eyes perceived it in the moment he stood staring.

"Yes'm, I guess we can," he said and leaned over the senseless fellow on the floor.

"How very small you are!" said the lady in surprise, as if seeing him for the first time. "I don't believe you can possibly lift him. Why, you must be very young."

"I'm going on thirteen, ma'am," said Reuben, drawing himself up and looking as tall as he could. There seemed no need to tell her that, but the day before had been his twelfth birthday!

Then he stooped to prove his lifting powers. The

lady bent over to help him. He told himself that if she had been *his* mother he would never let her lift like that. And, furthermore, that beautiful, white bed, fit for a prince, was no place for such a lump as this! Still they managed to put him there. He helped only by turning over just when he ought to have kept still, thereby nearly pitching himself out of bed, and muttered something about wanting to be left alone.

Oh, what a sigh that poor mother gave when it was finally accomplished, and she stood looking at him! It reached Reuben's heart and settled certain resolves which had been growing stronger every minute for the last few hours.

What was to be done next? The strange lady acted as if she had already forgotten him and stood gazing so mournfully upon her son that Reuben could hardly bear to watch.

"Is there anything else I can do for you, ma'am?" he asked at last.

Startled, she spun around toward him. "You poor boy!" she said pityingly. "How tired you look! Where do you live?"

When he had told her, she declared promptly that he must not think of going home. "It is more than three miles from here, and it's after midnight now. You are too cold and tired to *think* of going. It would be dangerous. You might freeze to death. Do you think I could let you go? I suppose you have saved my poor Edward's life. Boy, do you know what is the matter with him?"

"Yes'm," said Reuben simply. What else could he say?

"And have you a mother?"

"Yes'm, I have. I'm her only son, the man of the house, and I ought to be home this minute. She will be scared to death."

"It won't kill her. Many a time I have waited for my Edward until morning. You can make her heart glad over the whole story tomorrow. Look here, Reuben — did you say your name was Reuben? — well, do *never* go home to your mother as my only son has come home to me tonight!"

"No, ma'am," pledged Reuben solemnly, "I never will." Then he gave his attention to business. "What about Spunk, ma'am? He ought not to stand out there like this, after such a trip as he has had."

"True enough," sighed the lady. "I had forgotten the poor beast. I suppose I must try to rouse Mike to take care of him."

She evidently disliked Mike and dreaded to call him on the scene. "If you would like, ma'am, I think I can fix Spunk out all right for the rest of the night," Reuben volunteered. "We are pretty well acquainted — ought to be by this time."

"Are you sure you are not afraid of him?" the woman asked anxiously.

"Not a bit, ma'am."

As he slung the lantern on his arm and left in search of the barn, he said to Spunk, "Do you suppose I intend to be afraid of you or anything else, old fellow, after tonight?"

Reuben was much troubled about his mother and Beth. While he was bedding down Spunk, he felt so wide awake and ready for anything that he told himself he meant to go "right straight home."

But the lady was watching for him when he returned. She opened the door and then another door, pointed upstairs and told him to go right up to bed; he would find everything made comfortable for him. By this time, the long night's excitement had cooled down. The warm, quiet room and the thought of a bed made the poor boy feel so tired he knew he could not drag his feet over the frozen distance between him and Mother.

"I guess I shall have to give it up," he said wearily. "I meant to go home so Mother wouldn't be scared all night, but I'm afraid I couldn't get there."

"Of course you couldn't," his hostess assured him promptly. "It would just be committing suicide to try it. Go right upstairs and get some rest. In the morning bright and early you can make it all right with your mother. If I had anybody to send, I would let her know this minute that you are safe. But we have just lost our faithful hired man. This Mike is a new servant, and" — she came closer and spoke softly — "I think he drinks. Indeed I am sure he had been drinking tonight when he came home, and I am afraid of him."

"Ugh!" groaned Reuben aloud when he got safely to the upstairs room. "Two drunkards! I ought to stay all night to take care of her. Reuben Watson Stone, if you needed a temperance lecture, I think you have had one tonight."

"Hail, Columbia!" This remark followed his amazed stare around the beautiful room to which he had been directed. Soft carpet, soft curtains, soft bed, bright fire, bright gaslight! Reuben had never in his life been alone in such a room before. For fully five minutes he wandered up and down, examining, admiring, delighting his eyes with the sight of all that beauty. He tried to fill his memory with the details so he could describe it all to Beth.

Then the tears suddenly collected in his eyes as he thought of Beth watching, waiting, crying, and of his mother growing pale with watching and fear.

"I shouldn't have stayed!" he moaned. "I should have gone straight home, even if I froze." At that moment his eyes rested on a little stand which was carefully covered with a napkin showing odd-shaped bulges of something underneath. He raised the napkin curiously and beheld bread and butter, the wing and the leg of a chicken, a piece of frosted cake and a dish of canned strawberries!

Reuben discovered he was hungry. Why not? When did he eat that breakfast with Miss Hunter? "Seems three days ago, at the very least," he muttered. He felt in his pockets for the packages she had sent him to get. Yes, they were safe. "She'll think I went to Greenland to get 'em," he chuckled, "and I nearly did."

Tears and laughter both came easily for Reuben tonight. He fell to eating the bread and butter and decided that not even Miss Hunter's was quite equal to it. While he ate he pulled off his boots and realized his feet were *very* tired. Presently the jacket was thrown aside, and in less time than it takes me to tell it, he was in the middle of that nice bed. He thought he would rest himself just a little while and then get up and slip away home. He would not go to sleep at all, he told himself, for fear he should not be able to awaken in a few minutes. But the bed was so soft, the room so warm and inviting, and his head and feet and arms and hands so very, very tired!

He had just time to say to himself, What a lovely, scrumptious bed this is. If I *should* go to sleep I don't believe I could wake up again. That was the last he knew of himself for hours and hours.

CHAPTER VIII

TEMPTATION RESISTED

The next thing Reuben knew, the sun was shining directly into his eyes. He sat up straight and looked around.

"Halloo!" he exclaimed with utter amazement in his face. "What's all this? Where am I, and how did I get here? Beth!"

But, of course, Beth was three miles away and didn't answer.

"This is the biggest dream I ever had!" he said. Then his memory began to wake up and carry him back over that long, wild ride of the night before.

"I declare it's morning!" he said at last, much astonished. "And here I am in bed instead of being at home." Whereupon he hopped out to the middle of the floor and dressed in haste. His plan was to slip out and away and get home before the people in this grand house would know anything about it.

But the sad-faced mother downstairs did not intend any such thing. He opened his door very softly, but she also opened one on the opposite side of the hall and smiled a good morning.

"I want you to come in and have some breakfast with me," she said, as they went down the wide staircase together, "and after that my son would like to see you for a few minutes."

"I ought to get home just as fast as my feet will take me," declared Reuben, dismayed at this new delay. "I meant to go last night, after I had rested a little bit. But I fell asleep. I don't know how I did it, and I don't know what Mother will think."

"She will think you did just right when you tell her about it," the lady smiled. "You see if she doesn't. It won't take you long to eat some breakfast. By that time the southside cars will be running, and they will take you faster than your feet."

"Yes'm," agreed Reuben, "but my feet will do it cheaper." He followed her into the elegant dining room, since that seemed to be the only thing he could do just then. As he did so, the memory of his breakfast the morning before flashed over him.

I declare! I take my breakfasts out nowadays, he said to himself, laughing over the strangeness of it all.

This was a different dining room from Miss Hunter's. It was handsomely furnished, and the table was set with silver and china and glistened with a dozen pretty things of which Reuben did not know the name. It was set for two.

Reuben presently found himself seated opposite the pale lady and waited on by a deft servant to steak and toast and coffee and canned fruit and griddle cakes and maple syrup and, well, a number of other dishes with which he was unacquainted. Never had he taken breakfast in such style before.

Indeed, I may say he had never expected to be surrounded by such elegance. But, surveying it all, he decided in a second that he liked it. And, in about one second more, he had resolved to furnish his dining room in just this way when he became a man.

"So you are the man of the house?" said his hostess, as if she could read his thoughts.

"Yes'm," he said, blushing to think what she would say if she knew how he was planning to furnish his house. "I have a mother and sister to support. I haven't been able to do it yet. Mother has to work, and so does Beth. But then I help, and one of these days I expect to do it all."

"I believe you will," she said, looking at him earnestly. Those were much the same words Miss Priscilla Hunter had spoken to him the morning before. It was certainly very encouraging to find that these two women neither laughed at him nor were doubtful about it. They evidently believed in him.

I can't say that he enjoyed this breakfast quite so much as the one in Miss Hunter's south room. The truth was, he felt a little embarrassed by the expanse of his napkin and the weight of his silver fork and the careful attention of the servant. Still he managed to eat quite a hearty breakfast, in a hurry though he was. Of course, it would not do to leave until Spunk's master, or rather Spunk's owner, saw him, since he wanted to do so.

The somber-faced lady was pleasant and very interested in his mother and Beth. About the latter especially she asked many questions as to her age, size, appearance and the like. Reuben, who thought his sister was a beauty, had no objection to describing her, so the conversation went on nicely.

At last the lady arose from the table. "Now we will go in and see Edward a moment."

They passed through the hall across another large, elegant room into the same bright spot where he had landed the night before. Edward was still in the bed where he had been rolled and tumbled by Reuben himself, but all trace of disorder had disappeared. He was awake and alert, though very pale with heavy rings of black under his eyes.

"Well, my boy," he said as Reuben stood in the door. "I hear you and Spunk had a time of it last night. Ran away, did he? The scamp! I remember something about his being restless. One of my hard headaches came on in the afternoon, and I was soon beyond having much idea of what was going on. How did you come to be with me, my boy? I don't remember."

"You asked me to ride, sir," explained Reuben. "I remembered Spunk and thought I would like a ride with him."

"You remembered Spunk?"

"Yes, sir. I held him for you one day, and you gave me a shiner by mistake."

"Ah, yes, and you ran back to me with it. I remember your face now; I thought it looked familiar. Well, let me see, didn't you finally scud off before I paid you? Or didn't I go off? How was it? Anyway, I don't believe you got any pay. That was a regular cheat, wasn't it? Well, we must try and make it right. How far did you travel last night?"

Reuben, as well as he could, described the route and the plan of getting home.

Mr. Edward occasionally interrupted him to say, "Is it possible?"

"I declare!" he exclaimed when the story was finished. "You are a plucky fellow. Very few strangers can manage Spunk, though he is well behaved generally, too. Well, I owe you a great deal of thanks for your skill and good sense. Now what else do you need, besides thanks? Mother tells me you have a family to support."

"Yes, sir," said Reuben seriously, "a mother and sister."

"Pretty heavy burden at your age. What do you do for a living?"

"Hold horses, and all such things," answered Reuben with a twinkle in his eye.

"Then you have no regular employment."

"Yes, sir, my regular employment all winter has been to look for steady work. But I haven't found it yet."

His questioner interrupted him to laugh heartily and then said, "I'm disposed to think I can help you in that business. Are you particular as to what you do?"

"I am if I can get it to do. I've tried for the particular things first and stood ready to take the others, if the particular ones didn't come along."

"I see. Well, Mother, don't you believe this chap is just the one they need down at St. Mark's?"

"I shouldn't be surprised if he would suit them," the lady said.

"I think he will. I'll recommend you, my boy, and you will be pretty sure to secure the place if I do. I have some authority there. It will be a good place, steady work and good wages. You can begin to support that family of yours on a better plan than you have been doing lately."

"What is St. Mark's, if you please?" asked Reuben, his sparkling eyes saying "thank you" for him with every twinkle.

"Well, it's a wine parlor, one of the best in the city. You would be a sort of cash boy and a waiter in general. I hardly know what your duties would be. But I know the work is not hard, and the pay is good."

Then all the sparkle disappeared from Reuben's eyes. The memory of both his resolution and his positive promise made just the night before stalked up before him. "I'm very sorry," he began with a red face, "that is, I mean...I think...." He paused in great confusion.

"Well, what's the trouble? You need not be afraid you won't be able to suit them. You are just the quick-witted chap they need. I suppose I may as well say that you shall have the place, though I don't meddle with their hired help as a rule. I'll make this exception."

"I thank you," stammered Reuben, "but, if you please, I would rather not. That is — well, you see, sir," and having resolved to speak out, he held up his head and stated boldly, "the fact is, I have made a pledge never to work for *rum* in any shape — sell it, drink it or help other folks to drink it. So I can't work there, though I'm much obliged to you for the chance."

"Upon my word and honor!" said Spunk's owner, rising slowly on one elbow and staring at Reuben as though he were a curiosity. "You are really the coolest chap I ever came across. So you won't take the place, eh? Very well. Of course, if your wish for regular work is all a humbug, why, you can afford to throw away chances like this. I supposed you were really in earnest. Then I don't know of anything I can do for you. Mother, I guess you may as well let him go. He is simply impudent, and that is the most there is of him." The gentleman slowly lowered himself from his elbow, rolled over and shut his eyes.

Reuben did not speak at all. If he had had anything to say, he couldn't have said it then. His voice was choked with tears. It was a great and sore disappointment. To be so close to regular work and good wages and then to see them slip away from him was too much. He turned away and wiped two great tears from his eyes with his threadbare jacket sleeve.

"I am afraid you have been very foolish," the pale lady said sadly. "Edward had taken a liking to you and would have done well by you. He owns the saloon. People *will* sell liquor, and people will buy it. You might as well earn your living that way as in any other. Because you work in a wine parlor is no reason why you should drink liquor, you know. I hope you will *never* do that. But you must not throw away your chances to help your mother for the sake of mere notions."

Poor Reuben! The tears were dropping rapidly now. He was so ashamed of them and so angry about them — and *so* disappointed about Spunk's master.

"Never mind," the lady said kindly, seeing the tears. "I am very grateful to you for all that you did last night. So is Edward. He is a little vexed now. You must remember that you were rather rude to him, though I know you didn't mean to be. He will get over it. When you have had time to think about this and change your mind, come and see me. I think I can still secure the place for you — that is, if you are not too slow. But I think you do things in a hurry. Meanwhile, I want you to take this basket I've packed to your mother with my love. In this paper is something to help you support your family. Here is a streetcar ticket. You know to take the Blue Line on the south side."

Reuben, still in a daze over the rapid changes in his life during these days and almost before he realized what he was about, found himself signaling a Blue Line car. He had a large market basket — as much as he could carry — on his arm and a little bit of a paper package in his hand.

CHAPTER IX

Anxiety

rs. Stone and Beth will always remember that last night of the old year, when they sat up and watched and waited for Reuben and he did not appear. "Mother," Beth had said about a dozen times, "do you think anything has happened to him?"

"What *could* happen to him, child?" Mrs. Stone would reply, her voice almost cross. "Reuben knows the way through the city as well as a policeman. He is a careful boy, and a great many of the policemen know him. If there had been any kind of an accident, we should have heard of it by this time." But she peered out of the window into the darkness and started at every sound. She grew so pale and dizzy when she heard a strange step and a knock at her door that she had to sit down in the nearest chair and send Beth to the door.

It was only a blundering errand boy who had

mistaken the house number. Beth felt as if she would have enjoyed shaking him to pay him for giving her mother such a fright.

They set the little table out for three as usual, and the teakettle sang merrily. Beth prepared to toast the bread for a treat. As a rule they did not toast the bread because they were so apt to eat a great deal more than they needed. It took a certain kind of fire that was not economical, but for New Year's Eve Beth decided to venture. On this night the coals glowed beautifully, then dimmed, then died out almost entirely. On discovering it, Beth built them up again with sticks from the morning's stock of kindlings. She cried silently while she wondered what they would do if Reuben were not there to kindle the morning fire. Then, indeed, they would be sure that something *awful* had happened.

"Mother," she said quietly, "don't you think you better eat your supper before the tea gets spoiled?"

"Not just yet, child. Eat your own supper, if you are hungry."

"Hungry!" Poor Beth swallowed and swallowed to hold back the tears. She wondered if she would ever be hungry again.

By and by, as it grew later, the mother took her turn at advice. "Come, Beth, you may as well eat your bread and milk. Reuben must have had some supper by this time. He has stayed late to help somewhere, and they have given him his supper."

"I will eat if you will," Beth said wistfully. Her mother looked so pale and heavy-eyed that she felt able to push back her own anxiety and try to comfort her.

"I'm not hungry just now," Mrs. Stone said. She dropped the corner of the curtain she held up to peer out into the darkness, then returned to her sewing.

After a little while, Beth of her own accord put away the bread and the milk and the little bit of butter, untasted, and came and sat down beside her mother. As her eyes rested on Reuben's slate and arithmetic, her brave little heart gave out; she leaned her head on the book and cried outright.

"I wouldn't be so foolish," Mrs. Stone reproved. "Crying won't do any good. It's likely that something is keeping him."

Beth felt sure of that. But the awful question was, What was it? She had her head hidden in her apron and did not see the tears her mother brushed away as she spoke.

Meanwhile, Miss Priscilla Hunter had been bustling about all day, accomplishing no end of work in her new home. By night her sweet-smelling south room was in complete order and shone like a picture. Miss Priscilla did much besides work that day — or, at least, much besides arranging her room and tacking down her carpet that was yet in the line of ordinary work for her. She studied her neighbors.

Miss Priscilla was not one who would live for three months next door to a family and not know what their names were, what they did for a living, where they went to church and whether they belonged to her Captain or not. She was always interested in her neighbors.

Beth Stone interested her exceedingly. She had glimpses of her a number of times during the short, busy day. "That must be Beth," she said aloud to herself, with a sagacious nod of her gray head while she stood at the upper landing, and Beth tripped down the stairs.

"A spry little girl and as bright as a cricket, I'll venture. She ought to be — to be the sister of such a brother. I wonder how the brave young man is getting on and whether he sees his way clearer toward supporting his family. He'll support them yet. He will have to see to it that that little sister wears thicker clothing though, with this cold weather — calico, and rather thin at that. Calico is cheap, I know, but cold stuff, and always and forever wanting to go into the washtub. I like it in summer for that very reason. But there's my blue merino tucked away doing good to nobody. It would be just the thing for a New Year's dress for the child. If the 'man of the house' didn't object — but he would. The child might earn it. I wonder what she can do — several things, I'll venture. I wonder what kind of a mother she has — a good mother, I think. A boy and a girl with such faces are apt to have a good mother — not always, but it is more than likely."

So Miss Priscilla talked to herself and planned and watched and waited. By night it really seemed to her that she was pretty well acquainted with the Stones. By dark she too began to be somewhat anxious because the man of the house did not appear.

"I'm sorry he is out so late," she said, stopping frequently to peer out of the window. "I hope it isn't his custom. It won't do for a man with heavy responsibilities like his."

As it grew later, her anxiety gave way to positive alarm, mingled with a great pity for the mother and sister across the hall. If he was what she thought him, a trustworthy boy, this must be a new thing, and their anxiety must be great. She listened for sounds from the north room. At last when she heard an actual outburst of tears from poor Beth, she seized a cup from her little corner cupboard and started.

Just as Mrs. Stone was saying reprovingly, "I wouldn't be so foolish," a tap came at the door. The mother's face paled suddenly again, and Beth sprang to answer the knock.

"It is only your neighbor, Priscilla Hunter," said a cheery voice whose owner walked in without an invitation. "I've come to prove that I am a neighbor, and one of the borrowing kind, too. Could you let me have a little speck of soda? I've a bit of sour milk. If I hadn't been so foolish as to forget to buy soda, I could have some griddle cakes for New Year's."

Mrs. Stone arose civilly and took the cup. She got the soda, handed it back to her neighbor and stood waiting as though she expected her to thank her and go.

Such was not Miss Priscilla's intention. "Thank you," she said heartily. Then she set the cup down on the stand and commented, "Why, your room isn't quite so large as mine, is it? That is cozier for winter. So *you* are Beth? I've wanted to see you all day. Reuben took breakfast with me this morning, and he talked a great deal about you. By the way, he is late tonight, isn't he?"

Beth could stand it no longer. At the mention of the dear name she burst into tears again.

"Elizabeth, I am ashamed of you," said her mother sharply but with a quivering lip. Then in a few words she explained their nameless terror. "He has never been so late before," she said trembling, "and I don't know what to think."

"I'm glad of it," Miss Priscilla said in the cheeriest of tones, helping herself to a chair. "If he were in the habit of being so late, why, then, Miss Beth, you might cry for a purpose. It would be pretty certain that some awful habit had gotten hold of him. But a boy who *always* comes home early isn't going to stay late without a good reason. He went off this morning to support his family as ambitious as if he were the president. I daresay, with its being the last day of the year, business has been brisk. He has found himself late at night so far from home that his good common sense has told him to stay all night. It is piercing cold, and he is a prudent boy as well as a brave one. I kind of think you won't see him till morning."

Beth wiped the tears from her eyes and looked at her mother. A dozen times over she had said to herself in the last hour, Oh, what if he *shouldn't* come all night? What should we do! *What should we do?* She had not dared to put it into words for fear it would sound so awful! Yet here it was in plain English, and it actually had a comforting sound. Something of the same thought was in the mother's heart.

"I don't know," she said, shaking her head at their visitor. But her voice was somewhat thawed from its civil coldness. "Reuben is a prudent and thoughtful boy for his years. He would think of Beth and me the first thing and know that we would be frightened about him. I doubt if he could be persuaded to stay."

"Yes, he could," Miss Priscilla insisted, still in that positive way which somehow on this night was so reassuring. "You see, his very thoughtfulness would help him. Suppose he is four or five miles away at this minute. It is bitter cold. If he undertook to walk it, he might almost freeze and put himself in danger of sickness. Being a boy of unusual common sense, he knows it and would say, 'They'll be a little worried about me, of course. But I can make it all right in the morning. That will be better than walking home late in the cold and getting sick. Mother wouldn't like that.' "

Was Miss Priscilla a prophet? Her voice was so cheery and so definite. It actually comforted the mother to hear such possibilities suggested. "He always thinks of his mother," she said gratefully. She told herself that if Reuben did come home safely, and nothing dreadful happened, she would enjoy this new neighbor who looked on the bright side of things.

Miss Hunter seemed bent on making herself agreeable. She chatted on about Reuben regarding what he had said and how he had helped her in the morning. She told them of the plans they had made about milk and how careful he had been to say that Beth must only go for it when the weather was pleasant. She would like the walk, he said. And so by dint of busy talking she contrived to make the next hour pass more quickly than the last two had done. But now it was very late indeed, and the mother could no longer control her strong desire to find her boy.

"If I could only go out and look for him," she said in a wistful tone to her new friend. "But where could I go?"

"Sure enough. You see you have no means of knowing which way he went nor where he is sheltered now. You would just get your death from cold and do him no good. I feel it all over me that the boy is safe and comfortable somewhere. Now I'll just tell you the truth. I took a great liking to that boy of yours this morning, and I've thought about him a good deal all day. He seemed almost like kin to me somehow. Tonight I found myself watching for him. When I discovered he didn't come home, I got worried about him. So I just got down on my knees and asked the Lord to take him in His care and make sure he got through all right. He kind of sent me the answer that He would do just that thing. Do you often have such out and out answers to prayer as that?"

"No," Reuben's mother admitted with conviction. "I *never* have."

As for Beth, she dried her eyes, lifted up her head and looked at Miss Hunter in amazement. How could God have told her that He would take care of Reuben? she wondered.

"Well, now, I do real often, and they always come out right, of course. I never had a clearer answer than I did tonight, so I feel real safe and comfortable about him. You don't know what a relief it is to go right to the Lord with your worries. Oh, yes, I hope you *do* know all about it. But if you haven't tried it tonight, I know it will help you. Now I propose that we three kneel right down now and speak to the Lord about Reuben. It will kind of rest and help us to hear Him say over again that He will attend to it. For sure, Beth will be helped by it ever so much. Don't you want to try it, my dear?"

Beth's knowledge of praying was confined to the few Sundays in which she had been to church. She had seen the minister close his eyes, fold his hands and talk to God. But she still knew enough to be aware that it was a respectable thing to do. In fact, she dimly remembered when her little sister was sick and had died years ago; the minister came two or three times and always prayed. So she did not at all like the idea of praying about Reuben because prayer in a home was associated in her mind with awful trouble. But she still said, "Yes, ma'am," faintly.

Without more ado Miss Hunter slipped on her knees. Mrs. Stone sat bolt upright, but she stopped her needle and rested her head on her hand. Beth put her weary little head on the table, and Miss Hunter prayed.

It was not like the prayers Beth had heard in the church. She couldn't explain the difference, but she *felt* it — so much so that once she raised her head softly and looked around the room. It seemed as if Miss Hunter was talking with somebody who was standing right beside her. It was a very cheery prayer without a hint of possible danger to Reuben. It simply asked that he might be taken care of all through the cold night, that he might sleep safely and sweetly and arrive home early in the morning. Then there was a sentence or two of thanksgiving because she had been heard and answered. Again Beth glanced about her and wondered who could have brought an answer.

"Do you know anything about that poor old lady who has the room in back of ours?" inquired Miss Hunter as soon as she arose from her knees. She had concluded that they had talked enough about Reuben. "Her door was ajar as I passed by there this afternoon, and I thought she seemed very feeble. Who takes care of her?"

Mrs. Stone uttered an exclamation of dismay. "Why, that is old Mother Perkins," she said hastily. "I declare, I forgot all about her in my anxiety over Reuben. I haven't been near her tonight. I always check on her these cold nights, tuck her in and see that she is as comfortable as I can make her. Nobody takes care of her, ma'am, except us neighbors. The city furnishes her enough to keep her from starving, and she has a son who manages to pay the rent on that room. He comes home once a month to see her. She has been bedridden for a week and has needed more care than usual. I ought to go in there this minute." And she quickly rolled up her sewing.

"If that is the case, she belongs to me, too," Miss Hunter said in the same tone she might have used if she had discovered a little fortune left to her. "I'll just stay with Beth while you see if she is all right. Tomorrow I'll get acquainted with her and take my turn. I shouldn't wonder if she would like one of my nice griddle cakes for her breakfast."

But Mrs. Stone returned in haste. Poor old Mother Perkins was tossing from one side of her bed to the other and groaning in pain. She needed all the help she could get and as soon as possible. Now there was work for the two families.

Beth coaxed up the dying coals and added more. Miss Hunter dashed into her own room for a scuttleful and heaped them on recklessly. Between them they filled the two teakettles and a large iron pot with water. They ran from room to room, first hunting for the mustard. Beth held the light while Miss Hunter's deft fingers rummaged through a still unpacked basket. Then they searched in the green-covered trunk for flannel. They wrung out strips of cloth scalding hot from the water and fed the fire and fed the kettles and did a dozen other things. The night passed quickly away.

Reuben was by no means forgotten, but Beth's heart was lighter. It had been ever since that prayer when she had peeped to try to see the messenger, for someone had certainly come with an answer. Hadn't Miss Hunter thanked God for it? And if the answer was a joyful one, as she seemed to be sure it was, why should there be any more worry? Beth was getting some new ideas tonight.

As for her mother, her heart had smitten her for forgetting poor old Mother Perkins and letting her get cold enough to bring on those dreadful cramping pains. She put Reuben and everyone else aside and gave herself entirely to fighting the pain.

It was not until the faint gray dawn of a new day was glimmering in the east that the three families settled into quiet.

At one point Miss Hunter said, "Now I declare if I'm not afraid your 'man of the house' will come and find that his mother has been up all night without a wink of sleep. Then I don't know what he would do. You just go and lie down for a bit, you and Beth. Poor child, how she has trotted back and forth and up and down. I'll shade the light and sit here by Mother Perkins. She is so quiet now that I think she can sleep a little, too. Then we will all be chipper for New Year's morning."

"Oh, dear," said Mrs. Stone. She could not help wondering what New Year's morning would bring her. She had not felt the presence of the messenger with the answer to Miss Hunter's prayer as plainly as Beth had. But she was so tired out that it was not hard to persuade her to lie down on the bed.

She only waited to say, "As soon as it is light enough to pick my way out, I'm going to the corner police to notify him about Reuben." Then she fell into a heavy sleep.

Beth held her eyes open long enough to whisper softly to herself, "I don't believe he will need the police. I believe he will come in the morning. I'm sure she was answered." Then she too slept.

CHAPTER X

THE RETURN

appy New Year!" said a voice close to Beth's ear. She dreamed it was Reuben and that he came to her with his hands full of gold pieces with which he meant to buy a cow and a chair and a farm in the country. She awakened with a start to find the sun of New Year's morning flooding the world — and Reuben in truth standing beside her.

"Is it really and truly you?" she said, sitting up straight and rubbing her bewildered eyes. "Oh, Mother, Mother! Here he is, and he is alive, and nothing is the matter!"

Mrs. Stone opened her own heavy eyes, and New Year's morning began.

"My sakes!" said Miss Hunter. She opened the door softly, so as not to disturb the sleepers, and shut it suddenly and softly, so as not to disturb the people who were wide awake and holding a family council. Then she rushed away to make her griddle cakes.

Miss Hunter must have been hungry. She whisked the cover from her little stone jar and poured out a full bowl of nice, creamy-looking sour milk.

Priscilla! Don't you know that a bowl *full* of sour milk will make cakes enough for five or six people, and there is only one of you?

But Miss Hunter gave no heed, if any voice whispered that to her, but measured her soda with care and sprinkled it into the milk. It presently made quite a hissing noise. One who didn't understand the work of soda when it meets with anything sour might have thought a miniature steam engine had set up business in the bowl. At last the milk gurgled, changing its tone entirely.

Miss Hunter, who had been stirring it briskly all the while, commented with a satisfied air, "Oh, you're sweet, are you? All right...pity *folks* can't be made sweet-tempered as easily as that."

She broke an egg into another bowl and whisked it frantically with a fork until it was bubbling suds. Then she mixed the yellow foam into the white foam and stirred in little tin shovels of flour, adding salt. By and by she mercilessly dropped a spoonful of the mass onto a hot griddle — and lo! a lovely, round, brown cake, puffy and flaky.

"As nice as the nicest," smiled Miss Hunter.

She drew out her table and spread it with a clean cloth. Then she dashed over to her tiny cupboard and brought out four plates. Had she forgotten that she was only one person? If she had, she was happy over the mistake. She added spoons, forks, knives and cups, four of each, and made a ridiculous quantity of coffee for one woman.

When everything was ready, even to the baking of a great many of the puffy cakes, some of which she buttered and sugared and some of which she only buttered, she set four chairs around her table. Then she slipped across the hall once more and knocked boldly at the north door. Reuben answered the knock. He laughed when he saw Miss Hunter.

"Good morning," he greeted her. "I've got 'em. They're here in my pocket, safe and sound," he said as he dived down for the things she had ordered. "I didn't know but you'd think I went to the North Pole for them. And I started — I guess."

"Dear me," said Miss Hunter, "I'd forgotten about the things. It was so long ago — last year sometime, wasn't it? Happy New Year to you. We began ours early in this house. Now have they told you that you were going out to breakfast for New Year's morning?"

"Why, no, ma'am!" said Reuben, astonished. He was just about to introduce his mother to Miss Hunter. Then he laughed. "I'm not getting used to going out to breakfast — even though I've been doing it lately."

"Well," said Miss Hunter, joining in his laugh and turning to his mother. "It's the strangest thing. You know I was up some last night. Since I was kind of sleepy this morning, what did I do but go and mix up the whole of my sour milk. The result is, I've cakes enough for half a dozen families the size of mine. So you'll have to come and help me eat them for New Year's."

Of course, they understood her little pretense of being absentminded. And of course they were polite enough to step over to her pleasant room for breakfast and indeed grateful for her kindness and to be happy and enjoy those cakes and those cups of coffee. Mrs. Stone, at least, had not enjoyed such a meal in many a day.

"What did I do with my basket?" asked Reuben suddenly, as Miss Hunter helped him to the seventh cake. Strange to say, in spite of his elegant breakfast eaten from real china dishes and with a solid silver fork and spoon, Reuben was hungry. "I had a basket when I came in. Where did I put it?"

"You set it behind the stove in our room," said Beth. "I saw it and wondered what was in it."

"I don't know myself," declared Reuben, "except it's something that is awful heavy. I didn't know but what it would break my arm after I left the car. I guess I better bring it in and see what it is."

A wonderful basket it was! You should have heard the exclamations as Reuben drew out the parcels one by one. He found mince pie cuddled nicely among rows of doughnuts on the top layer; a turkey, dressed and even stuffed, ready for the oven; a dish of cooked cranberries, looking like a great mound of trembling jelly as Reuben uncovered the dish; a large, round frosted cake; and a chicken pie. Each little niche in the basket was filled in with nuts and candies.

On the bottom lay a smooth, thick package that Reuben guessed must be a quilt for the turkey to sleep on. But a paper was pinned to the string, and on the paper in delicate handwriting were the words "For Beth."

Beth's trembling fingers picked at the knot until Reuben gave in to her impatience and his own and cut the string. Behold, there was a lovely little fur hood and cape. The cape was not so little either, for it reached below Beth's waist.

It was curious to watch how the different members of this family reacted to the surprise.

"Oh! oh! oh!" squealed Beth. She jumped up and down and clapped her hands. As a rule she was a quiet little thing. But she had never in her life had a soft, furry garment to wear, and she thought the hood and cape were *so* lovely.

Mrs. Stone wiped her eyes and said nothing. She was very surprised and glad. She wondered if Miss Hunter's prayer of the night before could have had anything to do with all this.

"My sake!" exclaimed Miss Hunter. "Isn't that splendid!"

She thought, but did not say, how well the merino in her trunk, when it was made to fit Beth, would look alongside the fur hood and cape.

As for Reuben, his eyes held a sparkle that was pleasant to see, when one remembered they were shining because of his sister's gift.

"She must have been expecting me for at least a week and been getting ready," he said soberly.

They all laughed.

"We must have New Year's dinner," Mrs. Stone said, rising to the occasion. Then they began to plan. As soon as Miss Hunter found herself counted in, as if she were one of the family, she had her plan ready.

"Now I'll tell you what it is. Your mother was foolish enough to sit up for you last night, and you know you did not get in very early (calling it night). It stands to reason that she doesn't feel quite chipper this morning. What she needs is a good long nap, and she can have it as well as not, while I am cooking the dinner. Here's Beth to help me, and you, and we'll get the dinner fit for the president — if he needs one more than we do. What do you say?"

But here Mrs. Stone shook her head and reminded Miss Hunter that she, too, was up all night taking care of Mother Perkins. She must be quite as tired as any of them.

This, Miss Hunter assured her, was not the case. She was used to it; there was nothing like getting used to things. Her poor father was sick for years and couldn't sleep nights. She would stay up with him part of every night, sometimes all night. She grew so accustomed to having her rest broken that it seemed almost foolish to lie in bed all night. She often got up and sat in a chair awhile, just because she could not sleep.

She had her own way — the truth is, she was very apt to have — and in another hour or two the north room was darkened, and poor, tired Mrs. Stone was sound asleep on the bed. She could hardly remember any other weekday when she had actually gone to bed in the middle of the day.

In the south room a delicious smell was already escaping from the oven where the great turkey began to make little sputtery comments. Beth and Miss Hunter were washing the dishes used for cooking and chatting together as if they had always known and liked each other.

A royal dinner they had in that south room about two o'clock on the same day. Miss Hunter did not tell them of the great dinners she had been in the habit of managing on New Year's Days. But her cooking told the story to Mrs. Stone just as well as though she had spoken.

Not until late in the afternoon, when the dishes were washed, the party over and the guest had returned home, did Reuben unfold the piece of paper and show his mother what was hidden away in it. He had looked before and been so astonished that he had closed it quickly and shoved it down to the bottom of his pocket. Since then he had gone over every inch of the night, up to the time when he fell into that bed made of down to rest a minute. He had answered a hundred questions from the curious Beth about the rooms and the table and the pictures and the piano.

So now at last he said, "And see here, Mother. Here's something else I got." Then he placed the paper in her lap and slowly unfolded it. And, behold, a ten-dollar gold piece lay shining in it! On the inside of the paper, in the same pretty hand that had written Beth's name, was penned: "For the brave 'man of the house' to help him in the support of his family."

"I told her," Reuben explained, "that I had a family to support. I said you had to work hard now, but one of these days I meant for you to sit in a silk dress in a big armchair and not do a single thing. Well, of course, I didn't tell her *exactly* that, but she asked me questions, and I told her what I wanted to do."

The Stone family had more planning to do. It actually took hours to decide about that wonderful gleaming bit of gold. Reuben was in favor of paying a great deal of rent in advance and thus having that off their minds for a while.

"I hate rents," he said with energy. "You won't catch me paying any when I'm a man."

Then he was for buying a ton of coal and a barrel of flour. But his mother reminded him that it was growing late in the season. If the rest of the winter should be mild, they might not need a whole ton to carry them through to the days when chips and blocks of wood from new buildings would help boil their potatoes. And there was certainly no place for a barrel of flour to stand. So finally, with a little sigh, which he covered up as soon as possible, he laid the ten dollars in her hands.

"Well, Mother, there it is. I suppose the best way is to keep it and use it when you need it, just as you have always done. Only I would like to get the mean old rent paid off for a few weeks ahead. I'd just like the fun of going to Mr. Grimsby, handing it out and getting a receipt. He always acts as though he was sure we were going to cheat him out of it this time."

One other thing made Reuben sigh, even on that happy New Year's Day. Of course, he told his mother about the saloon and the offer of business. When he had finished his story, she looked sober. Something in her face disappointed him. "Didn't I do right, Mother?" he asked her eagerly. "You wouldn't have me go into such a business — would you?"

"Oh, I don't know," she admitted in a troubled tone. "We are very poor, and you and Beth both need clothes. We need almost everything in the way of provisions. It is the first chance you have had. Poor folks mustn't be too particular, I suppose. It will do for the rich to have principles, but it costs too much for us."

"Yes, but, Mother," Reuben said with a distressed face, "I should have had to wait on men with brandy and wine and all those vile things. You surely wouldn't have had me do that."

"Why, you needn't have drunk any yourself. As for waiting on other people, somebody will do that, if you don't. There will be just as much of it drunk. I don't see but that you might as well get the pay as anyone."

Poor, troubled Reuben! His mother's words did not shake his resolution in the least. Miss Hunter had burst that bubble by what she said about selling poison. But it was hard not to have her approve of his actions, as she had almost always done before this.

"I thought you would be glad," he muttered quietly. "But I couldn't have done it anyhow because I made a promise about it."

"A promise?" said his mother. "Who did you promise?"

"I promised myself last night, when I was riding along beside that drunken man, just before we crossed the track." In spite of its being broad daylight, with him safe at home with his mother, Reuben gave a little shiver.

"Besides," he said even more soberly, after a moment's hesitation, "I guess I promised God. I asked Him to take care of me, and He did, I think. And I said down in my heart that I would never taste a drop of rum and never do a single thing to help anybody else take any. He heard it, of course, and I guess maybe it is the same thing as a promise."

Here Beth, who had been a silent, attentive listener, suddenly burst forth: "I wouldn't wear any clothes that were bought with their mean old money, nor eat anything that was got by selling rum, not if I starved!"

"Dear me," said the mother, "what a couple of temperance fanatics I live with." But she said it pleasantly, and a smile brightened her face. "I suppose you are right, Reuben," she agreed after a minute. "I was a little troubled about your having lost a chance to earn some money on your and Beth's account, not on my own. But I guess it is best to keep clear of the business altogether. You are a good boy anyway, and I shall never have to worry about you as some mothers do. I don't suppose we shall starve. We never have yet, and today we have been a long way from starving."

She leaned over and kissed him in a motherly fashion. But Reuben could not forget that troubled look. He went in to make sure Miss Hunter was comfortable for the night before going to bed. It looked so cozy there that he couldn't help sitting down a minute to tell her some more about this strange day. He felt as if he had known her all his life.

"What do you think?" he said, leaning over her little table and gazing up into her kind, hazel eyes. "I had that chance we were talking about yesterday offered to me this very morning."

"What chance?" asked Miss Hunter with complete attention.

"Why, to 'hold out the poison' for other folks to drink, you know, and get good pay for it, too."

"You don't say so! And you refused it?"

"Yes'm," said Reuben gravely. "But then I had a great long temperance lecture last night from a drunken man. I couldn't go into any such business after that."

I suppose Miss Hunter saw a connection between what he had told her and the verse she quoted, although Reuben couldn't quite understand what it was. But this was what she said: "He shall give his angels charge concerning thee, to keep thee in all thy ways."

CHAPTER XI

LOOKING FOR WORK

Despite his wonderful last day of the year and the rather remarkable opening of the New Year, our young man of the house did not feel much richer than usual as he trudged down Second Street the next morning, wrapped in the old red shawl. It was very cold. Ten dollars to pay the rent and supply coal and other provisions would not last long. That very morning his mother had been refused work at the tailor's because the New Year's hurry was over. The last half of a hard winter was still before them. If he could only find some regular work!

There was St. Mark's. "No, there isn't," he said out loud stoutly to himself. "So far as I am concerned, it is just exactly as though there *wasn't* any such place. I'm not going there, that's sure! Even if I starve, I don't believe I could do it. You see, Mother didn't take that ride with me the other night. If she had, she would feel different."

Still he could not help feeling dreary. If tailoring was slack, it was quite likely that other work would be the same, and he had failed in finding any all winter thus far. Could he hope to be more successful now?

"Never you mind," Miss Hunter had said to him in a cheery way as he left that morning. "It will all come out right. You'll see. If you ought to have some work to do today, don't you suppose the Father up there will see to it that you find it?"

This was a new doctrine to Reuben, but he thought about it as he trudged along and felt somewhat comforted. God had taken so many pains to save his life during that dangerous night. He must think a little about me, thought the boy, and it would be just as easy for Him to find me some work as it was to take care of me.

"That is a manly looking chap," observed a gentleman who stood leaning against the glass door of a downtown grocery, nodding his head toward Reuben as he passed.

"Yes," agreed the young gentleman who stood near. "He is an odd sort of a genius. I became quite interested in him and tried to help him a little when I found he was looking for work. But I guess there is more talk than actual desire about it. I found him hard to suit."

"Is that so? I talked with him a few minutes the other day, and I thought him a particularly alert boy. He said he had a family to support."

"Yes, that's a favorite remark of his. I offered him work only yesterday, and he refused it."

"What sort of work?"

"Steady, and good pay. Mother ran across him accidentally and took a fancy to him. For her sake

I tried to help him. I could have gotten him in at St. Mark's as a waiter, but he declined the place because they sell liquor there." Spunk's master laughed as though that were a good joke.

"Good for him! I like his pluck," exclaimed the gentleman leaning against the door. He opened it and looked out after Reuben.

"I'm almost tempted to take him home with me if that is the sort of chap he is," the man said as he peered down the street. "I wonder what became of him? Do you know where to find him?"

"Not I. Mother does, I presume. She took a fancy to him and sent a basket of things home to his family, I believe. But, Mr. Barrows, I think you would be disappointed in him. He strikes me as having impudence rather than goodness."

"I didn't think so," said Mr. Barrows. "When I ran across him day before yesterday, I thought him a remarkably bright, civil fellow. And an out-and-out temperance boy is hard to find these days. It isn't the busy season with us, especially for boys. But if I could get hold of one of the right sort it would be a rarity, and I would take him along."

Meanwhile, unaware that Spunk's master was at work getting him a situation, Reuben forlornly left the store he had just entered in order to warm his fingers and try to find an errand to do. He glanced up and down the street, uncertain which way to turn.

"I just wonder which way I *ought* to go?" he mused aloud. "I suppose it makes a difference. If I am to find any work today, of *course* it makes a difference. The question is, At which end of the city is it to be found? It's odd now to think that God knows all about it. I wonder if He won't tell me which way to travel. I s'pose if I belonged to

Him, He would find some way of showing me just what to do and how to do it. Miss Hunter talks just as if He did that for her."

This bewildered boy stood there undecided. Which way should he turn? Was there work for him somewhere? Did God mean for him to have it? Would He show him how to find it?

Reuben had never had such strange ideas before. His recent experience, as well as his new friend, Miss Hunter, had made an impression on him from which he could not escape. At last he turned and headed back up Second Street; he could not have told you why. He had certainly hunted carefully on either side as he came down and saw no sign of "Boys Wanted" for anything. Still something made him feel that he was to go back, so back he went.

It was well he did. Mr. Barrows was keeping a lookout and spotted him as soon as he appeared in sight. He opened the door and motioned him in.

"How do you do, sir?" Reuben greeted Spunk's master. His respectful bow was not lost on Mr. Barrows. Whatever the boy had done to annoy that young gentleman, it was clear that he was not ashamed of it.

"Well, sir," returned Spunk's owner, "found any work yet?"

"No, sir, but I guess I will. I'm beginning to feel like it."

"I doubt it. You are too particular. Do you really *want* work, now, upon your honor?"

"Try me and see," Reuben said with a quiet good nature, ignoring the sneer that was hiding in the question. "Is Spunk well this morning, sir?" Nothing was to be accomplished by sneering at him.

The young man, with a careless answer to this earnest question, left the store.

Now it was Mr. Barrows's turn. "So you are still looking for work?"

"Yes, sir. A body would think there was nothing for boys to do. I've been miles since I saw you and not found much of anything."

"How did you fall in with Mr. Harrison?"

"Who is he, sir?"

"Why, that young man who just left the store. I heard you inquiring after his horse."

"Oh, I didn't know his name. We took a ride together the other night, and Spunk got afraid and ran away. We didn't get home until 'most morning."

"How did you come to ride with Mr. Harrison?"

"Why, he told me to jump in, so I did — and a wild time we had of it. You see," said Reuben, stepping nearer and dropping his voice, "he had been drinking, and he whipped Spunk. The horse wouldn't bear it and just flew away — went straight ahead in his fright, instead of making a turn, and got scared worse at the railroad crossing. The gentleman fell asleep. It was dark and windy, and we had an *awful* time — Spunk and I. I thought none of us would ever get home alive, but we did."

"I should have thought that would have been a good temperance lesson for you, my boy," Mr. Barrows said, his face very serious.

"Yes, sir," Reuben said simply and gravely.

Mr. Barrows scrutinized him closely and thought, I don't believe he needed any. I believe he is a good boy. "How would you like to get work out of town?" he asked suddenly.

"I wouldn't mind, sir, whether it was out of

town, or in, if I could take my family. I couldn't go without them, you know."

"Couldn't!" repeated Mr. Barrows. He began to feel that the boy's family was a reality to be considered on all occasions.

"Why, no," Reuben said earnestly. "They have only me to depend on. There ought to be some man around to see after a woman and a little girl. I do a great many things that I wouldn't like to have either my mother or my sister do."

There was no mistake about it; he was a manly boy. Evan Barrows was stirred by these responses.

"I'm not sure," he said, "but that the best thing you could do would be to move your family right out to our town. Your mother and sister could get nice work and good wages. As for you, though I told you the other day I had no place for boys, I shall need one in the spring. If you happen to be the one I want, why, I could find you something to do now. I guess your wisest course would be to move. It is cheaper supporting a family in the country."

"Could I get a house, do you suppose?" questioned Reuben. His heart beat wildly over the thought of country life, such as his mother had described in the stories she had told him. He and Beth had never seen green grass or pink clover or even yellow dandelions. These were among their daydreams.

"Oh, yes, there are houses enough. There is one now, just at the foot of my lot — a nice little place for a small family. The man who lived in it has just moved out, because it was such a cold house, he said. But the real reason was, he was a shiftless fellow and didn't like to take the trouble to bank it up and put it in shape for winter. It is no colder than any other home."

"What is the rent?" asked Reuben. He could feel his heart beat clearly while he waited. He even thought he could hear it thumping when Mr. Barrows named a sum only a bit more than they paid for the north room and the big clothespress!

"I'll talk with Mother," he said eagerly. "She doesn't like the city on Beth's account. If she will agree to it, I'll move."

"Suppose I go and see her?" suggested Mr. Barrows. He liked Reuben better every minute and began to be quite anxious to have him move to the country. "I could explain some things to her better perhaps than you could."

Of course, Reuben had sense enough to be grateful for this offer. So it happened that the morning was not half spent when he appeared at the north room with a stranger.

What has that boy done now? the mother wondered as she gazed out of the window and watched Reuben crossing the street with long strides, the stranger close at his heels.

Toward the close of the talk, Mr. Barrows made a startling proposal. "Suppose the boy goes up with me and tries the work for a few days? He can look around and see the house. By that time he will know whether he wants to have you move or not. He seems to be a boy of uncommon good judgment. I have a couple of round-trip tickets here. One of them is of no use to me; it is dated, and the time will run out before I am able to use it. I bought it and then changed my mind. I'll pass Reuben back without any expense to him. It is a short distance, you see."

I wish someone could have made a picture for you of Reuben's eyes just then. A journey on the cars was another of his dreams—but a journey alone, sent off like any other businessman to look after the interests of his family! He had not expected this for years.

"Reuben!" exclaimed his mother in dismay. "Why, he is only a boy!"

"He's an unusually smart boy, though. I'll venture he could look after himself on a forty-mile journey as well as anybody could do it for him."

Considering the importance of the subject, everything was arranged quite as soon as could be expected. Reuben was to go that very afternoon on the four o'clock train to inspect his possible new home. To be sure, Mrs. Stone changed her mind ten times after Mr. Barrows left and declared she could not have Reuben going off alone. Why, he had never spent a night away from home in his life!

"Yes, I have, Mother," he said with twinkling eyes. "Spent it with a crazy horse and a crazy man."

Miss Hunter came in to hear the news and took Reuben's side with earnestness. She had no doubt that he would have a good time and a successful journey.

"It seems kind of a wild thing to do," the mother said, looking doubtfully at Reuben. "But then it doesn't cost anything, and perhaps he ought to know whether he could do the work they expect of him before we make any move. We must do *something*. I'd like to get into the country, if I could, before another summer, and this is the first shadow of a chance I've had."

She bustled around getting him ready. You would be surprised at how long it took! This family was not used to packing. Miss Hunter lent Reuben an old-fashioned carpetbag for him to carry his clothes in, and Beth packed them. There were not so many that she had any trouble in getting them in, but serious questions had to be settled.

"Reuben," she said, as he carried in an armload of kindlings (he had been piling up enough to last until he returned), "do you want to take your Bible?"

"Why, no," his mother answered. "It isn't likely he will have any time to read, and it isn't worthwhile to make the carpetbag any heavier than is necessary."

"But there will be a Sunday," Reuben said, "and I might want to read a chapter. I guess I'll take it. It isn't very heavy." So the little Bible was packed.

And there stood Reuben, by half past three, with his Sunday shirt on, his carpetbag on his arm, his cap in hand, about to bid his mother good-bye for the first time in his life.

"I'll be back in a week," he said cheerily. "And if it's all right, we'll move there, won't we? Take care of yourself, Mother. If it snows, Jimmy Briggs will come and clear your path. I spoke to him about it. He owes me a good turn or two. Beth, don't you go after milk unless it is real pleasant. Jimmy Briggs said he would as soon go as not. He hasn't much to do. Times are slack. I guess I've fixed all the kindlings you'll need, and I put some coal in my bedroom, Mother, so you won't have to go after it. Well, good-bye."

His voice choked a little over the word. Never mind if it was only for a week. He was fond enough of his mother and sister not to be ashamed at having a tear over bidding them good-bye. Beth cried outright, and Mrs. Stone wiped her eyes on her apron two or three times while she stood at the window watching her boy go down the street.

Mr. Barrows was pacing back and forth on the platform and watching for him when he reached the depot. "Here you are, eh? I began to think you would be left."

"No, sir," Reuben said with the gravity and precision of a train dispatcher. "There are four minutes yet before train time."

Whereupon the gentleman laughed, and two other gentlemen nearby nodded their heads and conjectured, "Good business talent there."

But Reuben did not hear this. He followed Mr. Barrows and took a seat with him on the train. The engine snorted and shrieked and groaned. Finally it started with such a spiteful jerk as to throw a small boy entirely from his seat, and they were off.

Reuben's first ride on the cars! You wouldn't have known it if you had been watching him. He was quiet and at ease. He had stood outside and watched the train off so many times that its way of starting was no novelty to him. So he gave his entire attention to the way things were managed inside.

Mr. Barrows found an acquaintance soon after they left the depot and went to talk to him.

Left to himself, Reuben made good use of his time. A young, pretty lady just in front of him tugged at her window to bring the blind down. The blind was obstinate and would not budge. The warm rays of the afternoon sun streamed in on the lady, making her uncomfortable, so she tried again, but to no avail. Two or three gentlemen gazed at her sleepily but did not stir.

If I had ever seen such a concern as that before, Reuben thought indignantly, I'd try to make it come down. I wonder how it is fixed, anyhow?

He leaned forward and studied it. By the time the lady had gathered enough courage to try again, he had figured out that she didn't pinch the spring at the right point. He decided to try it himself. Down came the blind, settling into place with the promptness of one that had admitted itself mastered.

"Thank you," said the young lady. "What a thing it is to know how, isn't it?" She gave him a handful of peanuts.

He felt very good. It was pleasant to have conquered that blind. He believed he would now know how to raise and lower all car blinds.

A boy in front of him, younger than he was, next attracted our traveler's attention. The boy's mother was with him. You would have said so, if you had seen them. You would never have thought of saying he was with his mother; it was so evident that *she* was with him! He took such excellent care of her. He watched the sun to keep the blind just right, fixed up the shawl strap for a pillow to support her head and put a satchel at her feet. He brought her a glass of water, never spilling a drop. When the conductor passed through the car, the boy handed him the tickets from his hat. In short, he was the protector of the lady by his side.

Reuben noticed and was pleased. When he moved his mother out to live in Monroe, he would take just such fine care of her. By and by, finding himself too near the stove, he secured a seat with a boy somewhat older than he, who was chuckling about something; it was not quite clear what.

Two seats in front of them was a neat, trim old lady with a black dress and bonnet, who must have been a good grandmother to some boy or girl. Once there had been a grandmother in Reuben's home; he remembered her.

This woman was in some sort of trouble. She seemed to be frightened. She turned first one pocket inside out and then another. She removed the contents of her little black bag one by one, turned each over carefully and shook them. Then she shook her gray head. Meanwhile, the boy chuckled.

CHAPTER XII

REUBEN ON THE RAIL

ust look at that old woman!" snickered the boy, nudging Reuben's elbow. "She has been going on that way for the last half hour. She has turned every one of those pockets inside out at least six times. And of all the funny things that she's got in them — dried leaves, papers of pins, a box of pills, a stick of licorice and a ball of red yarn, and I don't know what all."

"What is she hunting for?" asked Reuben, his tone full of something besides amusement. He felt sorry for the bewildered lady.

"Why, that's part of the fun. She has lost her ticket. We changed conductors a few stations back, and ever since this new one came on she's had spells of hunting for the ticket. She can't find it high nor low. Between you and me, the conductor has about concluded she is fooling him and never had a ticket."

"Poor thing!" said Reuben. "What will he do about it?"

"Why, he'll put her off. I shouldn't wonder if he does it at the next station. He has about run out of patience with her. It is great fun to see her fumbling there. Wouldn't it be rich to see him put her off?"

"I think it would be horrid!" countered Reuben. "Didn't any of the passengers see her with a ticket?"

"Oh, you're green. Of course she had one. She has been on the cars all day. More than that, I know where it is. There's a little hole right behind her seat — a sort of crack. It slipped in there two hours ago. I saw it drop, and I can see the end of it peeking out when I stoop down. I should think she would get down on the floor and take a look through the cracks. But she hasn't seemed to think of that at all."

Reuben waited only to flash one indignant glance at the boy from his dark brown eyes. Then he darted forward. The other boy, guessing his purpose, tried to hold him. But Reuben jerked his sleeve away and in a moment was by the old lady's side.

"I can find your ticket for you, ma'am," he said. He dodged under the seat, pushed his hand up through the hole behind and brought out the ugly pink ticket that had caused the poor lady such trouble.

"Oh, thank you!" she said, seizing it eagerly. "You are a good boy to your mother, I know. What a world of trouble you have helped me out of. I was more sorry than you can imagine, to lose the ticket. It wasn't so much the money, though that was enough. But I believe I would have been put off the cars in disgrace, and they would never have let this old lady travel alone again."

"Oh, ho! Aren't you the green one?" sneered the boy when Reuben returned to his seat. "I didn't know that was your granny, or I'd have been more careful of your feelings. I wonder she didn't throw her arms around your neck and kiss you. I say, bub, are you sure your mother knows you're out?"

"Are you from the poorhouse?" Reuben eyed him soberly.

"From the poorhouse!" repeated the other, thrown off guard by the suddenness of the question. "Not much I ain't. What do you mean by that?"

"I heard they took a couple of idiots there last week, and I thought maybe you might be one of them."

This was the beginning of a series of persecutions Reuben had to endure. The ill-behaved boy beside him used his tongue as a weapon and made all kinds of disagreeable speeches as the train whizzed along. Twice Reuben changed his seat. But the boy immediately followed him, saying he must not think of being separated from the dear little fellow for a moment; he or his granny might come to harm if left to themselves. Beyond the first question Reuben had asked, as to whether the boy was from the poorhouse—of which, to tell you the truth, he was now a little ashamed—he took no further notice of his enemy and tried hard to control his temper.

Presently a boy passed through the car with huge oranges, the largest Reuben had ever seen. He wondered what Beth would say if she had one of them and if he would ever be able to earn enough money to buy her an orange every once in a while. Then a strange thing happened. The little old woman in front of him reached for her purse and bought two of the nicest oranges in the basket. Then she trotted over to where Reuben sat and placed one in his hand.

"I hope it's sweet and juicy and will keep saying, 'Thank you!' for me all the time you are eating it," she said heartily.

Reuben stammered his thanks and blushed, not so much for the orange as for the boy, who broke into a laugh.

Before the old woman was out of hearing range, the rude boy began, "Did granny give it an orange? Nice boy — should have an orange, so it should. And it should have a nice bib tied under its chin, so it wouldn't muss its little coatie-toatie. Yes, so it should." He seized Reuben's handkerchief that lay on the window seat, made a bib and began to tuck it under Reuben's chin.

A good deal to his surprise, Reuben sat perfectly still, allowing the tucking to continue without disturbance, only saying in the most good natured tones, "You're an awkward fellow. I guess you are not much used to doing a kindness."

Then he began to peel his orange skillfully. He had watched the process too often not to be skillful. Just as he had halved it nicely, his seatmate jostled his elbow, almost sending the orange onto the tobacco-stained floor. Had it not been for a quick movement from Reuben, much as a boy would put out his hand to catch a ball, the orange would have gone.

"Dear me!" said the rude boy in mock surprise. "What a narrow escape."

"Very," said Reuben. "It would have been bad for you if it had escaped, as that is the half I meant for you. Have it?"

"You are a strange chap," the other eyed him closely, apparently speaking in earnest for the first time. But he took the orange and sucked it with relish.

"I do say it is a sweet one," he declared. "The old lady knows how to pick them out. Say, honor bright, *is* she any relation to you?"

"Not that I ever heard of," said Reuben, sucking at his orange and reflecting upon the old woman. He wondered who he would have been and in what way his life would have been different if she *had* been a relation of his.

"Where're you going, anyhow?" pursued his new acquaintance. "Is that man over there in the corner your uncle or what?"

" 'What,' I guess," Reuben laughed. "You seem resolved on giving me some relations."

"Well, I know that old chap. If I were you, I'd be glad he wasn't your uncle, or nothing of that kind."

"Why?"

"Oh, because he's a skinflint. I worked for him once upon a time. Stayed three weeks — the meanest three weeks of my life."

"Perhaps he thinks the same about his life for those three weeks," Reuben laughed again and glanced over to the man whose character was being discussed. He still liked his face and believed in him, and he did not have a high opinion of the boy who sat beside him.

"Maybe he did!" said the boy, nodding his head with the air of one who could tell a hard story if he chose. "And maybe you don't know anything about it. I live in the same town, and I know all about him. There isn't a boy in town who likes him

— not one."

Reuben instantly decided he was sorry the boy lived in the same town where he was going. He resolved not to say a word about his own expectations and plans. Still, it could do no harm to learn what fault all the boys had to find with the man he liked so well.

"Why don't they?" he asked.

"Oh, because they don't. He's a mean man to work for — never wants a fellow to have any fun. He's always calling out, 'Come, step spry! Be sharp! Don't let the grass grow under your feet,' and all such mean things. He docks a fellow's wages if he's five minutes late, and he expects you to work right straight through from morning till night without stopping for breath."

"Nor for dinner?" asked Reuben.

"Oh, botheration! You know what I mean. It isn't likely you're so green as all that. Halloo! I declare! I've got home. Where are you going?"

"I'm going here, I suppose," said Reuben, springing to his feet and seizing Mr. Barrows's satchel before he had time to hunt about for it.

Then began one of those familiar crowding, shoving scenes in which an express train stops at a way station and lets thirty passengers disembark in two minutes. It's plenty of time. Only nobody seems to think so, and each one is determined to be the first one out.

Mr. Barrows stepped onto the platform, then he turned suddenly and said, "I have left my overcoat."

"Here it is, sir," Reuben said, just at his side. The gentleman who had been talking with Mr. Barrows remarked, "You have an alert boy there."

"I believe I have," said Mr. Barrows, and he

smiled at Reuben.

Among those who were struggling to get out was the little old lady with her arms full of bundles. Perhaps it was nothing but carelessness that caused Reuben's new acquaintance to jostle against her just as she was climbing down the steep steps, sending her bundles flying hither and thither. If it had been an accident, wouldn't you think he'd have picked up the bundles with a red face and said, "Excuse me"? Instead he shoved his hands in his pockets to keep them from the nippy air and laughed.

Reuben handed the coat and satchel hastily to Mr. Barrows and then stooped down to gather the bundles.

The gentleman fixed a pair of keen eyes on the snickering boy. "Andrew," he said, "you have not improved a bit in the last year, have you?"

"Yes, sir," returned the boy promptly. "I'm three inches taller than I was this time last year." But he blushed just a little, or else the north wind made his cheeks grow redder.

There was always something new for Reuben during this winter day. The next thing was a great, high coach with broad leather bands for the backs of the seats. Each of the four seats could take three passengers, and, indeed, four, if need be. The coach was drawn by four eager-looking horses, whose restless feet pawed the ground as if they were in a hurry to be off. During all his ten years of city life Reuben had never seen such a coach before.

"Pile in," shouted someone, and a great many people ran across the snowy walk to obey the call, among them the little old woman. By the time Reuben (who was really practicing on her a little, trying to show himself how he would take care of his mother) had held open the door for her and handed in her bundle after her, it became clear that only one seat was left in the coach.

"One of you youngsters will have to sit outside," said a stout man, drawing his overcoat about him and eyeing Reuben and Andrew. The last-named "youngster" had been watching a fight between two dogs and so was the last one at the coach.

"I know *I* won't this cold night," he said briskly and, hopping past Reuben as he spoke, claimed the vacant seat.

Reuben laughed good-naturedly. "You needn't be in such a hurry," he said. "I'd just as soon ride outside." So, although the little old woman snuggled herself into a very small corner and declared that they could make room for *that* boy, Reuben closed the coach door and climbed to the driver's seat, pleased to be so close to those four noble-looking horses.

What a ride it was! Snow was piled in some places higher than the fences and drifted in great white heaps on either side, leaving almost bare places. It made what Reuben learned to know by the name of "pitch holes," for the runners to drop into every few minutes. In spite of the jolting and the sudden descents and the little squeals which came from inside the coach, Reuben enjoyed the ride. In fact it was almost impossible for him not to enjoy a ride of any kind; he had so few of them, and he loved horses so dearly.

"How far is it to the village?" he presently asked the driver, a great burly man, who was half buried in a fur overcoat.

No answer.

Well, thought Reuben, you are a gruff old fellow. Why couldn't you just as well be nice and tell me about things? What is the use of folks being cross? This old fellow knows ever so much that I'd like to know, I suppose, and here he means to keep the whole of it to himself. Maybe he is half frozen! I mean to try to thaw him. I wonder if he likes his horses. I'll see if I can find out.

"What splendid horses you have!" he said in a loud, admiring tone. He liked the horses so much that he did not have to pretend in the least. But the bundle of fur beside him might as well have been a polar bear for all the answer he received.

He *is* a bear, and no mistake, said Reuben again to himself, trying in vain to get a glimpse of the man's face. Then he kept still. On plowed the horses through the snowy road, which was growing more difficult at every step.

Reuben began to watch things with wide-open eyes. It quickly became clear that the man who was holding the reins was not driving. He didn't make the slightest attempt at guiding the horses into the best parts of the road, nor in checking their speed as they traversed down a steep hill.

"If they didn't know how to drive themselves so wonderfully, we would all be pitched into a snowdrift," said Reuben. He peered curiously into the face of the cross and silent driver. He was more than cross. No sooner had Reuben gotten one glimpse when he leaned forward and gave a decided pull to the man's fur coat. Then he exclaimed, "Well, I never in all my life — never!"

CHAPTER XIII

The New Home

f you had been there to get a glimpse of the red face and had been Reuben Watson Stone, I presume you would have said, "Well, I never!" The words seemed almost to take Reuben's breath away: he sat quite still for a full minute. Another ride with a drunken man! Over a wild road with four horses and rows of men, women and children inside the great coach!

I should like to know, Reuben thought in his quick mind, why *I'm* having all this time with drunken folks? I don't need so many examples, I'm sure. I don't believe there ever was a fellow less likely to grow up a drunkard than I am. But, see here, what am I going to do?

I'll tell you what he wanted to do. He believed in his heart that he could slip those reins from that stupid, sleepy man's hands and manage those four horses as skillfully as he had managed Spunk but a few nights before. Only to think how splendid it would be to drive into the village with a grand flourish, having guided the four horses through all the snowdrifts and brought the people home safely! Four horses! What would his old city acquaintance Tony Phelps, who boasted of the time when he once drove two, think of that story! It made Reuben's heart beat fast to think of the possibility. Why shouldn't he do it? Why wouldn't it be a grand thing to do?

He managed Spunk in the night and darkness with a railroad track to cross; here was nothing but snow, and daylight to see it with. But — and here Reuben's heart beat faster — who helped him the other night? Who was it who had heard the words he spoke in his terror, quieted his heart, given him courage and brought him through in safety? Well, would not the same great Helper give him aid now?

What made the difference? Reuben felt rather than reasoned out the difference. He knew very well that, in the other case, he was doing right, doing his best — doing the thing that Mother, and everyone else who knew of it, could commend him for.

But suppose he should trust in his own small knowledge of horses and undertake to manage this whole thing without the help of any of those men inside — would Mother think he had done right? Suppose he got through safely — would *that* make it a right thing to do? Could he look up with fearless eyes to God and ask His help for such a work?

Thoughts like these ran rapidly through Reuben's mind. He covered the whole ground much faster than I have been able to tell you. And he decided not only what was right to do but just exactly what he *meant* to do. He turned himself around in his high seat, stooped down, lifted the leather flap that served as a sort of window to the front of the coach and, putting his mouth to the opening, spoke these words: "See here! This fellow out here has gone to sleep."

"What fellow?" asked two or three startled voices inside.

"Why, the driver — he has been drinking, and the motion of the sleigh has put him to sleep. He doesn't know what he is about. I've got the reins, but the road is awful."

Then there was a commotion inside. Two or three of the women screamed, and the little old woman grasped her umbrella tighter and looked as though she would like to use it on the driver.

"*You* go, Dick," said one frightened woman, laying her hand on the shoulder of a rough-looking man who sat beside her. "You can manage any horses that were ever made, and I'm sure I shall die of fright if *you* aren't driving."

Thus coaxed, the rough-looking man smiled kindly, shook his brawny shoulders and slowly clambered out, saying nothing except to Reuben, "Tumble in there, boy, in my seat and get warm."

"Ho!" snickered Andrew the minute Reuben was comfortably seated. "You got a scare, did you? I wish *I* had been outside. I'd have kept hold of the reins and said nothing. And you'd have seen us come into town with a dash. I can drive four horses as easy as I can one. I just wish I had taken the outside seat."

"Thank heaven you did not!" This was what a pale-faced young lady said. Not carelessly, as some speak their thanks, but with a grave, earnest face.

Mr. Barrows answered, "I think as much! It is fortunate for us that we had a trustworthy boy on the front seat."

"Humph!" Andrew said with a chuckle. "A *coward* on the front seat, you better say."

No one in the coach knew how great a temptation Reuben had met and conquered when he gave those reins into the hands of another. Never mind. He did not like to be called a coward, it is true. Who does? But in spite of that, a happy feeling took possession of his heart. He could not have explained the feeling; he hardly knew why it was there. Any boy who wants to understand just what it was like has only to persist in doing what he *knows* to be right — especially when he doesn't want to do it but would fifty times rather do what he believes to be just a little bit wrong.

That was a busy day for our man of the house. In the first place, there was dinner to eat at Mr. Barrows's house — a large, brick house with a beautiful yard in front, filled with trees and snow-covered mounds, which Reuben knew must be flower beds, and a barn in the rear which he privately thought was nice enough for a house.

The dinner, though not served in as elegant a style as at Spunk's home, was still much finer than anything Reuben had seen apart from there, and he did full justice to it. He was a little flurried, it is true, by the fact that Miss Grace Barrows, who was only eight, had not yet learned that it was rude to stare and gave him a good deal of curious attention.

"Now we will go to the shop," Mr. Barrows said after dinner. Reuben, who was fond of all shops or places where machinery could be seen, found plenty to keep his eyes busy.

"What in the world are they all for?" he asked at last in great astonishment, after he had been taken through two or three rooms, piled from floor to ceiling with pasteboard boxes of all sizes and colors. "What can anybody possibly want of so many of them?"

"A good *many* people want them," laughed Mr. Barrows. "Gloves and mittens for all the world are packed in those boxes. Since there are a good many people to wear those, of course, a good many boxes are needed."

From the warerooms where the finished boxes were kept, they proceeded to the workrooms. Here were boxes in all stages of manufacture. Reuben stood before the huge shears and saw its jaws, like some great monster, pounce down on sheet after sheet of pasteboard and bite them into two smooth pieces. He stepped over to one side and stood by a boy who was seizing two pieces and glueing them into one so fast that you could hardly see the way in which it was done. He crossed to a little machine in one corner and was astonished and delighted to see the rapid way in which it was biting out the corners of box covers. A boy about his own size was quickly creasing these same covers, and still another was bending them into the right shape.

"Well," said Mr. Barrows, watching the eager eyes that were taking in so many new things, "which of all these things would you like best to work at?"

"Me?" said Reuben, charmed at the idea of anything so new and strange. "Why, I think I should like to work at every one of them and know everything there is to know about them all."

"I shouldn't wonder," laughed Mr. Barrows again.

Then they went upstairs to the pasting room. At the door stood a barrel of paste. Reuben had seen his mother make a cup of paste to paper the shelves of her cupboard, but he stopped and gazed at this barrelful almost in dismay. He had not realized that so much was made at *once* anywhere in the world.

Two girls were at work in the pasting room, each at her own table, covering a great sheet of thin white paper, four feet long and more than two feet wide, with paste. Then they spread it skillfully on a sheet of pasteboard of the same size and smoothed it down.

"It will tear all to pieces!" exclaimed Reuben. He watched the reckless girl seize the wet paper by what seemed to be two careless hands and flip it over. "She will never get it turned in the world." But even while he spoke, the paper lay down gently and smoothly and was patted skillfully into place.

"I don't see how she did it!" he said in astonishment.

Mr. Barrows laughed pleasantly. He liked the boy's keen interest in everything he saw.

In the trimming room, just as wonderful things were going on. Lovely blue and red and green strips of paper, looking for all the world like ribbon, were being spread over a table, twenty strips at a time, each strip about half an inch wide and forty inches long. When all were laid in smooth rows, to Reuben's utter dismay, a brisk girl daubed them with paste!

"They are ruined!" he said breathlessly.

No sooner was this dire act finished than she seized upon one of them. Reuben expected to see it drop into a dozen pieces. Instead she whisked it around a box, covered the rough edges and made it look like a brilliant treasure box.

So many marvelous things were going on here. After a few minutes Reuben ceased his exclamations and gave silent and eager attention, bobbing his head from right to left, to take in all the sights. He was much astonished all the while at the reckless way in which boxes that were just pasted together with flimsy-looking bits of cloth were tossed about and piled on top of each other, five, ten, fifteen feet high. He expected every minute to see them fall apart and tumble around the room, but none did. And he could not help thinking of what Beth would say to such quick fingers and astonishing work — so much prettier than taking little bits of stitches in long, gray seams!

"Would you like to learn the trade?" Mr. Barrows asked him as they walked down the stairs. For a short time Reuben had silently watched the movements of a boy who was feeding a machine for trimming the edges of the pasteboards.

"Yes, sir," said Reuben promptly. "I would."

Whereupon Mr. Barrows said it was about time they checked up on the little house. This recalled Reuben to a sense of his responsibility. He followed with eager steps across the street and behind a great snowdrift to a trim little house. It was situated in a yard with a massive tree before the door. The huge branches of the tree stretched out leafless now and snow-covered, but Reuben could picture it dressed in green with a bird building her nest right in front of his mother's window.

Oh, those cunning little rooms! I don't suppose you can imagine how delightful they seemed to the boy who had spent most of his life in the north chamber.

"This is the parlor," said Mr. Barrows. He opened a door that led from the bit of a hall into a pleasant room which was small and square and papered with a light-colored, figured pattern. A mantle stood at one end, along with a south window into which the sun even then was shining.

Reuben, as he gazed about him, chuckled inwardly at the idea of their having a parlor! What would Beth think of that! Besides the parlor was what Mr. Barrows called a dining room. There were also a kitchen, a nice pantry lined with shelves and three beautiful rooms upstairs, each with a clothespress.

"They are rather small, all of them," said Mr. Barrows. "But, then, for a small family, I should think they would do very well."

And then Reuben stared at him, almost in indignation. What did he mean by calling those lovely rooms small?

One — a south room — made him think of Miss Hunter, and he sighed a little. It was the one bit that he did not like about this pleasant prospect of moving and living in a whole house, instead of one room and a clothespress — leaving Miss Hunter, the new friend who seemed so much like an old one.

That south room, with the bit of a bedroom on the side that Mr. Barrows did not count as a room at all, would be just the thing for Miss Hunter. How wonderful it would be if she should take a fancy to move, too, and make gloves instead of vests! Then they might almost hope to pay the rent of this grand house! Especially since there was actually a garden and a place to keep hens and an apple tree and a pear tree in the backyard!

"There is a woman who lives on the south side

of our hall," he said, speaking some of his thoughts aloud. "She is one of the best women who ever lived. She sews on vests and things, for the tailors. If she should move here too, could she find work to do, do you think?"

"Plenty of work at making gloves and mittens. There isn't much call for women tailors in this direction. But she can make better wages at gloves than she can in tailoring. This is a good time to come here and get started. Fact is, some of the hands, a large number of them, right in the busiest season before last fall, struck for higher wages. They were getting pretty good wages too, but they thought they would like more; so they struck. The manufacturers decided that, as soon as the new year opened, they would hire new hands and prepare for the next hurrying season before it came. So they are all advertising for workers. That is what people get who aren't willing to let well enough alone."

"What is the rent of this house?" It was a quiet little question, but it took Reuben nearly ten minutes to gather up the courage to ask it; he fully expected to have his hopes dashed to the ground by the answer.

"Well," said Mr. Barrows, rubbing his chin, "that would depend a little on who rented it. If your mother wants it, I think I could get it for her for a hundred dollars a year."

"That's only a little over eight dollars a month," Reuben said with crimson cheeks and bright eyes. It actually was only a trifle more than they had to pay every month for the north room and the clothespress! Now, if he could just earn enough to make up the difference and have a little left over to buy coal, they might try the new home!

"What could I earn in a week, do you suppose?"

Mr. Barrows could hardly keep from smiling over the boy's eagerness. "Well, now, my man, that would depend entirely on you. Some boys don't earn the salt that they eat with their potatoes; I wouldn't promise to furnish it, for all they do. Then again there are boys who earn good wages and help their mothers right straight through. I had a boy last year who earned his three dollars a week all through the year."

"In the box business?"

"In the box business."

"How old was he?"

"About your age—a trifle older perhaps. But what he did, he could have done just as well if he had been a year younger."

"Was he a *very* smart boy — smarter than I could be?"

Mr. Barrows laughed. "How can I tell? No, if you mean, was he a remarkable boy — he wasn't. He was just a good, faithful fellow doing his best."

"If I should do my best, could I earn as much as that?"

"I shouldn't wonder at all."

"For how many months in the year?"

Mr. Barrows laughed. "You will make a good businessman, I think," he said pleasantly. "You remember to look closely into things. Well, the season — that is, the *busy* season — lasts for about nine months in the year. If I were you I would plan to work hard for those nine months and go to school the other three—and do odd jobs out of school hours to earn your board. For nine months I think you could earn from two to three dollars a week at the box business without any trouble, and I would give you your board for what you could do after school during the other three months."

"I think Mother will come," said Reuben, his eyes shining, "and I shall tell Miss Hunter what you said about the glove business."

"All right," said Mr. Barrows. "I advertised for hands for my brother-in-law. He is a manufacturer, and he runs those little machines I was telling you about. If you say so, we will go now and see them."

So they left, and Reuben locked the door of the neat little house, all the while wondering whether it could possibly work out for him to lock it many times in the future. He was in such a hurry to tell his mother about it that he was almost sorry the last plan had been for him to spend the week at Mr. Barrows's and then return home. Still, if they were really going to *move*, there were ever so many things he was man enough to know needed looking after.

The little machines, one of which Mr. Barrows seemed to think Beth might manage, seemed to be next in order.

"The strangest-looking creatures I ever saw in my life!" This was how Reuben would have described them had he been talking to his mother or Beth. They seemed too small to be called machines. A round board about the size of a barrel head with a shaft of wood about three feet long stood upright from the center of the barrel head, finished at the top by a brass mouth about four inches long. This mouth had rows of tiny teeth on either side, matching exactly. It opened its jaws whenever the spring at the bottom was touched and seized, and it held firmly whatever was placed inside.

Reuben watched while a girl of about fourteen picked up a kid glove about the right size for his mother, folded it carefully across the back, made the little creature open its brass mouth and take it in. Then with a fine needle and silk thread she stitched down the length of the brass mouth, tucking the needle between each tooth, making a little clicking noise with her thimble against the brass and performing it all so rapidly that Reuben was lost in amazement. When the jaws opened, and the glove was drawn out, he leaned forward eagerly to discover a long, smooth row of the daintiest stitches, somewhat like those that his mother took in shirt bosoms!

"It is beautiful!" he said admiringly. "And how fast she did it!"

"How would the sister at home like that sort of work?" asked Mr. Barrows.

Reuben had not imagined setting Beth to work; for the first time he thought that perhaps such work as this might do for even Beth.

When he heard that industrious young girls actually earned sometimes a dollar a day and that his mother would have no trouble in earning that sum, he said emphatically, "I *know* Mother will move."

At last the exciting day was over. Reuben had accomplished a great deal of business. He had visited the freight depot and learned the price of freight and the exact way of marking it. He had learned the price of butter, meat, flour, milk and wood. In short, he had done everything he could think of that a man with a family to provide for would most likely have done.

Mr. Barrows observed him, sometimes amused and sometimes touched almost to tears by the young boy's thoughtful planning for his mother and sister. Where he needed help he got it; but for most of the work Mr. Barrows left him alone, curious to see how he would carry out his plans.

"The boy has the wisest head on his young shoulders that I ever saw in my life!" he confided to his wife that evening, after Reuben had gone to bed. "He hasn't done anything extraordinary either. I don't know that he is any smarter than most boys his age. He simply has used the brains that fellows like Andrew Porter spend in mischief, to help him in supporting his family. The notion he has that he is the man of the house and must look after the comfort of his folks like any other man is worth a fortune to him. I believe the boy will be a rich man, while he is a young one."

"You have taken one of your tremendous likings to him," Mrs. Barrows laughed. "I don't wonder. I am fond of him myself. As for Grace, she wants to teach him music and drawing right away. I hope the rest of the family is half as nice. Do you believe they will come?"

"I do if Reuben can bring it about, and I think he can. I set the rent of the little house at a hundred dollars. I'd have made it lower if the boy's bright eyes hadn't been fixed right on me. I knew he would suspect something; he isn't after charity. I hope I shall not be disappointed in him. If he doesn't grow up to be a smart businessman, as well as a good man, I shall wonder at it."

CHAPTER XIV

IN THE BOX FACTORY

euben Watson Stone sat on the side of his bed and gazed about him. There was plenty to gaze at. He had never seen a lovelier room in his life. The carpet was soft and bright; the gaslight caused the flowers on it to glow so it seemed to the boy as if he might stoop and pick them. He thought of his sister, Beth, and wished she could see the pretty carpet and the stylish furniture and the fancy curtains and everything.

"I suppose this is me," he said aloud to himself. "It doesn't seem as though it could be. This is just the most peculiar kind of world. Just think of the things that are happening to me! Ever so many of them have fallen into one week. I lived 'most twelve years without any happenings, and then they all came and tumbled themselves into a week! I wonder how we'll get money to move! Mother will surely move here, when she hears how much money I can earn and how nice it will be for Beth. We can both go to school some. It is a splendid chance. Isn't it a strange thing, now, that all these opportunities came because I wouldn't go to that St. Mark's saloon to sell liquor? Mr. Barrows said he never would have thought of bringing me home with him if he hadn't heard about that."

There were so many exciting things to think about that Reuben was in danger of not getting to bed at all. He did not feel sleepy. In fact, he told himself he didn't believe he could sleep a wink that night.

At last, however, he heard the clock around the corner strike ten, and, surprised at the lateness of the hour, he jumped into bed. No sooner was the gas turned out, so that all the fine things were lost to sight, than he was off to dreamland. The next morning began a new life for Reuben Stone. He was to start that day to support his family.

Directly after breakfast — and a lovely breakfast it was! — he headed for the great box factory, eager to learn all he could about that amazing business.

On the way, while Mr. Barrows talked with a gentleman who had joined them, Reuben talked with himself: Here I am, going to begin business at last! I've been for 'most two years hunting something to do, and now I've got it. Not a thing I ever hunted for, or thought of, or even heard of — but something new and beautiful. Think of learning how to make boxes! I'll make a lot of them for Mother some day, if I learn how real well. Beth would like some bright, red-trimmed ones, like the ones I saw yesterday. Won't it be fun to show her how to do things?

You can see that Reuben Stone thought a great deal about his mother and his sister, Beth. It was well that he felt so full of business; for if he had had time, he might have felt a little bit homesick. It isn't easy for a boy to be away from his mother for the first time.

In the pasting room only boys were at work—five or six of them, a little older than Reuben. They were covering great sheets of pasteboard with wet paper. Reuben was anxious to try his skill and soon had a chance.

During the night he had dreamed he could accomplish marvelous deeds in the box business. Alas for dreams! Never had he undertaken anything so dreadful. Mr. Barrows left him in the charge of a boy named Wesley Dale, with directions to teach young Stone just what to do. So Wesley began a series of orders about what must and must not be done—all given so rapidly that poor Reuben was utterly bewildered.

"Won't you please slow down?" he asked at last. "I'm getting all mixed up." Then all the boys laughed loud and long, as if getting mixed up was a good joke.

"Very well," said Wesley. "I'll go as slow as a snail. First you spread a sheet of paper on the pasteboard—not on the floor or on the wall, but on the *pasteboard*. Do you understand that? Are you sure I'm not going too fast? Well, then you take the brush in your right hand—mind I say *right* hand, because if you take the left, it's all up with you, and you dip it in the paste. Is that plain? *Sure* you understand? Dip it *way* in—the more paste you get the better. In fact, if you don't spread the paste on thick the first time, you spoil the whole thing. If you should take the tubful and pour over it afterward, it would do no good. Well, dash in your brush and daub on the paste, half an inch thick or less. Wet every inch of the paper, then dip in your brush again and go all over it once more."

"Yesterday, when I watched you, you only dipped it in once," Reuben pointed out solemnly. He was sure he was being made sport of, but he didn't know enough about the business to be sure where the sport ended and the things he must do began.

"Oh, well, I was working on a different quality of paper. That makes all the difference in the world," said Wesley. "You mustn't judge by your eyes. If you let them rove around to look at other folks, you'll never learn how in the world. Mind what I say to you, and go ahead! When you get your paper *real* wet, whisk it over. The quicker you can do it the better, and then with this big brush smooth it down. You have to bear on it *with all your might*, or the thing goes and wrinkles. It is a ticklish job, I can tell you."

In much fear and trembling, Reuben set to the task. He could see his fellow workers giggling and nudging each other and acting as much like wretches as they could. Wesley stood at his elbow, talking all the time and contradicting his own directions. It was worse than driving Spunk. He wished Mr. Barrows had let him go in a room by himself — after watching the others for a while — and try it; he might have accomplished something. But there was no help for it now. He dipped the brush into the bed of paste.

"Dip lower, man," said Wesley. "What are you afraid of?"

So he dipped lower and, with a shiver, brought the dripping brush to the delicate white paper. Splash, splash, splash over the smooth surface — it reminded him of stepping with wet, muddy feet on a bank of fair morning snow. The paste lay in thick ridges all over the sheet. Then he took hold of the two corners carefully, at the same time remembering his instruction to be "as quick as a wink." Alas! It would not turn at all. It seemed to wilt into a soft, pulpy mass in his hands and lie in a discouraged heap in the middle of the wet board.

He looked up in utter dismay, while the boys shouted with laughter.

"It is ruined!" he gasped.

"I should think so!" laughed Wesley. "Isn't enough of it left to make a dishcloth. *Awful* expensive paper, too. You'll ruin the old chap if you keep on for long in this style. Try again!"

Reuben tried again and again and again, his face red and pale by turns, his eyes now bright with hope, now heavy with despair. Once his instructor kindly offered to show him how and twirled the dripping mass which Reuben tried in vain to catch. Then he tried his skill with the rubbing-down brush, remembering Wesley's repeated caution to bear on hard. The consequence was that the wet mass parted in the middle, half of it staying on the board and half of it rolling itself into a sticky ball and following the line of the brush. With the fifth trial, which was worse than all the others, Reuben quietly laid down both brushes and walked out of the room.

"Beaten, as sure as I'm alive!" shouted Wesley, doubling himself up with laughter and rolling over and over on a pile of pasteboards that stood near. "I didn't think it would be done so easily. Something in his face made me think he wasn't so chicken-hearted as you would suppose from his size."

"Too bad on the little fellow," said one boy who had laughed less than the others. "He's away from home and homesick, maybe. What was the point?"

"Oh, now don't you go to getting spooney!" said Wesley. "Serves him right. What business did he have to come slipping in here among us? A lot of fellows in town want the place. Barrows needn't think we are going to have any little ragbag from the city poked in among us."

While they discussed it, Reuben headed straight for the room marked "Office" and knocked at the door. Mr. Barrows's voice told him to come in. That gentleman was seated at his desk, studying a pile of letters; he seemed serious and busy. Reuben stood for fully five minutes before getting any attention.

At last Mr. Barrows looked up and said, "Well!" in a gruff tone, as though he did not care to be interrupted.

"I don't think I'll suit, sir," Reuben said. He tried to keep his voice from trembling, but it was hard to do, and his face was very pale.

"Sick of it already, eh?"

In spite of his disappointment and bitter sense of failure, Reuben could not keep a wan smile from creeping into his face as he answered: "No, sir, but it is sick of me. They tear just awfully! I've torn up and spoiled five of those great big beautiful sheets of paper, and I did my best."

"You have!" exclaimed Mr. Barrows. Reuben could not decide whether his voice held anger or only surprise and dismay. But he stood his ground manfully.

"Yes, sir, I have, and I'm awful sorry. I thought I could do it, and I tried. But it got worse and worse. Now if there was something you were *sure* I could do, to give me till I earned enough to pay for that paper, I'd work nights and all."

"Just so," said Mr. Barrows. "I'll think about it. You may sit down on that stool until I write a letter, then we'll attend to it."

So Reuben perched himself on a stool with his arms folded and his heart sad. He remained motionless until the rapid pen had dashed a dozen or more lines on the paper. At last the writer glanced up again.

"Now, my boy, the paper tore, did it?"

"All to pieces," replied Reuben mournfully. "Went all to *squash!* It isn't good for anything."

"And how did the other boys take it?"

"Well, sir, they laughed all the time."

"How did you like Wesley?"

Reuben looked down at the floor. What did that have to do with the torn paper and his failure in business?

But Mr. Barrows waited, and at last he stammered that he didn't think he liked him very well.

"Did the directions that he gave you about the work seem like common sense?"

"No, sir!" That answer was prompt enough.

"What was the matter with them?"

"Why, he said to dip the brush way in and spread on lots of paste. I didn't see how the paper could help tearing."

Mr. Barrows turned over some papers on his desk and seemed to be thinking about them for a few minutes. Then he said: "Suppose you had a present of fifty sheets of pasteboard and fifty sheets of that best white paper, and you could do what you wanted with them—what would you do?"

"I'd earn some paste somehow and find a place

to work in. And I'd learn how to put the papers on, if it took me all winter."

"Very well!" said Mr. Barrows. "I'll present you with fifty sheets of paper and pasteboard to spoil, if you have to, with the understanding that if they come out in good shape they are to be mine. If they are spoiled, they are yours to make your fortune out of. I'll even lend you the paste" — a curious smile lit up his face as he said this — "and a place to work in. You can pay me when you make your fortune. Now the sooner you get to work, the less time you will lose."

"Thank you," said Reuben, climbing down from his perch with his eyes shining. "I'll go right at it."

Back he hurried to the workroom and appeared before the boys, whose shouts of laughter were still echoing through the building. They stopped in astonishment at the sight of him.

"Dear me!" said Wesley. "You're still here? I thought you ran home to tell your mother. Poor little fellow! He looks pale, boys. I believe he fainted on the way. We shall have to put some paste in his face to revive him."

But the fun was cut short by the arrival of Mr. Barrows. In an instant every boy who had left his post to help in the joke at Reuben's expense was back at work.

"These doors are very thin, boys," was the only hint that the gentleman gave that he had heard every word. Then he called Wesley to him and told him to stand by his side and give the few general directions that were important in learning to spread the paper.

"Much paste or little, Wesley?"

"As little as possible, sir."

"You may tell Stone so, then."

And Wesley with a red face repeated this to Reuben.

"About the brush, Wesley. Should the touch with it be light or heavy?"

"*Very* light, sir."

This, too, he had to repeat to Reuben.

Then Mr. Barrows issued strict orders that no boy in the room should speak to or in any way interfere with the newcomer's way of doing things.

"Whether he uses a new way or an old one, right or wrong, I forbid any boy to interfere. He is going to experiment and is to be let alone. Remember, boys," he said in a significant tone, "I *forbid* it."

Then he departed, and Reuben had peace. The boys snickered, to be sure, and made funny speeches at his expense; he won their hearts by laughing at some of the speeches. Reuben was such a good-natured fellow that he could not help laughing at a joke, even when he was the victim. But his work was not meddled with, and after one or two failures, he began to catch the secret.

When Mr. Barrows peered in two hours later to see how the experiment was working, Reuben told him proudly that only seven of the pasteboards were his; he thought the others were as good as anybody's.

"All right!" the gentleman said with a satisfied smile. "Keep track of these seven boards, and make your fortune with them."

Instantly there flashed over Reuben a new idea. What if he should begin to make his fortune out of those seven pasteboards! What if he should!

CHAPTER XV

CLARKE MILLER

fter the pasting room Reuben was called downstairs to the marking and cutting room. The odd little machine that bit the corners out of the covers so skillfully had attracted him the day before, and to his great delight he was set to working it. Skill was required here as well as in pasting, but it was of a different sort. Reuben caught the movement of the machine at once. His eyes brightened with every turn of the bright shears.

"You have an accurate eye," Mr. Barrows told him. His face broadened into a smile.

His success was worse for him, in one sense, than his failure in the upper room had been, inasmuch as it moved certain of the others to envy. They did not approve of the city boy at the best — as if there were not fellows enough in the town to run the factory! This was how they felt, and this in some form was what they growled to each other from time to time. Reuben paid little attention to them; all he asked was that he could guide the skillful shears in biting out perfectly square corners. The very speed with which it worked was a delight to him. Reuben liked fast things.

Mr. Barrows was moving in and out, talking with first one workman then another, with a general eye to all that was going on. During one of his visits he was sharpening a pencil with a choice, four-bladed knife whose pearl handle and polished steel caught an admiring flash from the eye of every boy in the room. He laid both down for a moment near the busy shears while he explained to the man running the monstrous machine just how a certain kind of board was to be cut. Then a sudden call for him came from the office, and he left.

He hurried in perhaps an hour later and searched among the pile of chips that were piling up around the little shears as Reuben still successfully clipped out the corners.

"Boys, have any of you seen my knife?" Mr. Barrows asked. Half a dozen pairs of hands paused in their work, and as many pairs of eyes looked up to his — innocent eyes along with a few mischievous ones. But they shook their heads.

Before one of the others could speak, however, Reuben's clear voice was heard: "Yes, sir, I had a glimpse of it. It is in the upper pocket of my jacket, and the pencil you were sharpening is there too."

Mr. Barrows stared at him in surprise, it is true. But it did not compare with the shock on the faces of the boys.

"Reuben," inquired the gentleman soberly, "did you fear that the knife and pencil would get lost, so you put them in your pocket for safekeeping?"

"No, sir — didn't put them there at all. But I know they are there, for I saw them drop in." Then noticing that Mr. Barrows still waited with a grave and not altogether pleased face, he added: "I didn't touch them, sir, as true as I live."

"Will you explain, then, how they got into your pocket?"

"They were put in, sir."

"But not by your hands?"

"Not by my hands."

"Do you know anything about whose hands put them there?"

In that room at that moment, busy place though it generally was, you could have heard a pin drop. Every boy was listening. One of them had a red face.

For just a moment Reuben considered, then he spoke: "Yes, sir, I know just exactly whose hands put them there. But I kind of think it was done just for fun, without much thinking about or meaning any harm. And if you will take them away and excuse the hands that dropped them there, I will too."

"Boys," said Mr. Barrows, turning from Reuben, "you hear what this newcomer says. He is a stranger to all of you; but I know him a little, and I have some reason for trusting him. Still, I will be fair to every one of you and give you a chance to express an opinion. Do you believe he has told the truth about my knife and pencil?"

A chorus of voices answered him: "Yes, sir, we know he has."

"Very well, then, I'll claim my property." He stepped over to the threadbare jacket and pulled the four-bladed knife and pencil out of the pocket.

As he did so, he said, "Now there is at least one boy in the room who has been guilty of a mean trick and ought to be ashamed of himself. I don't know which one it is and don't want to. Since Reuben has asked it as a favor, I am willing to excuse the hands that put them in. I hope the owner of those hands will be manly enough to apologize for the mischief he tried to do and say, 'Thank you,' for the kindness shown him."

Then Mr. Barrows left.

Reuben made the little machine bite out the corners as fast as it could and did not raise his eyes. Not a boy spoke. After a little while one of them whistled, then several of them laughed. Reuben worked on.

It was not until the magnificent bell in the church tower rang out its six-o'clock call to come home to supper that the tongues of those boys were loosened. While they rushed for caps and coats and mittens, they all chattered at once — not loud enough for Reuben to understand what they said, but loud enough for him to know they were talking about the knife and the pencil.

One, the oldest and most lawless-looking, lingered while Reuben hunted among the chips he had created for a bright bit of paper he wanted to save for Beth.

"Honor bright," said the boy, "do you know who put the knife in your pocket?"

Reuben turned flashing eyes on him and answered quickly: "Know as well as though you had told me all about it beforehand — you did it yourself."

Whereupon the boy gave a sharp whistle. "What did I do it for?" he asked presently.

"I don't feel so sure of that. I thought maybe it

was just for what some fellows call 'fun.' I don't see much fun about it, but I thought perhaps you did. If you meant nothing but that, why there's no harm done."

"Suppose I meant a good deal more than that?"

"Then there's lots of harm done. You feel mean about it by this time, and folks don't like to feel mean — at least, I don't."

"Why didn't you tell Mr. Barrows which of us did it?"

"I didn't see any good in that. He got his property, and that was what he was after. And I proved all around that I had nothing to do with putting it where it didn't belong, and that was what I was after."

"Well," said the other, after a somewhat longer pause, "my name is Clarke Miller, and I didn't mean a single thing except to have some fun and tease you a bit. I thought you was a spooney little fellow away from his mother, and we might as well have a little fun with you as not."

"All right," returned Reuben gravely. "I'm a little fellow — that's a fact — and I'm away from my mother. As for being spooney, I don't feel any too sure that I know just what it means down here in the country. Perhaps I am a spooney, and perhaps I'm not — never mind. The knife is where it ought to be, and I guess you and I will be all right after this."

"I guess we will. I mean to stand up for you. Only I'd like to know this: are you one of the goody-goody sort?"

"Don't know them," said Reuben in good humor. "What are they like?"

"Oh, bother! You're not so green as all that. Are you one of them that thinks it is wrong to wink or sneeze or whistle and that tells your mother every time you turn around and says your prayers and all that?"

The merry twinkle vanished from Reuben's eyes. He gave Clarke Miller a clear, steady gaze and answered slowly: "I'm good at whistling, or bad, I don't know which to call it. Mother says I almost deafen her sometimes. I like to tell things to her first-rate, when I don't think they will worry her too much. You see, it is different with me from what it is with most boys. My father has been dead a long time, and I'm the only boy — in fact, I'm not a boy at all. I have to do what I can to support the family. I've been the man of the house for these three years, so I have to think about things. As for saying prayers, I never did much of that — forgot it, you know — after I got too old to say them with Mother. But one night a while ago I was in an awful danger — didn't expect to get home alive. I just asked God to help me, the same as if I could see Him, and He did it. Since then I've thought it would be a good plan to ask Him about things."

"You are a peculiar chap!" said Clarke. "A *very* peculiar chap indeed!" he added solemnly, after a slight pause. "But I'll stand up for you through thick and thin — I will. And when Clarke Miller makes a promise, it means something."

Work continued quietly after this for two days. The boys tried to tease Reuben occasionally, but two things hindered their doing much in this line. Reuben was hard to tease. He was good-natured over what would have angered many boys. He laughed when they expected him to frown and whistled when they had intended for him to growl. Besides, he soon discovered that Clarke Miller was sort of a leader among them. When he said, "Look here, fellows—if you know when you're well off, you'll let that little chap alone; he's a friend of mine!" the boys knew he meant it.

Reuben's success in the box business surprised even him. He learned rapidly. Not that he was any smarter than most alert boys his age, but he had a mind to do his best all the time. And the box trade is, like most others, easy to learn when a wide-awake fellow does his best.

He discovered from Mr. Barrows's manner, rather than from anything he said, that he was giving him satisfaction.

But on Saturday the gentleman spoke: "Reuben, Mrs. Barrows thinks it would be a good idea for you to hire a woman to clean the little house and get it ready for your mother. What do you think about it?"

Reuben's face brightened, then grew sober.

"I'd like it," he said with his usual promptness. "Only I don't know whether Mother would."

"Why, she's the very one we are trying to please! What's in the way?"

"Well, you see, sir, it takes a good deal of money to move, and we are pretty short in that line. I don't know but Mother would think I ought to have saved the money and let her and Beth do the cleaning."

"I see," said Mr. Barrows, and he looked by no means displeased. After a few quiet minutes he spoke again. "Down the lane from my house a woman lives who wants a cord of wood split and carried into her woodshed. She cleans houses and washes and all that sort of thing, and she can't afford to pay money for her work. How would it do to return the job? Or are you too tired when six o'clock comes to think of splitting wood by the light of a lantern?"

Now Reuben's face shone.

"It will do splendidly!" he said with the eagerness of a boy to whom a fortune had just been left. "If I can get the job, Mother shall come to a clean house."

"You shall have the job," Mr. Barrows said with great satisfaction. "I promised the woman this morning I would look out for a boy of the right sort."

An hour later Reuben was downstairs piling boxes in the hall, ready for the delivery wagon. Mr. Barrows drove up in his carriage and jumped out, leaving little Miss Grace in charge.

"Shall I hold your horse, sir?" asked Reuben, admiring the sleek coat of the handsome fellow.

"No, he is used to holding himself. He is better trained than most horses," Mr. Barrows answered and entered the office where he stood talking with his foreman and examining some papers that were handed to him.

Grace Barrows leaned out of the carriage and nodded to Reuben. "How do you like boxes by this time?"

"First-rate," he answered heartily, setting down ten of them at once with great care. "Don't you hold the reins when you are left in charge of a horse?"

"Oh, no, Samson never does anything but stand still until Papa wants him to go."

"Is that his name? What a strange name for a horse."

"Isn't it a nice name? We call him that because he is so big. *Isn't* he big?" she said with pride.

Just then a paper fluttered from the desk out the door and down the walk, landing at the wheel of the carriage.

"Catch that, Reuben!" commanded Mr. Barrows in a tone that said it was an important paper. Reuben sprang after it.

What caused a sudden twist of wind just at that moment to carry a page from a torn newspaper halfway across the street and fling it into Samson's eyes? Why should a torn newspaper frighten a horse out of his senses?

Many questions can be asked, but who can answer them? Not Samson, certainly, for he hadn't time. Away he flew as if he had suddenly discovered that his four legs were long and intended for running away. Not Reuben, either, for he had other business. His hand was on the hind spring, where he had placed it in the act of bending over to pick up the important paper. Since he did not let go, you can imagine perhaps just how fast he was traveling at that moment.

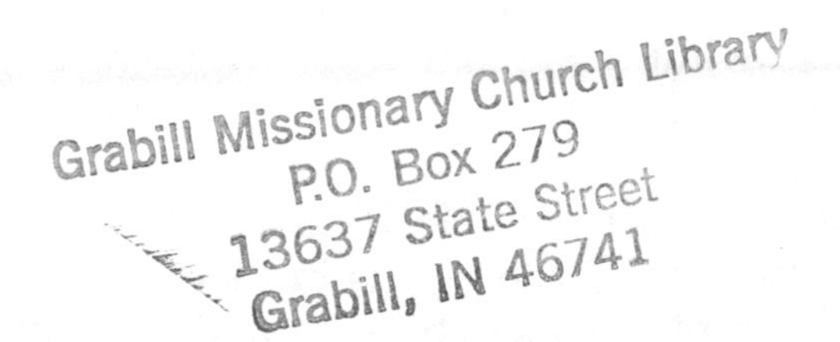
Grabill Missionary Church Library
P.O. Box 279
13637 State Street
Grabill, IN 46741

CHAPTER XVI

Reuben Conquers Samson

h, dear! Reuben was certainly one for getting himself into scrapes with horses! Here he was being whirled along too fast for thinking, one would suppose, while Mr. Barrows, without his hat and with his coattails flying in the air, followed on foot. He was shouting at the top of his lungs: "Stop that horse! Stop that horse!"

As if one could stop the wind! Men appeared in the doorways of their stores and stared and blinked. By that time Samson had passed them. Meanwhile a small white, frightened heap was curled up in the closet corner of the back seat — little Grace Barrows.

"Don't be frightened, Gracie. I'm coming."

She heard these words in the cheeriest of tones issuing from somewhere near the ground behind her. Sure enough! Reuben had not clung to the hind spring for nothing. He had climbed like a monkey to the back of the carriage and was busy with hands and teeth trying to unfasten the curtain. The whole time he worked, he kept up a lively conversation with Grace Barrows.

"Don't you be scared, Gracie. I'll be there in a jiff. Can't you catch hold of the reins? Then perhaps he will stop."

"I can't," said the white, trembling lips. "They have dropped away down at the side."

"In another second I'll be there, and I'll get the reins."

"Oh, Reuben! Do you suppose you can stop him?"

"Of course I can."

What lovely music Reuben Watson Stone's voice was to poor frightened little Gracie! Another vigorous twitch to the strap, and Reuben had clambered over the seat and was reaching over the dashboard for the reins. All the time he talked to Samson in a soothing tone: "Old fellow, good old fellow, don't be scared. Nothing is the matter."

At last he had collected the reins securely in his two brave young hands, climbed back to the seat and pressed his two stout feet against the dashboard. Then the tones of his voice suddenly changed, and Samson was greeted with a loud, firm "Whoa!" At the same moment the tug on the reins was steady and strong.

"Whew!" Samson said to no one in particular. "That means business! A minute ago I was my own master and was flying away from that awful white thing that came up to swallow me, and here I am being jerked at in the same old fashion. I wonder if I've got to stop! How he *does* jerk! I don't know his voice — it isn't my master. I don't believe I'll stop. It is rather pleasant, this running away. I never tried it before."

"Whoa!" said the firm voice again, and the tug on the reins was steady and strong.

"I do believe I've got to stop racing like the wind," Samson conjectured.

To be sure, I did not hear him say all this, but don't you know that actions speak louder than words? By the time they had reached the corner of the long square around which the town was built, Samson's wild run had steadied into a most respectable trot. The people who looked saw only a little boy and girl taking a ride. The boy wore no hat and rather a light jacket for such a frosty morning, but that, of course, concerned only him.

"Has he truly stopped running away?" asked Gracie, emerging from her little huddle in the corner.

"Of course he has — no danger of his doing any more of it very soon. He is beginning to be real ashamed of himself now; he feels mean. He wasn't exactly running away, only making up his mind he would. Now he is sorry he didn't behave better, so he could be trusted. I see by his ears that he is sorry."

"He ought to be," Gracie agreed, drawing a long breath and speaking in a voice that trembled. "He never did such a thing before. Papa has left me in the carriage lots of times and not tied him, and he always stood just as still!"

"Well, you see, he thought that piece of newspaper was a great white elephant come to swallow him. He isn't a literary horse, so he didn't recognize the morning paper." Reuben fumbled in his pocket. "I wonder if I've got that other paper safe! Yes, here it is. What a pity it isn't anything but a paper! It deserves a New Year's dinner or something for blowing out of the door just in the nick of time."

Whereupon he explained to Grace how the wind had suddenly lifted up the little piece of paper with a few words written on it and dropped it down by the carriage. Then he had been sent to fetch it and had just taken hold of the carriage to pick it up when Samson decided to leave.

"I said to myself, I'll hold on to the paper and you, too, old fellow. I'm fond of riding, and if you won't wait for me to get my hat, why, I can go without it. See here, Gracie, if I turn at this corner, will I reach the factory sooner? I'm in a hurry to see your father, or at least I imagine he is in a hurry to see you."

Do you expect me to tell you how Mr. Barrows felt as he saw that wicked horse whisking around the corner with his only little daughter alone in the carriage? He fairly flew through the street, but Samson flew faster. However, he remembered the cross street also, and with a wild hope that he might in some way head the horse off, he dashed across lots and reached the farther corner just as Reuben guided Samson skillfully around it — meek Samson, obedient to every touch of the harness.

"Whoa!" ordered Reuben again, and Samson stopped.

"Here we are, Mr. Barrows," said Reuben. "It's pretty cold this morning for riding; still we had a nice time."

"My little darling!" This was every word Mr. Barrows said as he threw his arms around Grace.

"I'm not hurt a bit, Papa — not a bit," she assured him. "Reuben tugged at the straps and got them loose and climbed in, and Samson minded him right away after a minute. Oh, Papa, aren't you glad you brought Reuben home with you?"

"Shall I drive on, sir?" asked Reuben. He had slipped into the front of the carriage and seemed to think the talk was getting too personal.

"Yes," said Mr. Barrows, his voice gentle and shaking. He did not speak again, except to ask Grace if she was much afraid and if she was quite warm now and over her fright.

After he had lifted her tenderly to the ground and watched her walk into the house, he turned to Reuben, who stood at Samson's bridle awaiting orders. "I shall never forget this morning, my boy."

Perhaps you think it was not much to say, but it sent the blood dancing through Reuben's veins and rollicking all over his face.

"Will you take the horse around to the stable for me and unharness him?"

This was Mr. Barrows's next sentence. Almost before it was finished, Reuben had bounded back again into the carriage with a delighted "Yes, sir."

"What a lark this is!" he told himself aloud as he drove through the avenue. "I shouldn't wonder if it would gain me the chance of taking care of this great big splendid horse now and then. Clarke Miller said Mr. Barrows wouldn't let one of the factory boys look at his old horse, but I've looked at him several times today, I'm thinking."

It was not until dinnertime that Mr. Barrows met Reuben again, just as he was leaving the box factory. "I suppose, my boy, the first piece of paper sailed off on the wind, did it?"

Then Reuben with a red face fumbled in his pocket. "I forgot to give it to you, sir. Samson and everything sent it right out of my mind."

"Then you really picked it up!" The surprise in

his voice gave Reuben a sense of delight that he could not have explained if he had tried. "It is worth a thousand dollars, my boy. But you saved something for me this morning that is worth a thousand worlds, if I had them."

"My!" exclaimed Reuben. It was his only way of expressing astonishment: not over the "thousand worlds" — he was prepared to believe that Grace Barrows was worth a great deal more than that — but over the fact that that simple-looking bit of paper could actually be worth a thousand dollars!

"I don't see how you got in," continued Mr. Barrows, staring down at the piece of paper. "Those buckles haven't been unfastened in six months, and I noticed yesterday that they were rusty."

Reuben answered respectfully: "Tugged at 'em, sir. You see, I knew they *had* to come unbuckled so I could get in. I didn't think I could climb over the top and get down that way in time to save mischief. Besides, there was the danger of scaring the horse more by doing that."

"My boy, did you know the lake was less than a quarter of a mile away in a straight line with the direction the horse took?" Mr. Barrows's voice was husky, and his eyes were dim.

"Yes, sir," said Reuben, glancing down so as not to appear to see the tears in the gentleman's eyes. "That was why I had to hurry so."

Mr. Barrows turned away abruptly; he could not trust himself to say any more just then.

On his way back from dinner, Reuben discovered that the cleaning had been started on the little house. The windows were open, two pails and a broom stood in the doorway, and thick smoke was puffing from the chimney.

I wonder where she got a stove to build a fire in,

Reuben mused as he stood with his hands in his pockets, staring up at it. Somehow that smoke seemed like a little piece of home.

He wanted to go in and look around, but the clock in the church tower gave a single, solemn stroke just then. He pulled his hands out of his pockets and ran.

Several things not mentioned before had occurred while Reuben was away from home. Among others, it had rained steadily for a day and a night, eliminating every bit of the sleighing. Then the ground had frozen, and the lake had skimmed over, as if it meant, if the weather did not change its mind too soon, to give the boys a chance at skating. Since the water was deep, this happened only in severe winters.

The boys discussed the chances as they worked. Further, they were about equally divided in their opinion of Reuben. Part of them were disposed to admire him, and the others to envy what they called his good luck.

"I'll tell you what it is," young Wesley said with an emphatic shake of his head, while Reuben was gone to the office. "It took something more than luck to climb into the back of that carriage and stop that horse. My father says there isn't one boy in ten who would have thought of it at all, and half of them would have been so scared they couldn't 'a done it. I think he showed himself to be a plucky fellow. I say, let's all give in and be friendly. I'm going to ask him to go skating with us tonight."

Not a boy approved of this. Some of them were really out of sorts about Reuben's coming, and some of them liked to disagree with whatever was proposed. So they argued the question hotly, declaring that Reuben was a little dried-up city dunce, and they would have nothing to do with him.

The more they talked, the more determined Wesley was to carry out his plan. The moment Reuben came back he said, "It's freezing hard. The ice will be prime tonight. Want to go to the lake and have a skate?"

Reuben's eyes glistened his thanks for the invitation, but his answer was prompt: "There are two reasons why I can't go: one is, I haven't any skates, and the other is, I never skated a rod in my life."

If you could have heard the shout of laughter that greeted this answer, you would have thought that the greatest oddity in life was a boy who could not skate.

"Poor little fellow!" mimicked one in a tone that he might have used to a boy of six. "Didn't his muvver ever let him go on the ice? It's a shame, so it is! Poor little boy! We'll stop on the way down and buy him a stick of red and white candy, so we will."

These were some of the sentences those rude boys sneered at Reuben. His cheeks flushed red. No boy likes to be laughed at. Still he answered good-naturedly: "You can't pity me any more than I've pitied myself. I s'pose you haven't much notion of how I've wanted a pair of skates. But the honest truth is, boys, it was a choice between skates or bread. When it comes to that, it doesn't take a fellow long to choose. Fact is, I'm poor. Always have been ever since Father died, and I haven't gotten around to skates yet. Maybe I shall some day."

Something in this manly little explanation pleased Wesley, although he had been laughing as hard as any of them. "Quit bothering him," he said. "He's a plucky fellow and a friend of mine. I won't have him abused."

Nevertheless the fun about the skating continued. Not to know how to skate was something so foreign to these country-bred boys that it seemed as though they could not get over laughing about it. Presently, Andrew Porter called on the boys, bringing news that turned their thoughts into another channel.

"You here yet!" he greeted Reuben in a tone of mock surprise. "I thought you would be gone home to your mother by this time. Had any more scares?" Then he told his version of the stagecoach story. "He came up in the four-in-hand with me and rode outside till he got so awful scared of the horses that he had to creep inside and let a fellow take his place."

The boys would have been more ready to believe this story if they had not known about Samson's performance that morning and Reuben's share in the matter. As it was, knowing Andrew as well as they did, not a boy believed that he had told the truth. Yet they laughed.

Then Andrew produced his news. "Say, boys, are any of you going to the thingamajig at the hall tonight? I peeked in there this afternoon and saw some of the pictures while they were fixing the canvas — just splendid, they are! Great big things! Cover all one end of the hall and just as natural as life. A hundred pictures! Don't you know about them? Why, it's the nicest thing that ever came along here. Everybody says so. Of course, I'm going. The tickets are only fifty cents."

Andrew talked exactly as though fifty-cent pieces grew on the bare branches of the winter trees. If the boys had only known how many twists and turns he had had to make, turns that were not even *quite* honest, in order to get that fifty cents, they might not have envied him so much. As it was, they pasted away, with some of them looking disgusted. Not a boy there could by any means afford to pay fifty cents to see pictures. Yet they were very fond of pictures. All boys are.

Andrew carried on with his extravagant account of the wonderful "peeps" he had taken that afternoon. Skating might be all well enough, but it was fast losing its charm for that evening. Every boy wanted to go to the Panorama.

In the midst of Andrew's description, Reuben was summoned to the office again. Andrew paused long enough to say, "Now, old fellow, you're going to get your walking paper. I heard Barrows as I was coming along, telling what an awful nuisance you were." Then he went on with his description.

Reuben left smiling. He was too sadly used to all sorts of bad boys in the city to be shocked with Andrew, and he could afford to smile on his own account. He knew very well how far Mr. Barrows was from considering him a nuisance. He returned with shining eyes and worked at double speed the rest of the afternoon.

If you had been in the office with him, you would have heard Mr. Barrows say, "My boy, here are a couple of tickets to the exhibition this evening at the Duan Street Hall. I think you will like to go. Perhaps there is some boy in the shop or out of it that you would like to take with you, since Beth isn't here. And, Reuben, one more thing — I would prefer you not go into the little house until after the cleaning is finished. Just wait until I give you permission, will you? The person working there doesn't like to be disturbed."

Over this last, Reuben pondered as he worked. He felt a great longing to see the little house with clean floors and windows. "She must be a touchy body," he said, thinking of the "person" who was hired to clean the house. "Just as if I would disturb her! But I suppose she thinks if I come the other boys will. I can wait." And he whistled over the thought of all his joys.

"Look here," he said to Wesley as the two proceeded down the hall together with a pack of pasteboard on their shoulders. "I'm real obliged to you for asking me to go skating tonight. I'd like no better fun. But since I can't, suppose you go with me."

"Go where?"

"To that picture exhibition at the hall."

"Just so. I'm agreed. Where shall we steal the tickets? Have you made your plans?" he asked with a mischievous twinkle in his black eyes.

"Yes, *sir,*" said Reuben. "Got 'em all made. Look here!" And he showed him the two green tickets.

Then Wesley whistled.

CHAPTER XVII

Some New Experiences

aturday night, just after the clock in the church tower had struck six, Mr. Barrows handed Reuben the key to the little house, with permission to inspect it and see that everything was all right.

He stood on the little stone doorstep and gazed about him a few minutes, key in hand. It seemed so new and businesslike to stand before a door which belonged to a house he had rented and into which he was to move his family so soon; for now he felt sure that his mother would come. He had often dreamed of the time when he would rent a house and move his family, but even his wildest waking dreams had placed the time a few years ahead. Yet here he stood, all prepared to do it.

"What a nice place this would be to keep a cow!" he said aloud to himself, surveying the bit of a yard with a neat shed at the back. He appeared to be wise and manly and tried not to notice that his heart was beating like a sledgehammer. "I wonder if we can manage to have our own cow one of these days! I wonder what Beth would say to that — whole tumblers filled with milk! I wonder what Beth will say to everything!"

He sighed. It seemed like such a long time to wait from now until Monday before telling Beth about things.

The night was old, so he soon decided it was foolish to stand outside when he might as well go in. How nicely the key fitted in the lock! He threw the door open and stepped into the bit of a hall. There was a neat oilcloth on the floor. He stopped and stared at it in surprise. He had not noticed it when he was there before.

"Maybe it goes with the house," he said aloud. "I hope it does. How nice it looks! Mother couldn't afford any now. I don't see where the money to move is coming from. That's what bothers me."

This he said as he was opening the parlor door. For the next few minutes he said nothing. If you could have seen his face, you would have wanted a picture of it to take home with you and keep. He swung his lantern aloft to gain from it all possible light on the scene and then stood still. On the floor lay a red and brown carpet with small bright leaves growing on a woodsy ground; it looked like the stories of the woods he and Beth had read about together.

Oh, how soft the carpet was. He lifted one foot carefully and set it down on a bright autumn leaf, then pulled it back. He could not have that leaf stepped on. Curtains hung at the windows, a warm, bright color that reminded him of sunshine. A little round stove occupied a place over by the mantel, and a fire burned cheerily in it. The room was warm. A round table was drawn out in the center of the room with some chairs around it as though people had just been sitting there and had left for a few minutes. There was even a little old-fashioned, cushioned lounge.

Reuben did not know it was old-fashioned, but he knew it was beautiful. Not a word did he say. He tiptoed through the room into the kitchen. How warm and inviting it was! The floor had been painted. He saw that at a glance — he saw everything at a glance. A stove was set up and glowing, with blacking outside and coals inside. The little cupboard stood open; dishes were arranged in rows, as if people had just eaten supper and washed and put away the dishes. How quietly and yet how brightly the fire burned in the stove! Reuben thought of the one at home that always smoked and sulked and glowered.

"Well!" he said at last. "Well, if this isn't the strangest way to clean!" Then he tried to whistle. He had always whistled before when anything surprised him, but something was the matter with his throat. He choked and coughed and tried to force out a clear sound. Then he actually sat down on one of the neat chairs, of which there were several in the room, and cried. What was he crying about? He couldn't have told you if you had been there and asked; in fact, I suppose if you had been there, he wouldn't have cried. But his heart was so full of surprised delight and some other peculiar feeling, of which he did not know the name, that the tears would not stay back.

"Reuben Watson Stone, you're just a simpleton — that's what you are!" he told himself at last, amazed over the tears. Then without more ado he climbed upstairs. What could it all mean? He began to fear that some dreadful mistake had been made and some other family not belonging to him had moved in. Here he found more carpet on the floor, a bedstead set up, curtains at the windows, a little rocking chair and a pretty oval table.

"Look here," said the boy at last, setting down his lantern on one chair and himself on another. "Wake up, can't you? I say, old fellow, you must be dreaming. This isn't your house! Where did all these things come from, and who are they for? *You* don't own any of them. What are you going to do about it? This is just the strangest world I ever heard of; there is never any telling what will happen next. I only wish Beth could see the flowers on this carpet! She would pick 'em as sure as the world." Then suddenly remembering the wonderful fact that Beth would see them very soon, that peculiar lump began to creep into his throat again. He jumped up suddenly, seized his lantern and hurried away. He didn't know what to make of himself, but he meant not to cry again.

"Well," said Mr. Barrows as he appeared at last in the kitchen where Reuben was hanging up his lantern, "been over to the new house, have you? Has the cleaning been done to your satisfaction?"

"Cleaning!" repeated Reuben. "I never heard of stoves and carpets and things being *cleaned* into a house before. Mr. Barrows, I don't know, I can't think —," and there he stopped.

That ridiculous lump began to swell in his throat again. How was he ever going to talk with that lump coming up to choke him?

"All right," smiled Mr. Barrows, "you needn't think anything about it. I'll guess all you were going to say."

"But, sir," said Reuben, "I meant, I didn't mean — you know, sir —," and Reuben stopped again.

"Of course," said Mr. Barrows. "I know all about it. You didn't mean anybody should help you support your family. You didn't expect any help, and you're quite right. I haven't a doubt you'll be able to do it nicely. But see here, my boy. Never be afraid to take a little hearty lifting from your friends, when they can do it as well as not and like to, and it will make things easier for your mother.

"Nothing very wonderful has been done. The carpet was some we had and didn't want to use. It might as well go down there and make things homelike. The stove in the kitchen is secondhand. We needed a larger one, and so we turned it out. It wouldn't bring much of anything for old iron, and yet it is a pretty good stove and will save your mother paying for moving hers. As for the stove in the parlor, it is out of use this winter and may as well stand there as anywhere. And the furniture is a present to your sister, Beth, from my little girl.

"My boy, you have done for me this week what all the stoves and carpets and furniture in all the world can never pay. And I didn't help furnish your new house for *pay,* but just because I wanted to. You can tell your mother you earned every cent of it and more too, for I put it there because she has a good, brave, trustworthy boy."

What was Reuben to say? He had never been so speechless in his life. At last he made a bold attempt. "I don't know how to thank you," he said, glancing up with frank, earnest eyes into Mr. Barrows's face. "I never learned how to thank folks, but I'm just as grateful as I can be, and I'll do the best I can."

"All right," Mr. Barrows said. It was a favorite

phrase of his. "When I have learned how to thank you for taking care of my Gracie, perhaps you will have learned how to thank me for a stove and a few things. You see, we are hardly even, my boy."

Reuben left the room with red cheeks. Of course, he was glad he had used his wits and been able to rescue Grace Barrows. But anybody who knew enough would have done that, he told himself as he prepared for bed. But there were lots and lots of people who wouldn't have put all those nice things in the little house for his mother. And I suppose that was true.

The next day Reuben attended church in a new fashion. His churchgoing had been very inconsistent. He had sometimes climbed into the gallery of the great building where he attended Sunday school in order to hear the organ play and see the well-dressed people, but he always felt out of place and uncomfortable. Very few people sat up there, and those few looked forlorn and friendless.

Nobody spoke to him or looked at him, and he paid little attention to what was happening after the organ was still. The minister may have preached good sermons; Reuben did not know. He was busy deciding how he would dress Mother and Beth when he became rich, which pew in the church he would hire and whether he would drive to church in his carriage. All these plans and many more Reuben had, and church was the place in which they grew faster than anywhere else.

In the first place he had a new overcoat.

"I wonder if Bennie's coat would fit him!" Mrs. Barrows had said at the breakfast table. Her startled husband had agreed that he shouldn't be surprised if it would; at least it might be tried if she said so.

After breakfast it was brought: a gray coat, long and heavy, with many pockets and handsome buttons. It fitted to a charm.

"It was my little boy's," Mrs. Barrows said, her eyes tender and sad. "We bought it for him only a few months before he went away. I have never wanted anybody to wear it. But if it hadn't been for you, perhaps we should have had no little girl in the house this morning. My Bennie was a good boy. I think I'll give you his coat."

All this brought the lump into Reuben's throat again, swelling even larger than ever. He resolved then and there he would never soil Bennie's overcoat by thinking a mean thought under it. It covered his worn and patched jacket to a nicety—even covered the patch on his trousers. With his shoes blacked and his hair combed, he felt as if his dreams were coming true, and he must attend to what was now going on instead of thinking about the somedays ahead. New things were pouring in on him so fast they needed all his present attention. So he sat straight up in the end of the Barrows pew beside Mr. Barrows. Though it was warm, he kept his overcoat on, tightly buttoned at his throat, and listened as well as he could to the sermon. But it was in the afternoon Sunday school that he did his best listening.

The class he visited was unlike any he had ever known about; at least the teacher was. In the first place she was a young, pretty lady. Reuben had a fondness for well-dressed people. He did not realize that he liked to look at them. He admired his teacher very much. The only other teacher with whom he had been acquainted was a man who read questions at him from a book, questions he did not understand or care about. This one did not seem to be discussing a Sunday school lesson at all.

"I wonder if any of you boys know how to manage a boat?" she began. Some of them did or thought they did, and others had questions to ask. Before he knew it, Reuben grew interested and forgot all about the lesson.

"What do you think you would do in a storm?" she asked the boy who said he knew how to manage a boat. That started talk afresh. One told what he would do, and another criticized it. At last when Reuben was appealed to, he had to admit that he knew nothing at all about boats.

"Well, in any case," said the teacher, "suppose you are in some place where you know there is danger. You have done the best you know. Yet you feel sure you are in great danger and know of no way to help yourself. What would you do next?"

"Why, there wouldn't be anything to do," declared one boy, "only to stand still and let it come."

"Or run away from it," said another.

"Suppose you couldn't run away from it?" said the teacher. "Suppose it would run away with you?"

"I'd find a way out somehow," said another.

"But we are supposing you had tried all your ways out and were *not* out, that you only felt yourself getting deeper and deeper into trouble. What then? Think, all of you. Is there one in the class who has ever been in a great trouble, out of which he could not help himself?"

Reuben's mind quickly returned to that wild ride with Spunk and his drunken master over dark and dangerous roads with the express train chasing them. He had kept still until then, an eager listener with little to say. But at the memory of his danger and his escape, he drew a long, half-shuddering sigh and said almost before he knew it: "I'll tell you what it is — I've been there."

The boys turned and looked at him, and the teacher smiled on him. "In danger, my boy?"

"Yes'm."

"And did you know what to do?"

"Some things I knew and did them. But there came a time when there wasn't anything left to do except hold on, and that I did with all my might. But it didn't seem to be doing any good."

"And then what?"

"And then," said Reuben in a slow, somber tone, his face paling over the memory of it all, "I told God about it."

"And did He answer?"

"Yes'm," said Reuben simply.

The boys looked at him respectfully. His face was flushed now, and he glanced down at the floor. He wasn't used to talking about such things.

"I am very glad," said the teacher brightly. "You can understand, perhaps, better than the rest of us how Peter felt when he climbed out of the boat onto that water, trying to walk on it, and found that he couldn't — found himself sinking. It wasn't until then that he called out to the Lord. I wonder, Reuben, if you waited until you had done for yourself everything you could think of before you called to Him."

"Yes'm," said Reuben, going swiftly back over his experience. "I did just that."

"People are apt to," she said. "Peter did so, too."

By this time every boy in the class wanted to know about Peter. Reuben had been placed in one of those trying classes where not a boy had studied his lesson, and of course he hadn't. He never dreamed of such a thing; so they were all ignorant together, but all eager to hear. Then began the story of the night ride on the lake with hard rowing and contrary wind and one walking on the water, of whom the sailors were afraid at first and to whom Peter tried to go and almost failed. It was a new story to Reuben; in fact, almost all Bible stories were new to him. He was intrigued and forgot he was a stranger, asking questions with such eagerness that the teacher found it a pleasure to teach.

But out of all this came something strange.

The last hymn was sung, the prayer was offered, and the young people were crowding out. The new teacher laid a small gloved hand on Reuben's shoulder and said in a voice that he never forgot: "I'm glad to see that you are a Christian, my boy."

Then Reuben was startled indeed. The blood rushed over his face, and he turned and gazed on her with astonished eyes.

"Ma'am?" he said at last, not knowing what to say.

"I am glad you love the Lord Jesus and look to Him for help and that you have found Him able and ready to help you."

"Oh, but," he said in great confusion, "that is a mistake. I don't know much about Him, and I don't belong to Him at all."

"Is it so?"

And Reuben felt his cheeks grow hotter over the sound of disappointed surprise in her voice.

"I'm so sorry. I thought since you knew where to go in trouble, you surely must be one who followed Him. Don't you think you ought to be a Christian, my boy?"

"I don't know what a Christian is."

He looked directly into her face and spoke the words with sincerity. He knew almost nothing about these things and had puzzled over them a good deal, especially since meeting Miss Hunter.

"A Christian is one who loves the Lord Jesus Christ and tries to do as He says."

"I don't know much about what He says, and as to loving Him, why, I never thought of it before."

Reuben was always honest, so now he spoke his exact thoughts.

"One thing He says is that everybody ought to make up his or her mind to obey His directions all the time."

"That mightn't be easy to do."

"No, sometimes it isn't. In fact, it can't be done at all without His help, but He is always ready with that. And the beauty of it is, the only safe and happy way is the one He points out."

"Then I shouldn't think it would be hard to mind Him."

"Not after we once decide the thing. Will you decide it now, Reuben?"

Reuben was startled. What a plain question this was! And the lady looked right at him with bright, earnest eyes and waited for his answer.

"I don't know," he said at last, glancing down.

"Aren't you a boy who always tries hard to do just as he says he will?"

"Yes'm." He didn't hesitate a minute over this answer. He felt so sure of his promises. In fact, he prided himself on doing just that.

"I thought so. I wish you would promise to do this thing."

"But I can't, you see. Maybe it is a promise I couldn't keep, and I don't want to make any like that."

"No, but you can certainly keep this if you choose. Won't you be willing to take my word for that?"

No, Reuben wouldn't. He did not say so, but he glanced down again with a troubled expression on his face and seemed not at all ready to answer. The lady waited.

"Well," she said at last, "will you promise this: that you will think about it the rest of this day — that as much as you can you will keep from all other thoughts and just give your mind to this?"

"To what?"

"To deciding whether you will take Jesus Christ for your master and obey Him in every little and great thing all the rest of your life."

"Yes'm," he said after another minute's hesitation. "I will promise to *think* about it."

Then she reached out her hand and took his little brown one in it for a moment. With a smile she said, "Thank you. I can't help thinking you are an honest boy with good common sense, and I'm not afraid of the way you will decide, if you only think."

CHAPTER XVIII

Reuben Takes Two Prisoners

hen Reuben walked home with Grace Barrows. She chattered like a magpie, but Reuben was quiet.

"What makes you so still?" she asked him at last.

Because he had something to think about, he told her.

"What is it? Oh, I know! You are thinking about going home tomorrow and getting the folks and coming back and riding on the cars and moving everything. You have a lot of things to think about."

"No," Reuben said with a serious face. "It would be easy enough to think of all that. But I mustn't do it today. You see, I promised I'd attend to something else."

"Promised whom? What must you attend to?"

But Reuben did not choose to answer any of these questions. Instead, he inquired about her class in Sunday school, what sort of a teacher they had, what they talked about and how much she had learned.

"Oh, we didn't talk about anything much!" said Grace. "Only a little about Peter, and some about Jesus. Miss Williams didn't tell us anything to remember. At least, I don't remember it, if she did. You had the best teacher in the school, Reuben. Everybody says Miss Parker is the best teacher in our school."

"I believe it," said Reuben sturdily. Then he was quiet again. He did not seem to be able to get on with his thinking. How was he ever to do it if this chattering little girl stayed by his side?

When they reached home, it was not much better. Mr. Barrows laid aside the newspaper he was reading and talked to Reuben, advising him on what train to take and planning how soon he could get back.

All the while Reuben sat with a sober, thoughtful face, wondering how he was to keep his promise. He tried to think just what he had promised — to keep as much as possible from thinking about anything else but the question of whether he would belong to Christ or not.

But I don't know how to belong to Him, he told himself. Then he remembered in the next second that it made no difference. He must decide whether he would belong. After that he could find out how to do it.

"Anything wrong?" Mr. Barrows asked at last with a kind smile, seeing Reuben so quiet.

"No, sir," said Reuben.

Then Grace came to the rescue. "He has something to think about, Papa — something he promised to decide."

"Indeed, what is that?"

"I don't know, Papa. It is a secret, I think, but Reuben promised to do it."

"Promised whom?"

"The teacher I had today," said Reuben, seeing that Grace was not going to answer for him.

"Yes, and, Papa, it must be a good promise, for Miss Parker was his teacher."

"I daresay it was," said Mr. Barrows with a curious glance at Reuben. "Do you need any help about it?"

"No," said Reuben thoughtfully. He had nearly said yes. Then he remembered that it was something to *decide*. How could anybody help him decide a question like that? After it was settled, he might need a great deal of help, but not before.

You would be surprised, perhaps, to know how that promise troubled Reuben all the rest of the day. He could not escape it, and he could not seem to settle the question. He wished for Beth. Things always seemed easier and plainer when he talked them over with Beth. But then he remembered that she knew nothing about this matter.

Then he looked over at Grace. She was a little girl, to be sure, but a very sensible one. He wondered whether she had ever made such a promise as this and settled the question. She was reading her Sunday school book; he didn't like to disturb her.

Presently she looked up. "I don't believe I like this book. It is for grown-up people."

"How do you know?"

"Why, it is all about folks being Christians — telling them how and why they ought to be and all that."

Reuben was astonished. How strange that

Grace's book should be about the very thing of which he had promised to think.

"Does it say there that folks needn't tend to such things until they grow up?"

"Why, no," said Gracie slowly. "No, it doesn't. It says that even little children ought to be Christians. But I don't see how they can."

"Why not?"

"Because they can't be sober all the time and think about dying and going to heaven."

"Does it say there that when folks are Christians they must be sober all the time and think about dying and going to heaven?"

"No," said Grace. This time she laughed. "But then grown-up folks who are good do, I suppose."

"I don't," said Reuben positively. "I know some good folks who think about their work and about making nice times for other people, and they look pleasant and laugh and talk." He thought of Miss Hunter. "What is being a Christian, Gracie?" He asked this after waiting for her a little while and getting no answer.

"Why, it is being good."

He shook his head. "No, it isn't. It is just loving Christ and trying to mind Him."

"Well, don't you have to be good before you can do that?"

"Do you have to be good before you can love your father and mother?"

"Oh, no!" she laughed again. "But that is different. Why, Reuben, Christian people are good people."

"Yes, I suppose they become good. They would have to, of course, if they tried to mind Jesus. But they don't have to be good before they can love Him, according to all that I ever heard of."

"No," said Grace, "of course not. I didn't mean that. People can't be good, of course, until they get new hearts. They won't get them without asking Jesus, and they wouldn't ask Him if they didn't love Him a little, I suppose."

Reuben turned toward her eagerly. He knew very little about this matter. He was not sure that anything had been said to him about a new heart. Maybe that was something to attend to before he could decide.

"What do you mean by that?" he asked her.

"By what?"

"By getting a new heart."

"Why, I mean just that. Jesus can give folks new hearts, and He does, of course, before they are Christians."

"How can He? Our hearts are inside us. How can God take them out while we are alive and give us new ones?"

"Why, Reuben Stone! Don't you know what I mean? Of course our hearts are not taken out of us! But Jesus puts new thoughts in them — makes them over in some way so we can like to do things that before we didn't like to. I don't know how He does it, but I know that is what a new heart means. And you've got to have one before you can be a Christian."

"And you get it for the asking?"

"Yes," said Grace confidentially — she had been well taught — "you get it for the asking. Then you are a great deal happier than you ever were before. You like to pray and read the Bible and go to church and all that — and you aren't afraid to die."

"Have you got one?"

"Why, no!" This time she blushed a little as well as laughed. "What a strange boy you are! I told you I thought it was for grown-up folks. How can little girls think about such things?"

"But little girls might have to die. The other day when Samson was running away with you, he was going straight toward the lake, and it wasn't frozen over then. He might have tumbled you in and drowned you."

"Don't," said Grace. "It makes me shiver all over." She hid her face in her hands.

A minute later she ran to her mother and told her Reuben Stone was the strangest boy she had ever talked with in her whole life.

Then Reuben, left alone, continued his thinking. Grace had certainly given him several reasons why he ought to decide this question. He thought she was peculiar to know so many reasons why it would be nice to be a Christian, know just how to become one and yet would rather wait until she was grown up.

I don't believe I would, he said to himself. I'd like to begin now. It's hard work, I suppose. All new things are hard to do, and some old ones. But it would be nice to feel that you weren't afraid of anything. Then there are lots of places where a fellow needs help, and He helped me once. I know a few things. I know I'll have to read the Bible. I don't like that very well, but I would if Gracie knows what she is talking about and I got that new heart.

Before him on the table lay a little bit of a blue-covered book not more than two inches wide and hardly three inches long. Reuben stretched out his hand to it, then drew it back. Hadn't he promised to think of nothing but this question all day? Still, it might be something that would help him. He would just glance at it. *Heavenly Manna* was the name of it. Reuben didn't know the meaning of *manna,* but the word *heavenly* seemed to fit the subject. He peeked inside and discovered it to be a book of prayers and promises, dated according to the days of the year. Of course, the most natural thing in the world was for him to turn to that day's date and read the verses. He could hardly believe his eyes. How very strange! These were the verses: "Create in me a clean heart, O God, and renew a right spirit within me."

"A new heart will I give you, and a new spirit will I put within you."

There's the prayer, and there's the answer, Reuben said to himself thoughtfully. The thing is now for me to do it.

But for some reason that he himself did not understand, he did not do it. He knew something about Satan. But Reuben did not, after all, know what an enemy he was—nor how anxious Satan was to keep him from deciding this important question once for all. If he could only get him to think of something else! Reuben wondered many times in the course of that day what could be the matter with his mind. It was so determined to think of everything but the question. He came back to it again and again because his promise called him. But it did not hold him steadily to the work.

When the day was gone, and Reuben was ready to lie down in his bed, he said aloud with a sigh: "Well, I've done my best, anyhow. I never knew it was so awful hard to keep thinking of the same thing. Nothing has come of it, either. I don't decide. Why don't I? It's odd now, but I can't tell why I don't. Gracie made me think she was a goose for not deciding. I suppose I'm a goose. I wonder what

Mother thinks! She must have had this question to decide ever so long ago. Maybe she is at it yet."

A feeling came over the boy that he wouldn't like to be so long settling the matter as his mother had been — in case she was still thinking about it. Then why didn't he kneel down then and there and ask Jesus Christ to take him? He didn't know what kept him from it, but Satan knew very well and laughed in triumph when the boy fell asleep without praying at all.

In the middle of the night Reuben opened his eyes and searched about him in the darkness, wondering what noise he had heard. He raised himself on one elbow and listened. There were certainly people talking. It couldn't be that the family was still up and around, for Reuben knew by the darkness that the moon was gone; he knew it did not set until after eleven o'clock. It must be about midnight. But the talking was growing more distinct.

"Where can that confounded key be, anyhow?"

"He always hangs it by the sink. I've seen him do it fifty times when I've been here with milk."

"Well, he didn't do it the fifty-first time, anyhow, for it ain't here. I've felt all around."

"You better not talk so loud. First thing you know, somebody will hear us."

"Somebody can't. That's Rupert's room over the kitchen, and I told you before we started that he was five miles away out in the country. Shut that door! I'm going to risk a match!"

Reuben heard all this as plainly as though he were in the kitchen. It took him much less time to hear it than it has taken to tell it. All the while he was thinking fast.

This was how it seemed to him: Somebody was in the kitchen hunting for the key to the barn. They either meant to steal Samson altogether or steal a ride on him that night. He also knew he had been the last one to have possession of the barn key. He hung it across the room from the sink over behind the closet door. He had come to the sink to hang it up, and Hannah had said: "You can't get here now. Put the key on the hook behind the door. Rupert does sometimes."

How did those fellows get into the kitchen? The door was open, for he had heard the order to shut it. He knew something about that too. He had been sitting by the kitchen window; Hannah had asked him if he wasn't going to bed tonight and said she was going to lock up. Then he had said with a sudden start: "Oh, Hannah, the kitchen key is upstairs in my room! You gave it to me this morning, you know, to unlock the washroom door, and I carried it up there. I'll run and get it."

Hannah had answered: "No, you needn't. I'll slip the bolt. It's better than the key anyhow."

But she must have forgotten to slip the bolt.

Now how did he happen to be in the room over the kitchen, hearing all this? Mrs. Barrows had said just before he went up to bed: "It's bitterly cold tonight, Reuben. I think I will send you to Rupert's room to sleep. That little north room where I put you is pretty cold, and it is quite warm in the kitchen chamber. Rupert won't return until tomorrow night."

Reuben assured her he did not mind the cold, and the little north room was splendid. But he scurried off well pleased to the hired man's comfortable quarters and rejoiced that Rupert had been given a holiday and traveled into the country to see his mother.

That was how he ended up being last at the barn

and to know about the key.

Don't you know how fast people can think? All this flashed through Reuben's mind like lightning. He even thought how strange it was that all these apparently insignificant events should have happened, one after another, so that he knew the whole story. More than that, he knew what he meant to try to do. To go down the front stairs and knock at Mr. Barrows's door and carry on a conversation with him would likely warn the thieves, if they were thieves — and they acted like it. Then they would slip away with whatever they chose to carry, and no one would be the wiser. The family might think he dreamed out the whole story. And perhaps the thieves would come the next night and carry out their plans. He would do no such thing as that.

He slipped out of bed and pushed up his window. Below him lay the roof of the outer kitchen or shed. It was easy enough for a surefooted boy like Reuben to let himself down to that and swing off to the coal box below and from there to the ground. What then? Why, then he had the kitchen key in his hand, and the visitors had shut the door. What was to hinder him from slipping around and making them prisoners by turning the key in the lock?

The windows were secured by strong shutters with fastenings which had a trick of not opening except for those who knew how to touch just the right spring. Grace had amused herself for fifteen minutes on Saturday by watching him try to find the secret of that spring. Reuben thought of that as another little thing that had been planned to fit this night's work.

He was out of the window like a cat, not even

waiting for clothes — waiting only to get the key from the little table where he had laid it when he went to the north room for his jacket. Why he brought the key back with him he did not know. He was standing on the frozen ground now. It was bitterly cold, and his little shirt was not the warmest. He wished he had wrapped himself in a quilt, but that would have hindered his quick, light steps perhaps. His bare feet made no sound on the snow, and in a minute more he stood before the kitchen door, key in hand.

Could he find the keyhole? Would the key slip in easily without noise? What if the fellows inside should hear him and should rush to the door and open it and seize him, choking him before he could cry out?

CHAPTER XIX

In the Little House at Home

ark!" exclaimed a voice inside. "What was that?""

"The wind, I s'pose. I didn't hear anything. I say, Jim, what a coward you are. If I'd known you was so scary, I'd never have undertaken this job with you."

"Well, hurry up, or the undertaking won't do you any good. I don't believe the key is here at all. That horse is a vixen anyhow. He won't let us touch him. What ails them matches? Why don't they burn?"

I don't believe he will, Reuben said to himself, in answer to their remark about Samson. So you are after *him,* you scamps. I'm glad I hung the key where it doesn't belong. Now for getting back.

The fact is, the little noise one of them had heard was the turning of the key in the lock. It slipped into place as noiselessly as anybody could wish with just the least bit of a click which the wind might have made in a dozen ways. Reuben drew it out again and tiptoed over the snow. Climbing to the coal box, he wound his spry young limbs around the gutter pipe, scuttled over the shed roof and was back in his room again in a jiffy. Moving softly still and not waiting for clothes even yet, he wrapped himself in the overcoat that had kept him warm all day. Then he opened the hall door and felt his way down the hall to the front stairs, down those stairs and another hall, carefully inching his way. Finally he knocked softly at what he guessed was Mr. Barrows's room.

There was no answer, so he had to knock a little louder.

"Halloo!" came at last from inside. "Who's there? What's the matter?"

"It's me," whispered Reuben. "Won't you please let me in? I want to speak to you."

A few words were said inside, then a little waiting, and finally Mr. Barrows threw open the door.

"What's up, my boy? Are you sick?"

"No, sir," said Reuben, stepping inside and quietly closing the door. "There's somebody in the house."

"Oh, no," said Mr. Barrows. "I'm sure not. You've been dreaming and got frightened."

Reuben knew by the sound of his voice that he was smiling.

"No, sir," said Reuben. "It's them that are scared, I guess, or will be pretty soon. I don't think they know yet. They're in the kitchen, sir, hunting for the barn key. I've locked 'em up, only they don't know it."

"In the kitchen! Who are? You've locked them up! Are you talking in your sleep?"

Mr. Barrows fumbled for his matches, touched the gas jet and scrutinized the boy buttoned up in an overcoat with bare feet and legs.

"No, sir," replied Reuben again and chuckled in spite of himself. He knew he looked funny. "It's quite a long story, sir. I heard 'em. I know they are there, and I don't quite see how they can get out until you or I let 'em. There's the key. They woke me up talking over their plans. I knew I had the kitchen key, so I slipped down the roof and locked the door. They thought I was the wind and kept on hunting for the barn key."

A more astonished man than Mr. Barrows it would have been hard to find. There was much about the story he did not understand, but it was plain to see that Reuben was wide awake and knew what he was talking about. So without more ado Mr. Barrows hurriedly dressed himself, while Reuben stepped quietly into the hall.

"Better go upstairs, my boy," Mr. Barrows said as he passed him. "You have done your share. If the scamps are young fellows, as I suspect, it will be better for you not to appear."

"I'll wait here," said Reuben, taking a seat in the hall.

Mr. Barrows passed through the hall and the dining room, pausing there to turn on the gas, which, when the door was opened, would send a flood of light into the kitchen. Then he quietly opened the door. "Well, boys, good morning!" he greeted them and sat down.

Reuben thought he would give almost anything to see their faces just then. He heard their smothered exclamations of dismay and terror and their dash for the door, which, of course, was locked.

Just what transpired in the kitchen after that,

Reuben does not know to this day. He heard the murmur of voices but could not make out any words. By and by he heard the key turn in the lock and heard Mr. Barrows say, "Good-bye!" Presently he returned to the hall.

"You have done a grand night's work, my boy," he said, laying his hand on Reuben's head, "one you can be glad about forever. Those fellows meant to take Samson and have an all-night frolic. They would doubtless have ruined him, but they would have done worse than that. Samson is a good horse when people know how to manage him and a bad one when they don't. They would have taken the whip to him, and then he would have been unmanageable at once. They probably would have been killed. Now come where it is warm and let me hear the whole story of how you found them out." He led the way to the sitting room.

"I don't suppose they meant to *steal?*" Reuben asked.

"I don't suppose they did," said Mr. Barrows. "At least they didn't call it that. Yet, you see, they were preparing to steal the use of my horse. People often fail to call things by their right names. Is your question decided yet, my boy?"

"No, sir," answered Reuben, glancing down.

Mr. Barrows caught sight of his bare feet and sent him to bed with directions to sleep as late as he could in the morning.

When Reuben had tucked himself into bed again, his eyes were wider open than they had ever been before. He reviewed every little circumstance connected with the night and wondered for the twentieth time who those fellows could be. He thought of all the little things that had happened beforehand to make it possible for him to prevent the mischief.

"Exactly as if somebody knew all about what was going to happen and had planned all the other things and made them fit," he said.

Then he gave a little start, and his eyes opened wider as he remembered that God knew about all things before they came to pass. What a wonderful kind of friend to have, he thought — someone who truly cared for him.

"I'll give myself to Him," he said with resolve. "I'll decide that question now, this minute. And I'll tell Him so and ask Him to take me."

A second time on that cold winter night Reuben Stone climbed out of his warm bed — this time to get on his knees.

In the little house at home, things were not progressing any too well during Reuben's absence. The mother was secretly astounded over the number of things one boy could do to make the days pass more easily. She had not realized before just what a help and comfort her "man of the house" was.

But missing him was not the only trouble. Work suddenly grew very scarce. Whether all the boys in the world were supplied with shirts, Mrs. Stone did not know. She only knew that when she returned the last bundle, a thing she was not used to doing — Reuben had not let her carry any bundles through the streets for two years — the foreman told her the package to carry home would be lighter; he had only a small one. Work was scarce. It had been all they could do to divide it among their faithful workers equally.

This saddened Mrs. Stone; it was all they could

do to manage when she sewed every minute. The little that Reuben had been able to earn — so little she had not supposed she could miss it — was really missed a great deal. She trudged home slowly, saving the five cents it would have cost to ride part of the long way in the streetcar, and tried to contrive some way to save money or to earn a little more.

To make matters worse, Beth met her at the door with the news: "Oh, Mother, the agent has been here and given notice that the rent on this house will be raised a whole dollar the first of next month!"

"A whole dollar!" repeated Mrs. Stone. "Then we must starve."

Then she did what Beth had never seen her do before: She collapsed in the sewing chair behind the stove and cried. This occurred only two days after Reuben left. From that time mother and daughter scrimped and pinched, both with coal and potatoes, and tried in every conceivable way to save a penny.

Miss Hunter was as kind and gracious as she could be. She had invited them twice to dinner and once to tea, but the third time Mrs. Stone refused to go.

"We can't invite her back," she said grimly to Beth. "She does it out of charity anyway. I'm not used to charity. You can go if you want to, child, but her nice white bread would choke me."

Beth wouldn't go without her mother, not even to save an evening's meal.

So Miss Hunter could not do much for them. In fact, she could not find out how much they needed doing for, though she suspected, for Beth's eyes were often red. She knew, too, that work had failed. But that was no more than had happened to her, skilled worker that she was. She shed no tears over it for two reasons: In the first place, she had a snug bit of money laid aside for future use; and, in the second place, it gave her time to make over the blue merino into a perfect fit for Beth. She got the exact measure by offering to cut out a calico for her that the mother was making out of hers.

"There's that ten dollars, Mother," Beth said as they sat together in the evening, commiserating about the future.

"Yes." That one word conveyed Mrs. Stone's gloomiest thoughts.

She didn't often feel so sad, but it seemed a dreadful thing for work to fail her, especially with rent being raised the same week. It was Sunday evening after a dreary day. A good deal of it had been spent in bed.

To be sure, Beth ventured out to Sunday school with Miss Hunter, and in her new calico and the lovely fur cape and hood she looked as neat as wax. Miss Hunter wanted her to wear the blue merino, but she had not found a good excuse for giving it to her yet. She was waiting for Reuben to return to pave the way for such a nice present.

"If I'd known about her birthday and had it ready, I might have given it to her then," she mused out loud. "But, then, dear me! I wasn't acquainted with them then."

After Sunday school, which Beth had not enjoyed as much as Reuben did his (she had sat beside two little girls who whispered and giggled over the strangeness of wearing fur hoods and capes and calico dresses), she came home to discover the fire out and her mother in bed.

"It died out," the mother said, raising herself on

her elbow to speak to the little girl. "I thought I would let it go until it was time to fix something to eat. It would save coal, and the coal is getting very low. Come and lie down and take a nap."

But Beth had slept well all night, and she was wide awake. The last thing she wanted to do was to take a nap. She thought of the glimpse she had had into Miss Hunter's cheery room; an intense longing came over her to sit down inside and read her Sunday school book.

"Mother," she said, "couldn't I go into Miss Hunter's room? She asked me to come, and it is so nice and warm in there!"

But the mother rebuked her sharply. "No, child, no! Don't beg fire until you have to. Come and lie down."

So Beth, with a sigh, had put away her hood and cape and slipped under the quilts beside her mother. She lay very still so her mother could sleep but did not sleep herself. She wished the dreary day was done and that Reuben was at home again. It seemed at least a month since he had left them. So this evening they lingered dolefully over the dying coals, and Beth reminded her mother of Reuben's ten dollars.

"Yes," her mother had said. "I wanted to keep that to buy you and Reuben some spring clothes. I don't know how you will manage without some. He is in rags, and he outgrew every single thing he had last summer. But the money will have to go, of course, for coal and rent, and then how long will it last? Ten dollars isn't a fortune, I tell you. If I don't get more work this week, I shall have to spend some of it right away. These shirts won't buy potatoes and salt enough to last us through the week."

"Mother," said Beth, after another gloomy silence, "don't you truly think anything at all will come of Reuben's going out there to stay a week?"

The mother gave a provoked little "Humph!" as a beginning to her answer. "Of course not! What could come of it? He is nothing but a child. Small for his age, too. I don't see what possessed me to let him go off like that. I've had my pay for it. I haven't slept two good hours a night since he left. If he only gets home safe, without learning any dreadful habits, I shall be satisfied. It was a wild idea to think of our moving away out there. Where would we get the money to move? And just as though anybody would let us have a house without paying for it beforehand!"

"But the man said we could earn it," persisted Beth.

"Oh, yes, the man said a great many things. He took a liking to Reuben and felt good-natured just then, and he thought he would be doing him a kindness to let him take a little journey. He knew well enough, I suppose, that Reuben would find out he couldn't do the work and would give up and come home. I hope he will. I never want him to go out of my sight again."

Poor Beth sighed and proceeded to cover the coals and prepare for bed as her mother directed. Despite all that talk, she couldn't quite relinquish her faith in Reuben's journey and her belief that something would come of it.

It was high time for something to come. On Monday morning the shirts were carried back to the shop, and, behold, there was not one to carry back again.

"Miserable slack times!" the foreman said, as though he was really sorry. "We've never seen tighter times since we've been in the business. Had to turn away a good many of our hands three weeks ago. We've hung on to our best ones as long as we could. And you shall have work again as soon as we have it, maybe in three or four weeks, maybe not so soon. The pinch won't last long. It never does. Keep up a stout heart."

Yes, but on what? Three or four weeks was time enough to starve and freeze. Mrs. Stone did not really expect to do either. She believed she could beg enough to save her from death. And cheery Miss Hunter, who had already been so good to them, would find some way to keep them from starving. Why, for that matter, there was the ten-dollar gold piece, and the rent not due yet for a week. A good many things might arise in a week. But Mrs. Stone was not in the mood to cheer herself without any hope of the future. It all looked as dark as night to her. She did not cry again, but she moved about her room with such a sad face that Beth cried whenever she looked at it.

Once the child ventured a suggestion: "Mother, Reuben said he would come on the first train. He will be here by dinner time. Won't he be real hungry?"

"I suppose so, but we must give him some of the baked potatoes and bread. I don't dare to spend a cent for butter or meat now. We must save for the rent, child, or we'll be turned out into the street. This is a strange time to raise the rent on poor folks."

Just at that moment the train that was bringing Reuben home steamed in at the depot three miles away.

CHAPTER XX

A General Surprise

euben jumped from the platform as the engine gave its final yell. His cheeks were red as roses, and his eyes were bright. He had been gone a whole week — and what a week it had been! He looked taller and larger in every way than the boy who left that depot a week earlier. Not that he had grown so much, but a thick, heavily lined, well-fitting overcoat, buttoned up to the chin, can make a boy look as if he had.

He was carrying Miss Hunter's carpetbag. It was full too; he couldn't imagine of what. "Some lunch for you," Mrs. Barrows had smiled as she handed the heavy bag into his keeping. But the boy had not needed a lunch for a two hours' ride and decided not to open the bag until he got home. He signaled a downtown streetcar at once and found a seat. He was in too much of a hurry to walk. Besides, the carpetbag was wonderfully heavy.

He picked five pennies out of his pocket case for the fare. His face reddened, and his eyes sparkled. Whenever he thought of that pocket case he laughed. Grace Barrows had given it to him "to remember their ride by," she told him. It held a wonderful paper, an envelope. Mr. Barrows had given him the envelope just as he started away.

"Put it in your pocket case, my boy," he instructed him, "and don't open it on the cars. It is never a wise thing to handle money on the cars. It is yours, every cent of it. You will need it to help move your family.

"I wouldn't bring the stove, if I were you, nor some of the other things that will cost more than they will come to — better sell them. The things in the house are all a present to you from Mrs. Barrows, but the money in this envelope isn't a present. It belongs to you. If you hadn't picked up that paper I would have offered a reward for its return. You saved my horse for me, and he is worth a good deal of money. So you have fairly earned what you will find here.

"You just send me a telegram on what day you will get started, and we'll have a fire in the house and supper going, so your mother will feel at home. Now good-bye, sir, and success to you!" And Mr. Barrows had shaken hands with him as though he were already a man.

He laughed again over that carefully sealed white envelope. What if there should be as much as ten dollars in it? If there only were, he could see his way clear to move right away.

He fell to wording his telegram. Suppose Mother could get ready to go this week! Suppose it should be on Thursday. A good deal could be done in two and a half days. Then he would telegraph: "Dear Mr. Barrows: We will come on Thursday morning on the train that leaves here at twenty minutes after ten." He counted the words — twenty! How did people ever say anything with *ten* words, the usual number for dispatches?

He tried again and again. The first message didn't suit him anyway; it didn't sound business-like. He had stood by and listened to the reading of business dispatches many times and admired their short, sharp sound.

By the time the car turned into Ninth Street and he knew he must leave it at the next corner, he had planned his dispatch in a way that delighted his heart: "We take the ten-twenty A.M. train Thursday."

"It sounds just like 'em," he said half aloud in his joy as he pulled the strap.

A brisk walk of five minutes or so, and he reached home. The idea came to him to knock at his mother's door. Beth opened it, stood a moment and stared, and finally cried, "Mother!" And then she uttered an "Oh, oh!" and threw both arms around her brother's neck.

"I thought you were a messenger boy. I was *so scared* because of your coat," she explained breathlessly. "Why, Reuben, where *did* you get your coat? Oh, Mother, isn't it splendid?"

The mother who had never really hoped to see her son in anything so fine and warm and beautifully fitting could not help laughing a little too.

"You are just in time for dinner," explained Beth. "But I hope you are not awful hungry. Or, no — yes, I hope you are *dreadful* hungry, because then just potatoes will taste good. We haven't a speck of meat."

"I don't want meat," Reuben said, unbuttoning his coat. "I had steak for breakfast, plenty of it. But then maybe I've got some in my lunch. You pitch into the lunch, Beth, and see if there is something good for dinner." Whereupon he unlocked Miss Hunter's carpetbag, and Beth began to draw out the treasures with squeals of satisfaction.

"Mother, here is a whole chicken put in for Reuben's lunch! And, oh, here is a pie — two pies tied together, just slipped in whole, on the pie plates! And here is a loaf of bread. Oh, Mother, Mother, here is a cupful of the sweetest-smelling butter you ever saw!"

"I guess it is!" Reuben beamed. "Their butter tastes just like the roses you smell as you pass the greenhouse on North Street. I'm awful glad they sent you some."

It was a splendid dinner they at last sat down to. The potatoes were fixed deliciously, and the cold chicken, pie, cheese and butter tasted better than any they had ever had before.

"I declare, we ought to have Miss Hunter in, to share some of these good things!" Mrs. Stone said.

But Beth explained that she was up in Mother Perkins's room, serving her some tea and toast. She saw her go.

Then Reuben commenced: "Oh, Mother, do you suppose Miss Hunter will move with us? She could get ever so much more work there and better wages, a good deal better. Mr. Barrows told me to tell her so and to urge her to come. He said now was her time to get in with some of the best."

Beth glanced up quickly at her mother to see how she received this matter-of-fact way of speaking of moving, then turned to the man of the house with her startling bit of news: "Oh, Reuben, can you believe they have raised the rent of this house one whole dollar a month!"

"Raised the rent!" replied Reuben with contempt. "I hope they will get it, or else I hope they won't. Anyhow, I know they won't from us. But I do wish Miss Hunter would go with us. There is a room in the house that would be just right for her."

"Reuben," said Beth, the color ebbing and flowing on her face, "do you really and truly mean you think we are going to move?"

"Why, of course we are going to move. Haven't I been working all week to get things ready? Mother, could you go this week, do you think? There's lots of work waiting there, and Mr. Barrows needs me. If they've raised the house rent here, the sooner we get out the better."

Mrs. Stone looked as if she didn't know in the least what to say to her eager-faced boy and waiting girl. She glanced from one to the other, then she laughed. It had been more than a week since Beth had seen her laugh outright.

"Reuben," she said, "I believe you are forty instead of twelve. Do you really suppose we could get work right along if we were to move, find a place to live in, manage to pay the rent and all that?"

"Why, Mother, I *know* we could," he said, his bright eyes sparkling. "And I've seen the house we are to live in. The fact is, I've rented it and had it cleaned and all. And there is work waiting for all of us. The oddest little machines, Beth, you ever saw in your life! Brass, you know, with rows of tiny little teeth for you to put your needle through!"

"Put a needle through brass!" exclaimed Beth in amazement.

Reuben laughed and said he couldn't explain, but she would see for herself in a few days. He started in on his mother again about moving, along with advice for her to leave the stove behind. Mr. Barrows recommended it.

"Horrid old thing!" said Beth, bestowing glances of hatred on it. "I should be too happy to go away and leave it behind. Reuben, you can't think how hateful it has acted since you've been gone — twice as hateful as it does with you."

"I'll fix it tomorrow morning," Reuben said, nodding his head toward it. "But, Mother, don't you think it would be best to sell it for old iron? That is what Mr. Barrows advised. And, well, to tell you the truth — I was going to keep this for a surprise — he gave me a stove to use in the place of it, one that goes better than that."

"He *gave you...a stove!*" stammered Mrs. Stone.

"Yes, he did," Reuben said, his eyes dancing. He concluded there were surprises enough left without that one.

To tell you all the conversation and all the plans in the Stone family during the rest of that day would fill a book. Before three o'clock in the afternoon Mrs. Stone was saying: "If we *should* move, we ought to let the agent of this house know." By evening she said: "We ought to let Mrs. Bemus know about this room. I guess she would like to rent it."

Then Beth and Reuben glanced at each other and laughed; their mother had decided to move. I must tell you, though, of one thing.

"I don't know how we would ever get enough money together to buy what will have to be bought and get ourselves ready!" This was one of Mrs. Stone's objections. It made Reuben whisk out his pocket case, over which Beth exclaimed in delight.

"I've got some moving money here," he explained. "It isn't a present, Mother. Mr. Barrows said so. He said it was rightly mine because I had saved him a good deal. I don't know how much there is. He sealed it up and told me I had better not open it on the cars. But he said I would need it to move my family."

Then he broke the seal. Out came the bills, four of them. Reuben's breath all but left him, and the flush on his face deepened. One bill was a five. What if some of the others should be!

"If there *should* be as much as fifteen dollars here," he said, stopping and looking at his mother, "what would you say?"

"I'd say that you must have worked uncommon fast for a boy of twelve," she answered, and her tone was not altogether one of pleasure. She did not like for folks to take pity on them and give them money.

Reuben laughed and glanced down at his money. He had a story to tell that he guessed would satisfy his mother, even if there should be fifteen dollars. But he gave such a sudden jump in his chair that Beth held to the side of the rickety table. Then he leaned his head on the table and actually burst into tears.

"Why, Reuben Watson Stone!" Beth exclaimed. "What on *earth* is the matter?"

"My dear boy!" his mother exclaimed at the same moment. It was so strange to see Reuben cry.

He stepped over to his mother and buried his head in her lap—*after* he had dropped the four bills on the table before her. She counted them: two fives and two twenties. Fifty dollars!

I won't try to describe to you the brief commotion in that family.

To give a boy ten or even fifteen dollars for a week's work, because a rich man felt sorry for him and thought he had a great burden to carry, would be unusual enough. But whoever heard of one giving a twelve-year-old boy fifty dollars? Mrs. Stone thought some wicked plot was out to ruin her boy. She almost expected to see a policeman appear and arrest him on a charge of stealing.

But Reuben's tears did not last long. He had been taken by surprise, and following hard on so much excitement he had forgotten his dignity. Now he brushed back his hair from his hot forehead, wiped away all traces of tears and told his remarkable story. He commenced with the ride behind Samson and the paper worth a thousand dollars that tried to blow away and didn't. And he ended with the story of the locked kitchen door and the two boys who were prisoners.

It was a long story but well told. When it all began the mother was prepared to resent the fifty dollars almost as an insult offered to their honest poverty. But by the time it was finished she declared she didn't know that fifty dollars was any too much to show his gratitude.

As for Beth, she laughed and cried half a dozen times during the account and half-smothered Reuben with hugs and kisses when it was finished.

Moving expenses were settled then, and by night the Stone family was actually packing! Only one drawback remained. They couldn't quite make up their minds to leave Miss Hunter behind. She had heard the whole story repeated by Beth and enjoyed it as much as that small lady thought she ought. She had heard with pleasure about the room that would just suit her and the chance for plenty of work at good prices. Then she had grown thoughtful and finally had admitted that she couldn't see her way clear to leaving poor old Mother Perkins alone. To be sure, she had known her only a week, but the nice old lady was getting used to her. She liked for her to visit her, liked her toast and relished an egg dropped in water. Mother Perkins was getting pretty feeble. The long and short of it was, Miss Hunter didn't believe she ought to go and leave her.

"It is your duty to go, of course," she said to Mrs. Stone. "You've got Beth and Reuben to think of. At least, he has you two to plan for, and he's done it like a man, I'm sure — a first-class man at that. Of course it is your duty to go along with him. Likely enough I'll come trotting behind after a little while. Nothing hinders me but the poor old lady. But I can't make up my mind to leave her, and that is a fact."

Reuben and Beth moped all one evening because Miss Hunter couldn't see her way clear to leaving Mother Perkins. But they need not have wasted a sigh over that.

The fact was, their Father in heaven saw the way clear all the time. He meant to have Miss Hunter go with them, and He knew exactly what to do for Mother Perkins so that she should not miss the loving care of her new friend. I'll tell you what He did: That night in the silence and the darkness He sent His unseen angels. They arrived without sound of footfall or rattling of keys and passed swiftly and silently through the door Reuben himself had locked but two hours before. When they passed through the door again, they had Mother Perkins with them.

In the morning Miss Hunter found her still body with her wrinkled old face lying just where she had left it the night before. She called to Mrs. Stone and Reuben and Beth.

"Look," she said, her voice serious and yet sweet. "Come up here. Something has happened — something we don't often have the privilege to see. Study her face. Did she ever smile like that when she lived here? I'm glad I kissed her last night when I tucked her in. The Lord must have touched her a very short while after that. He left a little gleam of glory right here on her face, so we could feel sure of what had happened. Well, Reuben, there's nothing to hinder my moving along with you now. Since the Lord wants her in the palace, she doesn't need me to take care of her anymore."

So they stayed another day, and the funeral of Mother Perkins was held in the sunny south room. Miss Hunter bought a rose from a small boy on the street and laid it on the coffin, and Reuben bought a flower he saw in a greenhouse window.

"It looked kind of sweet," he said. "I couldn't help it; it only cost three cents. Will it do to put with the rose?"

"Why, it's a bit of life forever!" declared Miss Hunter. "And since she's gone up there to live forever, it is the very thing." So there were flowers and tears at Mother Perkins's funeral.

The next day the man of the house moved his family to the country.

CHAPTER XXI

SHOW YOUR COLORS

euben's telegram was sent — you may be sure of that. A young man like Reuben Watson Stone is not likely to forget his first telegram. So when the stage drew up with a flourish at the little house, Reuben saw with pleasure the smoke issuing from the chimney.

What fun he had leading his mother and Beth and Miss Hunter through the rooms and hearing their exclamations of surprise and delight. Beth tried to hug the stove, though it was so hot she couldn't. She declared that she would like to kiss that teakettle which didn't leak. His mother wondered out loud how he came to have this and who thought of that. When that busy evening was over and Reuben was settled in his new bed, he was sure he had never been so happy in his life.

The excitement remained at white heat the following day. Reuben had a holiday from the shop to help his mother get settled. But, truth to tell, the settling had been so thoroughly accomplished for her before she arrived, and she had so few possessions, that the work was not hard.

And there was the box factory with all its departments to guide the wide-eyed Beth through, explaining to her in detail with the confidence of one who had been familiar with the business for years. He showed her the glove factory, where she saw the machine with brass teeth and discovered she was to push her needle between them, instead of through them.

He also introduced his mother and Miss Hunter to the glove factory, where they hoped to get work. To crown the eventful day, Mrs. Barrows stopped by with Grace to get acquainted with his mother and was as friendly as if she had known her for years. The next day they all went to work in earnest.

The first Sunday in the new home was one Reuben always remembered with fondness. Many things made it memorable for him.

In the first place they all attended church together, and they sat in a pew which Mr. Barrows told Reuben they better keep for their own if they liked it. A little uncomfortable, Reuben asked how much it would cost a year. He learned a new lesson in church work when Mr. Barrows told him that pews in this church were not rented. People selected their seats and paid what they could toward the support of the church.

He told his mother before they were barely out of the building. "I like that," she answered heartily. "We can pay a little something ourselves. I've always sat in the gallery and felt like a pauper. If they've found a way to make poor people feel at home in their churches, I'm glad to hear it."

Then Reuben had escorted Beth to Sunday school and placed her in the care of Grace Barrows. In her new blue merino, which Miss Hunter had at last contrived an excuse for giving her, and her fur cape and hood, she looked as nice in his eyes as the best of them. In fact, he told his mother that their Beth was certainly the prettiest girl in the class.

In his own class he had much to think about and remember. Almost the first question his teacher asked was whether he had remembered his promise of the Sunday before. Embarrassed, he dropped his eyes to the floor, but he still answered firmly that he had remembered. When he told her he had decided the question, he never forgot the glow in her eyes.

She extended her hand to him. "I am very glad. Now, my boy, remember this: Show your colors everywhere."

He contemplated this sentence during the lesson. What chance was there for him to show his colors, he wondered. He was not quite sure what she meant. He thought he would like to know.

After the classes were over, he waited a few minutes for Beth, partly in the hope that his teacher would speak to him again. Sure enough, she faced him with that bright, glad smile and asked him one of her direct questions.

"Are you going to do it?"

"Do what, ma'am?"

"Why, show your colors everywhere and always."

Reuben glanced down at his plain gray clothes. They had very little color in them, and that little was rather dingy. He did not even own a bright necktie, like some of the boys.

"How'll I show them if I haven't got 'em?" he asked at last, a glimmer of a smile flickering across his face. He knew Miss Parker did not mean that sort of color, but he was puzzled all the same to know what she did mean.

"Reuben, do you know something about soldiers?"

"Yes'm." Reuben's thoughts scurried back to the story of his great grandfather and his brave fighting and his hat shaped like George Washington's. His mother had entertained Reuben and Beth in their childhood with stories she had heard while sitting on her grandfather's knee.

"Well, don't you know they wear their country's colors? A uniform, we call it. When we see them, we are never at a loss to know which side they are on, because their colors show us instantly. Now the Lord Jesus Christ has called you to be a soldier, and you have accepted the call. That's why I say to you, be sure you wear His colors always. Let nobody doubt on which side you are."

A pleased expression brightened Reuben's eyes. This was a new thought to him: He was actually a soldier like his great grandfather, of whom his mother had told him dozens of times he had reason to be proud. It was nice to think he wore the colors of his Captain. He understood in a flash what Miss Parker meant.

"Yes'm," he said, his voice showing his joy, "I'll try for it."

She realized he understood her and was turning away with a smile. Suddenly she came back. "Reuben, one thing more: Remember your Captain has had your orders written out for you in a book, and He expects you always to look for directions as to what He wants you to do. You can talk with

Him, to be sure, at any time. But He may not always repeat directions you can find by looking in your order book."

"That's the Bible!" exclaimed Reuben. "I never thought of it. Thank you — I'll remember."

Did he walk with a march-like step down the aisle to meet the waiting Beth? He may have, for he realized for the first time that he was a soldier.

That evening he and Beth sat together in the little parlor. It was so funny for the Stones to have a parlor! This speck of a room was delightful to Reuben and Beth. It chanced to be a mild day, and the door leading into the cozy kitchen had stood open all day. The sun had shone in at the east window all the morning, adding a pleasant warmth to the room. Beth and Reuben sat there together, reading their Sunday school books. At least Beth was reading. Reuben had closed his book and was deep in thought.

The story had been about a Christian girl who had prayed for and talked with and worked for her brother and led him at last to give his heart to Jesus. Reuben thought of his sister. Should he talk to her? He had prayed for her all week. Indeed, it was the first thing on his mind that Monday morning when he prayed — how much he would like for Beth to understand about this new, peaceful feeling that had entered his heart. Ever since then her name had crept into his prayer as naturally as his own.

Still all this week he had not mentioned a word to her on the subject. This astonished him a little; he always told Beth everything. She had heard about the boys in the shop, the spoiled pasteboards out of which he meant to make his fortune, the two tickets to see the pictures and, well, everything but this one experience. His talk with his teacher; his promise to her and the thought he had given to it all that Sunday afternoon; kneeling down at midnight and the strange new feeling that had stayed with him ever since — concerning all these things he had remained entirely silent. He was surprised to find that he shrank from telling Beth anything about it. Why should he?

Reuben did not know then as well as he did later about the enemy who longed for nothing more than to keep him from showing this new spirit to Beth and enlisting her at once as a soldier in the same army.

Tonight as he sat staring into the twilight, thinking of the book he had been reading, of Miss Parker's words about showing his colors, of his promise to try for it, suddenly these questions entered his heart: Has Beth seen your colors? Does she know about this new Captain of yours? Suppose you had never mentioned Mr. Barrows's name to her during all these days.

Oh, but Mr. Barrows has done so many things for me — I *had* to mention him, he responded inwardly.

Then Reuben's cheeks glowed in shame! Did he really mean that this new Captain had done nothing for him? Oh, no, no! He could never mean that, for he had pondered it a lot during this week. He felt certain it was this great Captain of his who had surely been leading him in these unusual new ways. He had done things for him all his life, perhaps, but certainly on that night he took that awful ride with Spunk and Spunk's master. Then he felt directed where to go and what to do, and the following weeks had been no less wonderful!

Oh, yes, Reuben was certain that a great deal

had been done for him. Then why didn't he tell Beth about it? He resolved that he would.

"Beth," he commenced, "it is too dark to read any longer. Let's talk."

"Well," said Beth, closing her book promptly, "talk!"

Reuben sat and stared out of the window.

"Why don't you talk?" said Beth. "Lots of things must have happened to you since we last had a long talk."

"There have — great big things. I'm trying to think where to begin."

"Begin at the biggest thing of them all and come down. Tell me all about it."

"The biggest thing that ever happened to me in my life," said Reuben slowly, "is that I am a soldier, and I have a Captain. I wear His colors and am bound to obey Him just exactly every time."

"Reuben, what in the world are you talking about?" said Beth. She dropped her book on the floor, came over and sat on the edge of the chair that was in front of Reuben's. She stared at him, astonishment showing in her voice and on her face.

"Why," said Reuben, fidgeting a little, "that's it, you see. I don't know how to tell you. It's a long story; that is, it's long to think it, but when you start to tell it there doesn't seem to be much that a fellow can tell. Look here, Beth — suppose you were tramping down this road." Reuben stood up and stepped careful steps on the bright flowers in the carpet toward the west window. "And you should meet somebody who said to you, 'I want you to turn right square around and go the other way,' and you should make up your mind to do it. Don't you see how different everything would be right away?" Whereupon Reuben wheeled around and headed toward the east window.

Beth watched him doubtfully. "I should want to be pretty sure who was talking to me, what he wanted me to turn around for and what good it would do anyway before I should make up my mind to do any such thing," she replied at last, since Reuben seemed to be waiting for her to answer.

"Exactly," he said, returning to his chair. "Well, the fact is, I found out that the One who met me wanted to do the best thing for me all along and knew what was the best. He *made* me in the first place and had a right to tell me which way to go. So I just turned around and made up my mind to follow Him the rest of my life."

"You must mean that you are a Christian!"

Reuben would always remember the surprise he heard in Beth's voice.

"I suppose I am," he said seriously. He had not put it into words before. "If a Christian means one who has made up his mind to follow the Lord Jesus Christ — take Him for Captain, you know — why, I'm one for sure."

"That is what it means," Beth nodded. "Miss Hunter told me so. She told me a good deal about it. She wanted me to go that same way, but I didn't think I wanted to do that. I didn't want to leave you behind. I wanted to keep right along with you and not go anywhere at all that you didn't. And now you've gone and left me!" Beth dropped her head on her arm and began to cry softly.

"Oh, Beth, I haven't!" he declared eagerly. "I've come back for you, don't you see? That's what I am trying to tell you — I want you along. I couldn't be a soldier without you! We've always been together.

Girls can be soldiers in this army just as well as boys; it's different from any other army. I say, Beth, won't you come right along? That's the very reason I wanted to tell you about it tonight."

Beth had already dried her tears and was listening.

"What did you mean about hearing somebody speak to you and ask you to turn around and all that? I don't understand what you mean."

So Reuben began at the story of that midnight ride, part of which she already knew. He described to her the terror and the prayer, the quiet that came to him and the sense of somebody's leading him and how he followed just where the somebody led. From there he jumped to the experiences of the Sunday before. He recounted the lesson and the teacher's question; her talk with him and his promise and how hard it was to keep it. He told her that Grace Barrows had helped him along without knowing it. Finally, after midnight, he had knelt down and settled it and had been certain ever since of the presence and help of his Leader. Then he told her how Miss Parker had reminded him that very day to be sure and show his colors. "I wanted to show you, Beth, the first thing and ask you to put them on."

It had been quite a long story. The twilight faded out entirely while he talked and left the room dark except for the glow of the firelight. Beth had listened in silence, but with the utmost attention. She drew a long sigh when he closed. If Reuben could have seen her face it would have told him that she felt left behind.

"You've been converted," she stated at last.

"Have I?" said Reuben. "I don't know. I don't even know what the word means."

"I do. Miss Hunter told me. She said there were two sides to it. God had one side, and folks the other. God called to people and asked them to *belong,* you know, just as you heard Him ask you — that is His side. Then they said either, 'I will,' or, 'I won't' — that's their side. She said even *God* couldn't do anything for them as long as they said, 'I won't.' He had promised Himself when He made them that they should have the right to decide things for themselves, and that was their side. Then she said just as soon as they made up their minds to say, 'I will,' He put new feelings into their hearts so that they wanted to do right; before they hadn't cared or hadn't thought anything about it. All at once they knew that the thing they wanted most was to follow the Lord Jesus and please Him. She said that new feeling in their hearts was called being converted, and there wasn't anybody else who could do it, just God. I know you have been converted."

"Well," said Reuben after a thoughtful silence, "I never heard it explained before, but it sounds like Miss Parker's talk and fits right in — and I guess it is all true. I've often wondered what it felt like to be converted; I'm glad I know. I'll tell you what it is, Beth: You do your part right away, won't you, so He can do His, and then we'll go on together."

"Does Mother know?" asked Beth.

"No, she doesn't. I wanted to tell you first. Fact is, I don't know how to tell such things. Do you suppose Mother will understand what I mean?"

"I guess so," said Beth. "She will have to be told anyhow, for things will have to be different now, you know."

"How different?"

"Why, every way. We'll have to read in the Bible every night and morning and kneel down and pray and say a prayer at the table every time we eat."

"How do you know?" asked Reuben, startled. "Who could read in the Bible and pray? People don't always do that."

"Oh, they do," Beth said confidently. "Miss Hunter told me about it. She told me about a bad man who was converted and began the next day to read in the Bible and pray. They all knelt down, and everything was different. And you know, Reuben, you are the man of our house."

CHAPTER XXII

HE TAKES A NEW STEP

here was no time to answer Beth, for a stream of light poured in just then from a new lamp. Behind it were Mother and Miss Hunter. Reuben poked the fire and added a fresh lump of coal, cheering up the lovely room. He was glad for the interruption, for in truth he had no answer ready. Beth's ideas of the Christian life were startling. Was he, Reuben Watson Stone, supposed to read in the Bible and pray before people?

What did Beth mean by saying, "They always do it"? Could she be right that because he was a Christian he must take up such duties as those?

"Well," said Miss Hunter briskly, setting down the new lamp on a colorful lamp mat she had fished from her box of treasures, "how did Sunday school go? Did you like it, Beth?"

"Some," said Beth absently. Rousing herself, she added, "Why, yes, ma'am, I liked it very much."

She was still contemplating Reuben's wonderful news.

"Something about this room makes me think of my old home," interrupted Mrs. Stone suddenly. "I can't tell what it is nor where it is, but the minute I get into it I think of the house we used to live in when I was a little girl, especially the sitting room where we used to sit on Sundays."

"Well, now," said Miss Hunter with hearty sympathy in her voice, "isn't that pleasant! I do think it is so nice to have something to remind us of our childhood. You must have had a real nice home if this reminds you of it, for I do think this is about as pleasant a room as I ever saw. And what did you do on Sunday nights when the twilight came?"

Both Reuben and Beth turned interested faces toward their mother and waited for her answer. They knew very little about her old home. She had never seemed fond of talking about it.

"Oh, we used to sing," she said slowly, as if it were hard work to revisit that long-ago past. "We had quite a family once, and we were all singers: Reuben and Kate were first-rate singers — they were the two youngest — and Father used to say they could earn their living with their voices. But they didn't need to earn a living; they both died before they found out what a hard thing it was to live. Father had enough and to spare in those days." Mrs. Stone gave the weary sigh Reuben and Beth were well acquainted with.

Miss Hunter didn't want her to sigh. "So they went to heaven to sing?" she asked brightly. "Well, that has a pleasant side to reflect on, I'm sure. Those things usually seem so sad when they first come. Sometimes I've thought I never in the world could feel it was for the best. 'I'll believe it,' I say, 'because the Lord says so.' I used to tell Him that on my knees. 'But as for understanding it, I don't think I ever can, not till I get to heaven.' And if you can believe it, I've gone to Him on my knees and told Him since that I saw it as plain as day about those very things; they were best! After the singing was finished, did somebody get out the old Bible and read, and then were there prayers said?"

Mrs. Stone caught her breath hard for a moment, then she whispered: "Yes, my father always did."

There they were, right back to the subject that had put Reuben in such a whirl! This was great news to him; he was eager to hear more about his grandfather. His mother had grown up in a home where the Bible was read every Sunday evening, at least — perhaps on other evenings, too. He wished he knew, but he did not like to ask her.

At this point in his thoughts his eye caught Beth's. She nodded her head, and her face communicated almost as plainly as words: I told you so. Grandfather was a Christian, you see, and he read in the Bible and prayed.

But then he was a man, Reuben thought.

"Well, what of that?" asked that other self who often in these days held conversations with him. "You will be a man if you live long enough, and you are the only man in this house now. You have to help pay the rent, buy the coal and do ever so many things now that you wouldn't if you had a father. Likely as not you would be in school instead of working hard every day to support your family. Why should you wait until you get to be a man before you read in the Bible and pray with your family, any more than you waited until then to do other things?"

Mother might not like it, Reuben thought.

"You will never know till you ask her," said the other self. "She may even like it, or at least she probably won't find any fault with it. She hardly ever finds fault with anything you do."

Maybe I'll do it next Sunday, thought Reuben.

"I should think it would be a great deal more sensible to do it now," said his other self. "Things don't grow easier by waiting. You know that because you've tried it. In fact, this first Sunday in a new home, when everything is starting over new in your family, is the easiest time you will ever have. If I were you, I'd do it this very night. Your mother doesn't know, to be sure, that you have become a soldier, but Beth does, and you see what she expects of you. Your mother might as well hear it now as at any time. You wondered how you would ever have a chance to show your colors. Are you going to shirk the very first chance?"

At this point Reuben gave up holding an argument with one half of himself against the other half and set himself to earnest thinking. The talk continued in the room, but he did not hear it. He had an important question to settle. It seemed strange to him that Beth, who was not a soldier at all, had roused him to duty and even pointed the way. But the more he thought about it, the more sure he felt that she was right and that here was a chance to stand by his colors. It seemed like hard work to him. But Reuben possessed a trait that made everyone who knew him believe in him and believe that he would make a man to be trusted. When he saw a plain duty, he never shirked it because it was hard. He did not mean to shirk this one.

"Mother," he said, breaking into the midst of something Beth was saying. He was so intent on what he was about to say that he had not heard

Beth at all. The earnestness in his voice caused his mother to turn toward him expectantly. "Mother, I've had something to tell you for a week, but I haven't told it. I've become a soldier, and I've got to stand by the colors all the time."

"A soldier!" repeated Mrs. Stone with dismay. This boy of hers had astonished her so much lately that she was prepared for almost anything. If he had told her there was a war with the Indians and he must march away the next morning, I don't know that she would have been much more bewildered than she was now. It was plain that she did not understand him any better than Beth had, and it was equally plain that Miss Hunter did. Her eyes flashed at him, warming his heart. He answered her smile and then turned to his mother.

"Yes, Mother, a soldier of the Lord Jesus. I'm bound to serve Him all my life. Since I'm the only man of the house, I was wondering if you would care if I read some verses in the Bible and prayed, as Grandfather used to do. I never knew before that Grandfather did so."

For the next minute or two it was so still in that room that you could have heard your own heart beat, I think. Then Mrs. Stone answered so quietly that Reuben had to bend his head to hear it: "Of course I wouldn't care, Reuben, if you want to."

Without another word Reuben reached for the Bible he had been studying only a little while earlier and read aloud the words he had been considering that afternoon: "Thou therefore, my son, be strong in the grace that is in Christ Jesus.

"And the things that thou hast heard of me among many witnesses, the same commit thou to faithful men who shall be able to teach others also.

"Thou therefore endure hardness as a good soldier of Jesus Christ.

"No man that warreth entangleth himself with the affairs of this life; that he may please him who hath chosen him to be a soldier."

Reuben did not understand a lot about these verses. Indeed they had caught his eye because the word *soldier* was repeated several times. That last sentence about pleasing Him who had chosen him to be a soldier filled him with joy. Reuben was sure of this, that he wanted nothing now so much as a chance to please Jesus.

During this reading he was much troubled as to what he should say when he knelt to pray. Remember, he had never heard his own voice in prayer, and indeed he had rarely heard anybody pray. But he was much surprised to discover that words came to him without any trouble. He prayed only a few simple sentences, but they expressed as plainly as words could his resolution to belong to the Lord Jesus and to serve Him in everything as well as he could from that time forth.

He was happy when he rose from his knees. Somehow he felt more like a soldier than ever before — as if he had put on his uniform. Besides, something in his mother's voice, low and husky though it was, made him feel that she did not dislike the reading and praying. She had knelt close to him, and he had heard her crying softly. Perhaps she was thinking of Grandfather; perhaps she had missed his prayers very much. Reuben resolved that she should never miss prayers again.

Even Miss Hunter's pleasant sentence, "Well, now, I thank the Lord that I belong to a family altar once more," was hardly needed to make him feel that he had done the right thing and that God would bless him in it.

CHAPTER XXIII

THEIR FIRST PARTY

ne evening the new house where the Stone family lived was athrob with excitement. For the first time in their lives, Beth and Reuben were invited to spend the evening out. Children who have attended a children's party or an entertainment of some sort as often as once a month ever since they can remember will find this hard to believe, but it is true. Hattie Turner, a young girl in Beth's Sunday school class, and her brother who was in Reuben's class, were planning to have a candy pull, with plenty of apples and nuts and games and a good time generally.

Beth was plaiting her hair with lovely silky braids and tying it with a blue ribbon to match her dress.

"You are much too dressed up for a candy pull, and that's a fact," her mother said, eyeing the blue merino doubtfully, and yet with satisfaction. Beth looked so nice in it!

Miss Hunter rushed to the rescue. She saw the look of alarm in Beth's eyes — if she would have to take the blue merino off and wear her brown calico, she felt as if it might break her heart. "Oh, she won't hurt her dress. That white apron covers the front nicely, and she can roll up her sleeves when she pulls candy. She is special company, you know, with being a stranger, so it will do for her to be dressed up pretty well."

Reuben couldn't help laughing a little as he inspected his new gray jacket and pants, cut just the right length and trimmed with as many buttons as the rest of the boys wore. The idea of Beth's being too dressed up to visit a place was new and quite funny.

"She must match my new jacket and trousers, you know, Mother," he added cheerily.

The mother thought that she would have to search far and wide to match her boy.

Reuben's thoughts, busy with contrasts, returned to the old home. "I wonder what Kate and Timmy Blake would say if they could see us, Beth?" He asked the question with a gleeful tone, but not one that you would call proud.

"I wonder how poor Mrs. Blake has managed in this cold winter?" Mrs. Stone sighed for her old neighbor and friend in the city. "Poor thing! I've thought of her a dozen times this winter and wished she could have a little bit of the comfort that we are having so much of."

"Couldn't we have them down here for a few days, Mother, and get them rested up? Maybe Timmy could get work here; Katie could anyhow and Mrs. Blake."

"Have company?" Mrs. Stone smiled at this new

and not altogether unpleasant idea. "Maybe we can, Reuben, when summer is fairly here. I doubt if they could get enough together to pay their fare though."

"Let's try for it," Miss Hunter nodded with the air of one who saw how to accomplish it.

So Beth and Reuben headed out to their first party, their hearts warm with the thought of what they in their happier circumstance might do for their friends.

Miss Hunter held the light at the side door and waited while Beth returned for a handkerchief. In this way she had a chance to speak that last word to Reuben.

"I suppose you mean to look out for your colors tonight, my boy?"

Then Reuben glanced down again at the neat gray suit and the trim necktie with a dash of red in it and smiled. He knew Miss Hunter did not mean those colors — no danger that he wouldn't look out for them. But he didn't quite see what she could mean.

"I don't know of any chance to show them tonight. It is just a few girls and boys to pull candy and eat apples and nuts. There won't be any way to show the colors that you mean."

"Humph!" countered Miss Hunter wisely. "Don't you believe it. I never heard of a parcel of boys and girls together for half an hour but what the Lord gave them a chance to show their colors. Why, Satan looks out for that, and you can depend on it. He is always throwing in words and actions to help folks go backward."

Reuben gazed at the side of the little table thoughtfully. "But, Miss Hunter," he began, "these are not rough fellows like some of the ones in our shop. They are well-behaved boys, real gentlemanly fellows always, and the girls will be there too. I don't believe I'll have any chances tonight."

"Just you keep watch and see if you don't. I've seen gentlemanly boys and nice girls set a whole nest of snares for careless feet. You make me think of a nephew of mine to whom I once gave the verse: 'My son, if sinners entice thee consent thou not.' He was going off to the woods with a party of boys. 'Auntie,' says he, 'the verse doesn't fit. There isn't a sinner among them. Those boys are ever so much better than I am.'

" 'You keep a lookout, my boy,' I said. 'It's my opinion you'll find sinners enticing you as hard as they can, before you are an hour older. You will need the verse if Satan is as smart as I have reason to think he is.' Well, in the evening he was pretty quiet and thoughtful. When I got a chance I asked him about the verse. 'Auntie,' said he, 'it just exactly fitted. I found a whole troop of sinners right in my own heart enticing me as hard as they could. I had to fight them with all my might. It would have been so easy to have consented to what they wanted.' "

"Whew!" said Reuben with a whistle. "I never thought of that."

Then Beth returned. "I thought I would never find my hemstitched one," she said in apology for having kept him so long. "I put it away so carefully I could not think what I did with it."

"You are not used to having places for your things," said Reuben, reaching for his cap. He felt that Beth had been gone none too long for him to get his colors righted.

"No," she said with a happy little laugh. "For that matter, I'm not used to having things. But,

Reuben, I'm getting used to it very fast. Now you know it isn't quite three months that we have been living here, and yet it seems to me as though I could not go back to the city and live in the old way; I think I should die. And it seems as though we had always known what we would have for dinner, could always have meat once a day and had never thought of such a thing as shivering over the stove to save coal. What makes people get used to things so fast, do you suppose? It isn't that I've forgotten the hard places; I guess I haven't! I wish I could, though. I wouldn't like to have the girls know how hard we used to have it."

"Why not?" Reuben wondered. "I should think you would like to have them know all about it, so they would understand better what hard times poor folks have, and what fun it is to help them. Why don't you?"

"Oh, because I don't," said Beth. She tossed her pretty brown head. Reuben did not have a streak of that kind of pride about him and could not understand.

It would be difficult to describe to you how much Beth Stone enjoyed the first part of her first evening out.

The girls were inclined to be especially kind to her. The fact was, they liked the little city girl with her pale cheeks and delicate looks and quiet, graceful ways, for Beth was one of those who had grown graceful by merely watching others at a distance. She had never had bright ribbons to wear in her hair before nor a lace ruffle for her dress; yet she knew as well how to tie the ribbons and how high to baste the ruffle as though she had worn them all her life. Hadn't she studied other little girls by the hour?

Well, the girls at the candy pull studied her and liked her very much; so did the boys. They gathered around her and asked questions.

She knew a lot about the city, to which some of them had never been. She had used her eyes to good purpose and could describe the park and the fountain and the huge store on Broadway that was like a good-sized town in itself. She could also describe many of the other wonders in a way that surprised the listeners, even Reuben, who had no idea Beth could talk so well.

It seems almost a pity that any other subject should have come up for discussion that evening.

It was Arthur Holmes who suddenly drew the attention on himself: "Oh, I've got the richest thing to tell you. Halley Parsons has come home. Did you know he had come? I was up there yesterday and saw him. Well, you know little Teddy, the washerwoman's boy that Judge Adams is sending up there to school? You don't know him, Reuben, do you? A funny little chap who is smart with his books. Judge Adams has taken a notion to him and sent him off with his son to school.

"Halley says they have the richest fun with him. He told me about one scrape this winter. They have big rooms in the boardinghouse with double beds and cots or something, and that brings six of the fellows in a room.

"Well, Teddy, you know, joined the church just before he went away. He's a real good little fellow, but he's an awful coward.

"Halley, it seems, thought he would have some fun, and he told the boys in Teddy's room about it. The first night they all talked and laughed a blue streak when they were getting ready for bed. They watched for Teddy's Bible to come out, because

Halley had told them that he read in the Bible and prayed every night as regular as the minister. But it seems they were too much for him that night; he left the Bible in the bottom of his trunk.

"Finally a boy named Case who slept nearest to the gaslight gave the word that it would be out in two minutes, and out it went. Almost, that is. He winked at the other fellows and left the least little glimmer of light — not so you would notice it at all, Hal said, but so he could turn it on again in a twinkling.

"Then for a few minutes everything was quiet, Teddy in bed with the rest. Pretty soon they heard a soft little motion, not more noise than a mouse would make. 'What's that?' asked Case, and he turned on a blaze of light. There sat Teddy on the foot of his bed, shivering as though he had an ague fit.

"Then Hal said you ought to have heard Case tell how sorry he was that he turned out the light before Teddy was in bed. 'I didn't notice,' he said. 'I thought everybody was ready. I ought to have paid attention to you, since you were a new boy.' Then he offered to help him and said it was a cold night. Finally he hopped out of bed and tucked poor Teddy up, head and ears, and turned down the light again.

"Then all was still, and pretty soon some of the fellows began to snore as if they were asleep. Then they heard that little creeping noise again. This time Case waited until he knew by the sound that Teddy must have slipped off the bed. Then he flashed the light up, and there stood Teddy shivering and looking like a goose. I'd have given a dollar to have seen him!"

Here Arthur stopped to laugh, with nearly all of

his listeners joining in. "Well, Case questioned him again, and he stammered and muttered something. He wouldn't admit, you know, that he wanted to say his prayers. Case said he was very sorry for him; was afraid he was sick; hoped he would be able to sleep and all that sort of thing. Then he tucked him into bed and turned out the light again, or rather didn't turn it out.

"After that, Halley said it was still so long that they began to think the little fellow had given up his prayers or said them with his head ducked under the bedclothes. One or two of them were just dozing off to sleep when that mouse-like noise was heard again; Teddy was evidently crawling out. This time Case waited until the youngster was fairly on his knees — in the middle of his prayer, maybe — then he flashed up the light, and all the fellows sat up in bed. There was Teddy out on the cold floor with his bare feet, nothing around him, kneeling down with his eyes shut tight and his lips going as if he were saying forty spelling lessons at once.

"Well, sir, Halley said you never saw anything so funny. He said if he had been expelled the next morning he'd have had to laugh. All the boys just roared. Teddy, he hopped up and jumped into bed and hid his head under the covers. Halley says they believe he cried half the night."

Now I really don't know how to account for the way in which those boys and girls listened to this story. There must have been among them those who thought that a shameful as well as a silly trick had been played on poor Teddy; yet every one of them joined in Arthur's laugh, except Reuben Stone.

He sat up straight, his cheeks red, his eyes flashing, so indignant, especially over the faint giggle from Beth, that he could hardly control his voice enough to say: "Well, I must say that I don't know if I ever heard of a meaner trick, with nothing to be got out of it, and I've heard of a good many. The newsboys and bootblacks are always getting up some sort of trick that is twice as bright as this, and not any meaner. If I were Halley Parsons I'd be ashamed of myself for telling it and calling it fun. I didn't know that rich gentlemen's sons with chances to learn and all that were so mean."

Then the girls glanced at one another and at Beth, whose cheeks flamed now like peonies. Two or three of the boys whistled. "A lecture on morals, one night only, admission two peanuts," Stephen Morgan said and began to pass them around. Then some of the other boys and girls laughed.

Arthur Holmes countered: "Pshaw. Nobody meant any harm; it was only a little fun. It didn't hurt the youngster, either. He needn't have been such a coward as to be afraid to say his prayers, if he wanted to."

"That is true," agreed Reuben more quietly. He already regretted that he had spoken so sharply. He did not believe he would have done so if Beth had not given that little laugh. "That is true. I'm sorry the little fellow hadn't more pluck. But I must say I can't see the fun in a lot of older fellows doing a mean thing because a young one has done a silly thing. I don't know how you folks who've had chances argue about such things. I've never been to school, and I've never been around many boys who could go. But I know there isn't a street boy in the city who would play as mean a trick on one of his own mates as that. They stick together and try to help each other. I supposed all boys did."

It had its effect on the boys — this frank confession that he had no opportunities and knew more about street boys than he did about those who were carefully reared in happy homes. If Reuben had offered his opinion without this explanation, some of those present might have been rude enough to ask him where he got his education, what boarding school he attended or whether they taught manners in the box factory or some such silly thing. Most of them were boys whose fathers took care of them and sent them to school, while he had to work hard for a living. They were becoming very uncomfortable and didn't know what to say.

I think perhaps some were cross over Reuben's hint that the city newsboys and bootblacks outranked them in politeness. But they seemed at a loss how to answer him. All were relieved, I think, that just at that moment the candy was announced to be ready to pull.

For one girl, however, the rest of the evening was almost spoiled, and that was Beth. But it was not because of her silly laugh, though she was a good deal ashamed of it — or would have been if she had given herself a chance to think about it. The story had not amused her at all. In fact, she thought it was a shameful, stupid trick. The truth was, poor Beth's pretty head was turned with a desire to be like other people. The boys and girls who had always worn nice clothes, had enjoyed evenings out at candy pulls and had spent pleasant times together in a hundred ways that were new to her, had laughed over the story. She, Beth Stone, must needs do so too; that is how she reasoned.

Of course, because she was in this frame of mind, Reuben's frank statement that he had never had any chances or attended school like others and that he was well-acquainted with newsboys and bootblacks and other dreadful creatures like them, fell like live coals on her comfort. How *could* Reuben talk so! All these uncomfortable thoughts raced through her brain as she pulled and pulled her candy. She was determined to have the whitest strand in the room.

The conversation continued happily enough. If Reuben had not noticed that most of the boys had very little to say to him, it would have been pleasant work pulling that candy. As it was, he found himself off in the corner somewhat, working alone. There was not a boy who did not resent being told that he had laughed over a mean trick.

At last the candy was pulled, and much of it eaten. Sticky hands were washed, and stray wads of candy were picked from the chairs and carpet. Then the whole company donned their winter wraps and coats and said their good-byes.

Beth and Reuben took the quietest walk home of their lives. Reuben was silent with disappointment over the evening: not for how the boys and girls laughed over the story about poor Teddy but because Beth had not acted as he thought she would.

The winter which was almost past had disappointed him in this regard. In his honest, earnest heart Reuben had fully expected Beth to join him as soon as she heard the great news that he was a soldier; indeed he had no thought of going without Beth.

But to his great dismay she did not seem interested in his new hopes and plans. Her head was full of pretty new dresses and ruffles and new ways of braiding her hair and in trying to look and act as much as possible like other girls her age.

She worked hard on her bright brass machine, driving the needle between the shining teeth in a way that astonished even her. And she earned more money each day than her mother had been able to earn in the city, laboring twelve hours a day. But her ambition was to save enough money to go to school, study French and perhaps later take music lessons.

Who knows? said Beth to herself. A great many wonderful things have happened this year. More things may happen before the year is out.

She was bright, eager and industrious and as ready as ever to enter into all of Reuben's plans for work or study. But on this one subject that was growing every day to be more important to Reuben than anything else, she was unconcerned. So they were both quiet on this moonlit evening as they walked home together from their first party. Neither was as blissfully happy as both had expected to be.

"Oh, Beth!" Reuben cried at last. "I didn't think you would laugh along with the others!"

"Why not, I wonder?" Beth said, defending herself, though secretly she was ashamed of the little laugh. "I think it was silly anyway and awfully proud of you, Reuben Stone, to set yourself up to be better than all those boys and girls who have been to school all their lives. If you had kept quiet I might have had a nice time. I didn't a bit, and I never want to go anywhere again, so there!"

Reuben had never in his life heard his sister talk in that fashion before. He did not know what to say. At last he tried to explain.

"But, Beth, I had to say something because, well, I am a soldier. And, oh, Beth, I thought you were going to be one!"

"Well, I'm not!" declared Beth sharply. "I don't want to be a soldier nor anything that makes me different from other people. I've been different all my life — never had things or gone places or done like other girls. And now, just when I've got a chance to be like them and have a good time, you go and spoil it all with your notions about its being wrong to laugh at a funny story, and wrong to do anything. And you go and tell them about your never having had any chances and about newsboys and bootblacks and everything! You never used to be so! Before you got these notions you would do anything for me, and now you spoil all the good times I might have. I never want to be a soldier at all, and I wish you weren't one, so there!"

Poor angry Beth burst into a passion of tears and dashed into the house like a comet.

And that was how their first evening out, to which they had looked forward, ended.

No, not quite that way. Beth went directly upstairs, but Reuben stopped in the little parlor a moment. No one was there but Miss Hunter. She greeted him with a cheery smile and a question: "Well, my boy, did you see anything of Satan tonight?"

"Oh, Miss Hunter! He was there all the time and busier than I ever saw him before."

"I'll warrant you: Get a party of boys and girls together, and he's bound to be on hand."

"And, Miss Hunter, he is after Beth."

"Of course he is. Do you think he is going to let such a pretty, bright girl as Beth alone and let her slip away from him without a hard fight? He is much too sharp for that. Don't you let him get her, my boy."

"I don't know," said Reuben doubtfully. "I don't believe I can help it. Down there in the city where there were fifty chances for going wrong for every one here, she was just the best girl! After I found out about it, I thought maybe she had been a soldier all the time and didn't know it. But up here, where everything is nice and pleasant, and it is as easy again to do right, she seems just as different. You can't imagine."

"Yes, I can imagine," Miss Hunter nodded her gray head. "Satan has different ways for different people, and he knows just how to catch a girl like our Beth. This is twice as hard a place for her to do right in as it was in that dingy north room of yours, shut up with her mother.

"But look here, my boy, *you* can't do much alone, to be sure. Isn't that Captain of yours strong enough to manage Satan in the country as well as in the city? Do you suppose he has any plans that your Captain doesn't understand? Well, then, you just go to Him about Beth. Tell Him the whole story, and ask Him to show you how to get her to wear your colors. If I were you, I would tell Him all about it this very night."

And Reuben did.

CHAPTER XXIV

AT BETH'S SUGGESTION

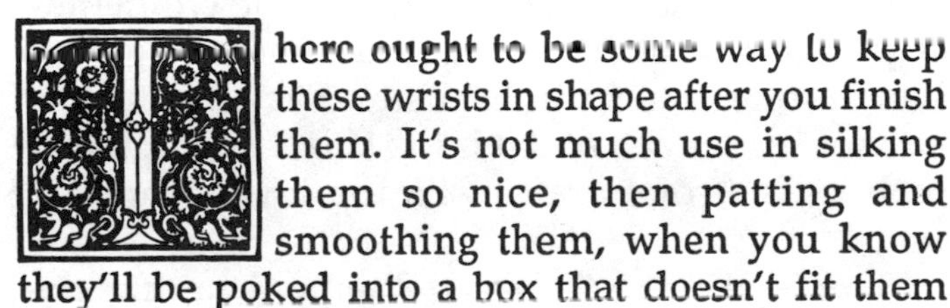

There ought to be some way to keep these wrists in shape after you finish them. It's not much use in silking them so nice, then patting and smoothing them, when you know they'll be poked into a box that doesn't fit them and be all rumpled up dreadfully."

Beth was talking off and on to herself while she inspected and added final touches on a dozen ladies' gauntlet gloves that she had taken unusual pains in silking.

At least she concluded she was talking to herself. Reuben was in the room and had been for an hour. Beth had said a good deal during the hour — at first to him. But then she found him wrapped up in the arithmetic lesson that was puzzling him and received only an absentminded "um" now and then, which he meant for yes. So Beth had tried to keep still.

Whether the subject had especially interested him or whether he had just conquered a troublesome example, I do not know. But as Beth finished her lecture about the gauntlets, he looked up from his slate and asked: "What did you say, Beth?"

"Oh," said Beth, "you've come back, have you? I've been talking to you by spells for the last half hour, and I might as well have talked to the lamp."

Reuben laughed, admitted that he had been bothered by the example but had beaten it and then asked again what she said about boxes.

"Oh," said Beth again, "it was that word that woke you up. Say anything about boxes, and if you are within a hundred miles you will hear. Well, I said that some of you ought to contrive better-shaped boxes for these beautiful gauntlet gloves than the ones you stuff them into. They must come out looking horrid, and it is too bad. Look at these, Reuben. Isn't that orange silk too lovely for anything?"

"That's an idea," agreed Reuben, taking the glove in his hand. He looked as if the orange silk was far from his thoughts, though he stared at it with wide-open, glazed eyes.

That was the beginning. The arithmetic suffered somewhat after that for days at a time. The mother, observing, was disturbed. She wanted Reuben to be a scholar. His grandfather had been. She had watched with great satisfaction when he brought out the arithmetic and expressed his determination to catch up with the rest of the boys so he could join the class by next fall. Now the question was, What had captured his attention so completely that for three evenings he did not open the arithmetic?

"Never you mind," Miss Hunter assured her.

"The boy has an idea, and he is planning to carry it out. I see him busy thinking, even while he is eating his supper. No mischief is brewing as long as he has such clear eyes as those and prays every evening the way he does. Don't you be afraid."

"You don't think he can do anything wrong," said Mrs. Stone, smiling. She was very proud of Reuben.

Now what was he about? Well, I suppose you have forgotten all about those seven pasteboards out of which he meant to make his fortune. But you may be sure he had not forgotten. All through the winter, which was now quite gone, he had thought about them more or less. He had often climbed up to the attic to look at them in the corner where they were stored. He had studied and cast aside several plans for creating something new and wonderful out of them. Nothing suited him. He wanted something different from what had ever been seen, and he could not decide what it should be. The moment Beth began to argue against the boxes now in use for her favorite gauntlets, he was interested. An idea entered his mind and developed as the days went by.

His first experiment did not succeed. In fact, he had spoiled one entire sheet of the seven before anything had come of his idea.

Meanwhile Beth became almost discouraged over his silence and dreaming.

"It is worse than arithmetic," she told Miss Hunter. "Then I could get him to say a word once in a while. But now he just sits and stares at the sky or the trees and doesn't open his mouth."

"You wait," said Miss Hunter. "Something will come of it, I know." Miss Hunter believed in Reuben.

Nearly two weeks had passed since the new idea had taken root when Reuben arrived home one evening with a radiant face. He could hardly eat his supper; in fact, he made them all laugh by trying to eat his syrup with a fork and stir his milk with a knife. He seized upon the bread dish the moment supper was over and followed Beth to the cellar for a confidential talk.

"Beth," he said, his face aglow with triumph, "I've got it!"

"Have you?" said Beth with cool indifference as she stooped over the cookie jar. "I hope it is worth having and that you will give me a piece of it."

Reuben laughed joyfully. "I'll do that," he said. "At least you shall have a piece of the 'thank you' that I feel sure Mr. Barrows will give me. I am going to tell him that you deserve the largest half of it, for you gave me the idea in the first place."

"Reuben," said Beth, setting her lamp on the potato box and seating herself on an overturned tub, "what *do* you mean?"

"Why, that night — don't you know, when you found fault with the boxes the gauntlets are packed in? I never thought before of how awkward they are, but that set me to thinking. I've fixed up the nicest kind of a box for them. I made one, a regular beauty — brought it home under my work apron and hid it in the parlor. I wanted you to see it before anybody else did so you can tell me what you think of it. Not a soul has laid eyes on it. Are there any gloves in the house?"

"Yes, I completed some lovely ones just this afternoon. The wrists are lined with dove-colored silk, and they are finished with the prettiest shade of blue silk! If you have a box as pretty as they are, it must be a beauty."

"Come, children," called Mrs. Stone. "What in the world keeps you so long in the cellar?"

It was not until the dishes were washed and the little kitchen in order that Reuben had a chance to show Beth his treasure. They hurried off to the parlor then, with Beth carrying a pair of the lovely gauntlets under her arm for a trial.

It was a perfect fit! The new box was fashioned with more care than usual in green and gold and appeared on the outside like all other boxes. But inside an ingenious piece of pasteboard had been fitted in such a way that it shaped the graceful wrist of the gauntlet exactly and kept it from being crushed.

Beth clapped her hands in delight. "They will be worth more money—I know they will! One day I said to Mr. Barrows that it was too bad to crumple them all up in that way; there ought to be boxes just for them. But he said that couldn't be done because they were such an odd shape that no machinery could cut them, and nobody could make them after they were cut. But this is easy enough, I should think, and it doesn't take up a speck more room than the other way. What a peculiar little twisty piece of pasteboard that is, Reuben. How did you ever get it to fit in as it should?"

"I had an awful time with it," admitted Reuben. "For a while I thought I would have to give it up, and I tell you I felt bad! I couldn't get to sleep at night for thinking of it. One night, don't you believe, I dreamed about it! You see, it wouldn't bend enough without breaking. But one day I hit upon this plan of cutting little niches at regular places, and it worked like a charm. I'll tell you what, Beth, this is the only one I have made, but I want to get half a dozen made up out of my sheets. I want them made beautifully with lovely colored paper and trimmed elegantly, and I want you to help me with it. I have enough money saved from what Mother let me have for the boots and hat to buy some elegant paper. I want them to be the handsomest boxes that ever were seen in our shop. And I want you to help me."

"Well," said Beth, "I will."

After that Reuben was busier than ever, but now Beth was in on the secret. They worked together evenings in the little kitchen as late as their mother would allow. She looked doleful, meanwhile, over the arithmetic but tried to take Miss Hunter's advice and wait.

At last they were ready for exhibition, the entire half-dozen, and handsome boxes they were. Along with her talent for pretty things, Beth was also fond of learning to do something just by watching. She paid many visits to Reuben in the box shop and kept her bright eyes open. Thus she was no mean hand at the box business. She worked slowly, of course, but neatly. And she knew how to choose her colors so as to harmonize them well, which was more than you could say for Mr. Barrows's foreman.

So the boxes were carried in triumph to Mother and Miss Hunter, with some handsomely made gauntlet gloves showing off their beauty in their new houses in a way they had never been able to do before.

But, dear me! I don't know how to tell you how pleased Mr. Barrows was with the new idea.

He visited the small house on purpose to take a more careful look at the boxes and inquire into their management. He questioned and cross-questioned Reuben as to how he did this and managed that. Beth listened, along with the mother and friend, well pleased at Reuben's eager explanations. They thought it not too high praise when Mr. Barrows concluded at last that it was a complete success: a hundred of them should be manufactured right away and placed in the salesroom on exhibition. It was a capital idea, and he believed manufacturers would all be willing to pay a trifle more for the boxes, since their goods would show to so much better advantage.

"You certainly deserve a great deal of credit," he said, turning to Reuben, "for thinking and carrying out this idea."

"I didn't do all the thinking," declared Reuben eagerly. "Beth made me think of it in the first place, or I don't suppose it would ever have entered my head."

"I!" exclaimed Beth, surprised out of her usual timidity before Mr. Barrows. "Why, Reuben, all I ever did was to grumble because they rumpled up the pretty gauntlets in the boxes that didn't fit them."

"Yes," Reuben said, "and that was exactly what set me to thinking about it!"

Everybody laughed over this, and Mr. Barrows said it would be a good thing if all grumbling could end up in such a fine account.

But the most surprising part of the conversation was yet to come. Mr. Barrows had chatted for some time with Mrs. Stone, then with Miss Hunter and a little with Beth herself. He suddenly turned to Reuben with a question: "Well, young man, what are you going to charge me for this invention of yours?"

"Why," exclaimed Reuben in great amazement and embarrassment, "nothing, sir, of course!"

"I'm sure I can't see why, provided you mean to let me have it at all. It is a good, useful thing, and I'm inclined to think it will please the manufacturers very much. It isn't mine, though, any more than that jacket you have on is mine or those new boots I saw you wearing the other day. The question is, What will you charge me for the use of it, if I am to have the use of it? Or do you mean to sell it to some of the other manufacturers?"

Reuben's face was red. "It is for you, of course, sir," he said eagerly. "And if it is of any good, I'm as glad as I can be."

"But, my boy, I thought those seven pasteboards were for you to make your fortune with. You won't make it very fast at that rate, I'm afraid."

But Reuben laughed with some embarrassment and declared that they had begun already to make his fortune. They had made him feel that maybe he could think of things and do them.

"Well," offered Mr. Barrows at last, "if you won't sell your brains to me, I'll tell you what we'll do. I'll have some boxes made up in our best style and put on exhibition. I believe the manufacturers will be delighted with them. We'll sell them for two dollars on a hundred more than the others. One of those dollars I'll have to pay for the additional trouble of making the boxes in this way, and the other dollar you shall have as a nest egg for that fortune we talked about."

Never was there a boy more astonished. It was plain that he had not been working for money, nor had he expected any. He was very sincere in his explanations. But Mr. Barrows assured him that it was all right. Of course he ought to be paid for his thought, if it proved worth paying for, and the manufacturers would soon decide that.

Then he explained how the accounts could be kept and the machinery set for cutting the ingenious little partitions. He mentioned who would be the best person to glue them in. From this, he confided why it would be best for Reuben not to let any of the other boys know about this private understanding between them. He was altogether so businesslike and yet so kind and talked with Reuben as if he were already a man indeed, as well as the man of that little house. Reuben's head was well nigh turned with business and pleasure by the time Mr. Barrows went away.

As for Beth, she professed not to be surprised at all. She declared that, of course, Mr. Barrows ought to pay for the idea. Why shouldn't he? It was a good one, and it wasn't his. She *knew* it would work. The manufacturers would like it; they couldn't help it. The way the gloves were being packed now got them all rumpled up —anybody could see that. And she shouldn't wonder if Reuben really *would* make his fortune out of it yet.

Their laughter and chatter filled the little house with great excitement that night. Finally the mother brought them back to everyday living with the sensible remark: "I hope, Reuben, now that you've got this plan well out of your head, that you'll return to your arithmetic with all of your might. If you are going to invent things or do much of anything else that is worth doing, you'll have to know a great deal that they learn out of books."

"That's true," said Reuben. "And I mean to *know* things, Mother, whether I invent things or not."

"Yes," said Beth, "and if I am to be the sister of an inventor, I must know things too."

So with laughter, though it was rather late, they

settled themselves to their arithmetic and worked an example that very evening that Reuben called a "tough fellow."

In thinking of it long afterward, it seemed strange to Reuben that his great trouble should have followed so soon after this first little success of his — almost as if it were jealous of the victory and meant to make him suffer for it at once.

He went to bed that night so happy that he told Beth not to be surprised if she should hear him burst out laughing in the middle of the night because he was so bubbled up with joy that he couldn't keep it in.

But the next night when he climbed into bed his heart felt as heavy as a lump of lead.

CHAPTER XXV

What Followed It

It was toward the middle of the next morning. Work was moving on very briskly in the box factory. The busy season was fairly upon them, and all hands were pushing things.

Reuben had not seen Mr. Barrows that morning, but he had seen and heard a great deal that made his heart beat high with pleasure. The half-dozen handsome boxes were arranged in a prominent place in the vast salesroom, and more than half a dozen of the leading manufacturers of the town had dropped in on business and had been shown the new invention by the foreman. Every one of them expressed satisfaction over the product, and, what was more to the point, they had all ordered a few for trial.

Reuben, keen-eyed and quick-witted as he was, felt almost sure now that they would succeed. It was great fun to march back and forth on errands, hear the scraps of talk, know that he was in on the secret and have none of the others know anything about it. He liked it better than he would have if people had known the thought was his. Of course, Beth was inclined to be indignant over this part of the arrangement and believed everybody ought to be told who invented the box.

Several times during the morning Reuben wondered where Mr. Barrows was and why he did not come to talk with the manufacturers. At last he heard the call to go to the office.

Mr. Barrows was at his desk, surrounded by files of papers and blank books. He looked very sober, and Reuben decided at once that something was troubling him. Some business matter, perhaps, had driven all thought of the new boxes from his mind. He seemed to have nothing to say to Reuben after all. Raising his eyes for a moment as the boy came in, he dropped them again on the column of figures before him, and Reuben waited.

"Have you nothing to say to me, sir?"

The boy did not ask the question, but the man, after Reuben had waited in respectful silence for some minutes.

"I!" Reuben was too much astonished to say more. Then he rallied. "Why, yes, sir, there is ever so much to say. Six of the manufacturers have been in, and Mr. Burnside is there now. They have all ordered boxes, and they said a good many nice things about them. Mr. Anderson said —"

An impatient gesture from Mr. Barrows stopped Reuben's eager tongue.

"I am not thinking about the boxes," said that gentleman, "nor do I want to hear anything about them. The question is, What have you to say to me about the horse?"

"The *horse,* sir!"

And now Reuben was not only too much astonished, but too thoroughly bewildered to say more. What could he possibly have to say about the horse? But Mr. Barrows waited until at last he stammered forth: "I don't know what you mean, sir. I don't know anything I ought to say about Samson."

"You don't?"

"No, sir."

"Well, it is my opinion you ought to know a good deal that should be said about him. Reuben, it is worse than idle to waste your time and my patience in this way. I have been waiting all morning in the hope that I was not so utterly deceived in you as the case appeared in the hope that you would come to me with some explanation or at least confession. But I waited in vain. And now after I send for you, I find nothing but an attempt to deceive me."

"Mr. Barrows, I haven't a thing to confess, and I don't know what you mean."

Reuben's large, frank eyes gazed steadily into the face of Mr. Barrows as he said these words, and the gentleman in his turn seemed bewildered. At last he said: "It cannot be, Reuben, after the trust I have placed in you, that you would be so entirely false. I must believe that you do not know how much injury you have done. I have to tell you, then, that the poor horse is hopelessly injured and is suffering greatly. We have great fears that we shall have to kill him to put him out of misery."

Then, indeed, did Reuben's face change; it grew pale. His voice was intense and filled with pain.

"Oh, poor Samson! How did it happen? Can't they do something for him? How did you find it out? Mr. Barrows, I heard the foreman tell yesterday of that new man on Main Street, how he cured a horse that was hurt awfully. Couldn't you have him try?"

"Everything is being done that is possible," Mr. Barrows said coldly. "And as to how it happened, I am waiting for you to tell me."

The words and the tone reminded Reuben that for some reason Mr. Barrows was displeased with him. Now it flashed over him that he was suspected of having hurt the horse. He was so surprised and grieved that he could hardly speak the words distinctly, yet he poured them forth: "Oh, Mr. Barrows, do you think — do you suppose — you *can't* believe that I would hurt Samson! Why, I love him!"

"Not intentionally, Reuben — I cannot think that you would. But, you see, the mischief is done. Now I want the whole story."

"Mr. Barrows, I haven't any story to tell. I don't know anything at all about how Samson got hurt."

Alas for poor Reuben! Mr. Barrows did not believe this was so. For the last three months the boy had been around the horse every day — watered him, fed him, petted him, driven him to the store and the office, driven around the block with him again and again while they waited for his master. He remained the only boy in his employ that the master had allowed to have anything to do with his valuable horse.

Since the night Reuben had spoiled the attempt to steal Samson for a ride, a padlock with a unique lock had been placed on the barn. To this lock belonged two keys — one for Mr. Barrows and one for Rupert, the trusted hired man. For nearly a week Rupert had been sick in his bed, and Reuben had taken more care than ever before of the horse. He had been trusted to carry the other key that he might visit Samson when necessary while Mr. Barrows was absent.

This morning the barn had been found locked as usual, but the poor horse was holding up one trembling leg and moaning pitifully. In thinking it all through, Mr. Barrows believed the temptation to take a horseback ride had been too much for Reuben. He had snuck out in the night and, running into trouble, had hurried the horse back to the stable, locked the door and left him in his misery. It had been a hard thing for him to forgive, but, as he talked with Reuben, he decided that the boy had not known earlier that Samson was injured. This was bad enough, but still not as dreadful as the other. Now, if he would only confess it all!

But here he stood, denying boldly that he knew anything of the trouble.

"Reuben," he asked after a moment of grave silence, "where is the padlock key I allowed you to carry?"

"In my jacket pocket, sir, that hangs by my corner in the workroom."

"I know it. I took pains to learn that it was there. And mine is in my pocket. You and I know that only those who have been carefully taught can turn that lock — Rupert and you and I know how. Rupert is sick in bed, and my key is here on my chain where it has been all the time. The lock is not broken, yet the horse has been out during the night. He has been ruined and then brought home and locked in alone in his misery. Now, Reuben, will you confess the whole story? I cannot believe I have frightened you so that you will not tell me the truth. I have loved you, my boy, because you reminded me of my own boy who is gone, but he was truthful and noble."

Not a word did Reuben say. If he had suddenly been turned to stone he could not have stood more still or been more silent.

Mr. Barrows watched him and waited. Reuben's face was pale and his eyes held a troubled look of one who does not see his way clear. One, two, five minutes, and they seemed to him afterward like hours. Finally he spoke: "Mr. Barrows, everything is against me. I don't see how you *can* believe me. I know I have that key safe in my pocket, and I know the lock can't be turned with any other kind of a key or by people who don't know how. I can't tell anything about it, only this: I never took Samson out of his stall. He was as well and happy as could be last night at eight o'clock when I locked him in for the night, and I haven't seen him since. I don't know how he got hurt, and, oh, I am so sorry for him! But, Mr. Barrows, everything is against me, and I don't see how you can believe me."

Mr. Barrows sighed with disappointment: "You are right, Reuben—I can't."

Then followed a sad time for Reuben. Samson had to be killed, and that almost broke the boy's heart. Worse than that, he found no way to prove that he had nothing to do with the trouble.

But you should have seen Beth. She was furious. The idea that Mr. Barrows should not believe every word Reuben said was to her mind an insult too deep to be borne. She urged Reuben not to work another hour for him but to tell him to look out for a boy that he thought he could trust. She urged her mother to move at once out of his house and to refuse to have anything more to do with him. She only burst into tears in response to the question of where they would go.

As for the mother, she did not help her boy very much. She believed in him. Oh, yes, indeed! It did not once occur to her to think that he had spoken other than the truth. She had known Reuben so long and trusted him so fully that the habit was formed. But she fretted and said some things that were hard to bear: "It serves you right, Reuben, for meddling with the horse at all. If you had kept away from him as the other boys did, you wouldn't have gotten into any trouble. Why doesn't he suspect them?"

Then Reuben tried to explain that his employer had given him duties about the horse and trusted him to his care. It was as much a part of his work at times to care for Samson as it was to go to the shop.

But Mrs. Stone answered: "Oh, yes, a part of your work! I know that, but if you hadn't always been hanging around the horse and petting him and showing yourself so eager and able to take care of him, Mr. Barrows would not have thought of such a thing, and you such a young fellow!"

Then Reuben sighed and looked utterly discouraged, and the mother hastened to say: "Not that I blame you — you did it all for the best, I daresay. If the man had common sense, he would know he could trust you. But it is all very hard — you had such a splendid chance, and I thought he would send you to school."

Meanwhile Miss Hunter was the cheeriest friend he had.

"It'll all come out right," she assured him, nodding her wise head. "Trust *Him*. He never makes mistakes or forgets. Just keep telling Him all about it, as though you knew He would take care of it, and He will."

Reuben smiled and felt his heart warm inside him at the remembrance of his powerful Friend.

Beth was apt to torment him with questions hard to answer. "Reuben, haven't you the least kind of a notion who might have taken the horse?"

"What's the use of notions without proof?" Reuben answered. "Notions are mean. They make a fellow suspicious."

"But, Reuben, I think you can guess who it might be. Somebody did it, of course. I wish he would get awful sick and afraid and have to confess it."

"That's like a story in a book," Reuben replied with a curl of his wiser lip. "Things like that don't happen outside of books."

But then Miss Hunter had a word to say: "Things don't 'happen' at all, my boy. God looks after them. He can take care of you and of the one who did the mischief, and He'll do it."

"But, Miss Hunter, don't you think it is awful *mean* in Mr. Barrows not to believe Reuben? He never told a lie in his life."

"I don't think it is strange that he doesn't believe me," declared Reuben. "You see, it is all against me. I've got the key, and it's the only key besides the one he carries himself. I know how to turn the lock, and I was the only one besides Rupert who did. Rupert was sick in bed, and somebody took the horse out and lamed him and then put him back there to suffer. I think that was the meanest."

When Reuben continued to try to clear Mr. Barrows of meanness for not trusting him, Beth's patience gave out entirely. She was apt to get almost as angry with Reuben as she was with his master. So among them all, Reuben had a sad time.

A large number of the handsome boxes were being manufactured, and all who saw them were pleased, but Reuben had almost entirely lost his pleasure in them. It seemed very strange to him that Mr. Barrows did not discharge him. Every morning he went to his work wondering whether it would not be his last day in the box shop.

The truth was that Mr. Barrows, though he still believed him guilty, felt sorry for him. He believed he had been led astray by a great temptation and frightened by the consequences into telling falsehood after falsehood. He thought by keeping him in his place and being kind to him, Reuben would grow ashamed of his silence and gather courage to confess the whole story; so he waited.

And Reuben waited and prayed and wondered how it would all end. In spite of his prompt answer to Beth, "What's the use of having notions?" he had one all the same. He could not dismiss the thought that his special torment, Andrew Porter, had something to do with the trouble. Not that he could even guess how it could have been done. He had never shown Andrew his key or boasted of it in any way. If he had, that would not have taught the boy how to use it. "And if he tried ninety-nine times to unlock it," Reuben mused aloud when he was alone one day, "he would have been as far away from doing it the hundredth time as he was the first. Besides, I had the key to the stable all the time in my pocket."

So he argued with himself, growing more and more puzzled as he thought it over and feeling more and more strongly that Mr. Barrows was not to blame in suspecting him. "But then," the boy continued, "somebody unlocked that barn and took out that horse — dear old fellow! — and brought him back again and locked him up. I *know*

I didn't do it, and that thing Mr. Barrows doesn't know. So there I have the advantage over him."

The days passed, and nothing occurred to help him out of his trouble. Mr. Barrows had questioned and cross-questioned Reuben and was growing every hour more bewildered and anxious.

"I loved the boy almost well enough to give him part of the place of our boy who is gone," he said to his wife. "I meant to do well by him if this thing hadn't come up. I don't understand it."

"Papa," Grace Barrows said, setting her lips firmly, "Reuben Stone never did it — never!"

The father smiled and found himself wondering if Grace was not right. But, then, who had done it?

Meanwhile Andrew traveled the streets as well and as strong as ever — though as often as Reuben looked at him he could not help remembering Beth's words: "I wish he would get awful sick and afraid and have to confess it."

Nothing looked more improbable than that Andrew Porter would get "awful sick." Reuben was thinking this as he overtook him one evening at the corner, and Andrew turned suddenly and set off the other way. As Reuben continued, he rehearsed again for the hundredth time the possible reasons he had for suspecting Andrew.

They were very weak ones. He was a mischievous and untruthful boy and was very fond of horses — and almost equally fond of teasing Reuben Stone. Yet Reuben had to admit that he saw no possible way for Andrew to have accomplished this teasing. If he did it, he told himself with a sigh, he will keep his secret. He is not the kind of boy to tell on himself. As for getting sick, there isn't a healthier looking boy in this town.

Yet the next morning news came.

CHAPTER XXVI

JUSTICE AT LAST

he boys were full of it when he reached the shop. Had Reuben heard? Did he know about the great fire? Surely he must have heard the fire bells.

Yes, Reuben had heard the fire bells, but his mother had objected to his going to the fire, so he had stayed in.

"Humph!" scoffed one of the boys. "I guess Andrew Porter wishes *his* mother had objected, and he had paid attention to her."

Reuben turned quickly.

"Why? What about him?"

"Why, he went to the fire. It was the machine shop, you know, burned to the ground — ever so much money lost. Andrew climbed up somewhere — he's always climbing — and the wall gave way, or the stairs or something, and he fell hundreds of feet, some say. Anyhow, they picked him up for dead, but he isn't dead. The doctor just left there, and I heard him tell Mr. Stuart that the boy was breathing, but that was about all."

Reuben stood silent for a full minute, trying to digest this at once wonderful and terrible news, before tackling his work. A curious, pained feeling crept over him that somehow he was to blame. Had he really wished Andrew to get "awful sick"? Oh, but he had not wanted him to die! Suppose he should die without ever speaking another word! And suppose he had done it! All day Reuben's heart was heavier than ever, but he prayed a great many times that day for the life of Andrew.

The boy did not die. As the days passed, it was found that his life was no longer in any immediate danger. But then further word was received that seemed to the boys almost as sad as death itself. A hush spread all around the shop all the morning after Clarke Miller brought the word. He himself had heard the doctor that very morning tell Andrew's uncle from Eastport that the fall had hurt his spine somehow — Clarke had not understood how. He knew only this: The doctor had said positively that the boy would never take another step.

Three days later Reuben decided to visit Andrew Porter. He had no hope of hearing news from him concerning poor Samson; in fact, he did not think of Samson when he decided to go. But Clarke said he heard that Andrew was awful lonesome and complained that the boys did not come to see him.

I really have not time to tell you much about the next three weeks, except in a general way. Reuben carried out his resolve, went that very evening to ask after Andrew and found him sick and suffering.

His mother, who had had orders to let "every fellow in who looked like a boy," took Reuben to his room without warning.

A short call he paid. But he felt so sorry for Andrew that on the next day he went again, and again after that. At last it grew to be a settled thing that not a day would pass without his spending every spare moment with Andrew.

The books suffered a little. Reuben learned a lesson every night. But the time spent was shorter than it used to be, and his mother wondered if he was going to "learn to nurse sick folks" instead of being a scholar.

Beth asked many questions as to why he had grown fond of "that Porter boy, all of a sudden." Reuben admitted he was not particularly fond of him, but few of the boys came to see him; he seemed not to have many friends and was so lonesome. "He is getting used to me now and likes to have me come. At first he didn't seem to want me." This was Reuben's only explanation. Beth tossed her head and said she thought it was very peculiar.

As for Mr. Barrows, the days passed, and Reuben continued to be faithful in his work and respectful. Yet the boy came no nearer to that confession for which the gentleman longed. He told himself that he did not know what to think. How could he trust a boy and do for him what he had meant to when he had deceived him? How *could* the trouble have happened in any other way than through him? Yet, on the other hand, how could a boy who was so faithful in all other things have so dreadfully deceived him even once?

Mr. Barrows was certainly troubled by it all.

Meanwhile, what Andrew thought as he lay day after day on his bed, much of the time alone, he kept to himself.

It was a lovely summer evening. The windows of Andrew's room were thrown wide open, and the bed on which he lay was wheeled as close to them as possible. He lay gazing out on the lovely fields, green and quiet, perhaps thinking what a strange, sad thing it was that he should never scamper over them again. His face was very sober.

Reuben, book in hand, waited to go on with the story he was reading to him, but Andrew raised his hand and waved the book away.

"No, I want to talk — that is, I've *got* to talk. I've made up my mind. It has taken me weeks to do it, and I never thought I should. I suppose I might have waited to hear the last of the story, for you won't want to read it to me when I'm through with my talk. But I'm going to tell it right now."

"All right," said Reuben, "talk away."

"But you won't say much more to me in that good-natured way, old fellow, when you've heard my talk. I've got something awful to tell you. Reuben, I took Samson out that night and brought him back again."

"I thought as much," said Reuben, his voice quiet and matter-of-fact. He had not thought over this whole thing for weeks without learning to keep his face quiet when there was need.

"You did!"

In spite of his ailing back the boy on the bed gave a slight start in response, sending a quiver of pain all through him.

"Yes, I did. Do be careful, Andrew! Don't move the least bit again. What will the doctor say if you get up a fever? I think I better read now."

"What made you think I did it?"

"Oh, I don't know. I just kind of felt maybe it

was you. Somebody had to do it, you see, and I knew I didn't."

"But how did I get in?"

"That's more than I know or can guess, and it is what made the whole thing seem foolish. But, you see, *somebody* got in, and it might as well have been you as anybody. Now shall I read?"

"No. I'm going to tell you all about it. I didn't mean any harm to you, Reuben — not a bit. I began to like you a little before this. I guess I kind of liked you all the time. I didn't mean to harm anybody. I thought he was dreadful afraid for his old horse, and I knew I could ride horseback. I thought he considered himself so smart about that key that I just longed to try my hand with it. I guessed it was like the locks Uncle James makes — he's my uncle up in Eastport. He makes all kinds of locks, and he had a real odd one that I learned how to manage. I thought this might be like it, and it was — oh, enough like it for me to catch the trick when I saw Rupert locking the barn one day! Well, I didn't mean to steal a key, you know, but he left his right on the desk that afternoon."

"Who did?"

"Mr. Barrows himself. He wears it on that chain, you know. And while I was waiting for him to read the note I brought, he glanced at his watch, and the chain got caught somehow. He worked at it a minute, then he unscrewed the chain and slipped off the keys and laid them down on the desk. Then that fellow tumbled through the elevator hole, you remember, and yelled. Mr. Barrows thought he was hurt and ran, and I just picked up the key and ran too."

"But how did it get back on the chain?" Reuben asked in utter bewilderment.

"That was easy enough. I didn't know how to do it. I thought I should have to lose the key. I wish now I had done it. Then he would have thought some fellow found it and broke in and wouldn't have blamed you. I never thought of his being such a moolly as to think you did it. I didn't, honest, Reuben."

"Never mind. What did you do?"

"Why, I went there after milk. Mr. Barrows was dressing. He had been up in Rupert's room taking care of him. There on the table lay his watch, his cuff buttons and all his fixings. I just slipped the key on the chain in a twinkling and left happy. I thought there wouldn't be any trouble to anybody."

"Then you didn't know Samson was hurt?"

"Not a bit of it. I knew he stumbled and caught his foot in that mean hole in the crosswalk and limped a little, but that was when we were just home. I hustled him into the barn and thought he would be all right in the morning. But it turned out just awful!"

"Oh," Reuben exclaimed with relief. "I'm so glad!"

"Glad of what?"

"Why, that you didn't know how poor Samson was hurt. It did seem too awful of anybody to leave him to suffer."

"Well, I didn't think much about his being hurt. I was cut up awfully when I heard the news next day. Then, next thing I heard, he thought it was you. He might have known better than that, seems to me. I'd have known it with my eyes shut—as many times as he has held you up to me for a pattern, too!"

Andrew's voice was full of contempt.

"I'll tell you what I did," he continued after a moment. "I watched to see if he would discharge you. Then I meant to own up, whatever it cost. But when things went on just as usual, I felt a little better."

"Oh!" said Reuben.

It was the only word he said. It all flashed over him — the folly of trying to make a boy like Andrew Porter understand what he had suffered and what his mother and Beth had suffered in bearing false blame.

There was more talk, a great deal of it. Now that Andrew's lips were open, he seemed to find comfort in telling all the particulars of those weeks. He told how "beat" he was to think that Reuben should have been the first boy to call on him, and the only one to come to him day after day. He had learned to watch for his coming. At last, when he made up his mind that he must tell the whole story or he should die, the worst was to think of not seeing him there anymore.

"I shall come all the same," said Reuben quietly. "But now I want to ask you one question more: When do you intend to tell Mr. Barrows?"

"I!" cried Andrew, and dark red washed over his face. "Why, you can tell him all about it! I'll take the consequences; they can't be very dreadful here on my back. Father would pay for the horse fast enough if he had anything to pay with — but he hasn't, and Mr. Barrows knows it."

"No," said Reuben firmly. "You're the one to tell."

And to that he held, despite Andrew's half-tearful arguments. It would be better, much better, both for him and for Andrew, that the confession should come from him.

"And until you tell it," he said, "I will keep still. I have done it so long, and I can keep on."

At last Andrew admitted it would be best, but he was sure he never could. If Reuben would wait, some day he would try; he could not tell when.

Truly it seemed to Reuben as the days passed that Andrew was very long in honoring his promise. He did not desert him. The readings continued, accompanied by the tender care and kindness. Because of the fever and delirium that followed this first talk, he did not hurry him or indeed utter a word more than his wistful eyes expressed every day. But all the time he could not help wishing and *wishing* that Andrew would gather the courage to do right. He could not bring himself to be willing to tell the story; he feared Mr. Barrows and others might think his only object in visiting Andrew in his trouble was to threaten the facts out of him.

One night, as soon as he rounded the corner that led to the little house and saw Beth standing at the gate, he knew something had happened. Sure enough, she rushed toward him.

"Oh, Reuben, such news! You can't think! Don't you believe that Andrew Porter did it all! And he has had Mr. Barrows there and told all about it and how good you were and all. And Mr. Barrows has been here. He cried and said he should never forgive himself for thinking badly of you. I'm sure I don't believe I can ever forgive him. But he was so nice, Reuben — you can't think. And he wants you to go to school all the time, and he is willing to send you to college, and — oh, dear! It is such a splendid long story. Reuben, aren't you awfully astonished?"

"No," said Reuben, his eyes shining. "Not

much. You see, I knew the most of it before."

Then it was Beth's turn to open her eyes. She stormed him with questions and exclamations for the next half hour. How could he possibly have kept still all these weeks, thinking that Andrew Porter was the boy? Why didn't he run right home and tell her the minute Andrew confessed it? What was the use in being thought so meanly of a minute longer than was necessary?

After much careful explaining, Reuben succeeded in getting his sister to understand something about the feelings that had kept him patient and quiet all these weeks.

"You see," he said, ending the story, "I could afford to wait, because I knew it would all come out right. I didn't see how, but I was sure of it because I'm a soldier. My Captain is bound to take care of me and see me safely through everything because He has promised to. It is likely I should trust Him when I've enlisted to fight under His flag forever. Oh, Beth, if only you were a soldier too!"

This silenced Beth.

I did mean to stop right here and not try to tell you anything more about Reuben Watson Stone, although, as you may imagine, there is plenty to tell. But I do feel as if I must tell you about one thing, because it seems to fit in so far back in the story.

Not a week after all these strange things had happened to Reuben, just as he was heading out for the shop one morning, a little brown and white cow came trotting up the street. A boy was guiding her, and a pleasant-faced older lady on the sidewalk walked toward Reuben.

"How do you do?" she greeted him heartily as

she caught a glimpse of him. "I was hoping I'd find you in. You remember me, don't you? You found my ticket on the cars and helped me to the stage afterward. Oh, I never forgot it, nor your nice, honest face. I learned your name and have kept an eye on you ever since, though what with sickness in my son's family and then being sick myself, I haven't gotten around before.

"I heard of your trouble, and I heard of your getting out of it. I knew you would, my boy. The Lord takes care of His own, and I knew you were one of His own. I know a good many things about you. Look here!"

She stepped closer to him and dropped her voice to a whisper. "You didn't know Spunk's master had anything to do with me, did you? It is peculiar, but I'm his grandmother. I've heard about midnight rides and saloons and all that. You did better work that time than you knew of. My grandson hasn't forgotten it — and can't. He is the 'man of the house' himself — all the son his mother has. He didn't like to think of the contrast that would be between you one of these days if he kept on and you kept on. So he has turned square around.

"Well, I oughtn't to hinder you from your work, my man. If you will just look after Molly here and tell the boy where you would like to have her put, I'll step along. Why, yes, of course she is yours. A man with a family to support needs a cow, and she is the nicest critter there ever was and gives *cream*, almost, instead of milk."

Now I am sure there is no use in trying to describe to you Reuben's astonishment. Isn't it a good place to stop?

And yet there came to him before that day closed what he called the best news he ever had in his life.

Beth, curled up in a little heap on the sofa beside him, brought it.

What do you suppose it was? Why, of course, at last she had decided to wear the colors of Reuben's Captain and fight under His flag. She had been led to consider it all carefully after seeing how well he bore the trouble that had happened to him. Before that she was beginning to feel that it was easy enough for Reuben to be good. Everyone praised him and trusted him. He did almost exactly as he liked, and there wasn't anything for him to be cross about. But afterward she found herself angry at Mr. Barrows and angry at that wicked somebody who brought all this trouble on him. She saw that Reuben was patient and unwilling to have Mr. Barrows blamed, and he seemed so cheerful. She finally started to see that something had made him different.

It was dusk when they had their lovely talk. Reuben had just visited the new Samson who lived in the barn and already knew him and liked him. He had fed Molly her evening meal, drunk a glassful of her rich, creamy milk and tucked her away for the night. All the day's duties were done.

Just then the parlor door opened, and Mother entered, carrying a lamp. Behind her Miss Hunter followed, looking twice glad, for Beth had given her the good news.

"Come, Reuben," said his mother. "Let's have prayers now. It's after eight o'clock. The evenings are growing very short."

So they all knelt down, and the man of the house, with a full heart, thanked God for all His benefits.

Grabill Missionary Church Library
P.O. Box 279
13637 State Street
Grabill, IN 46741

If you enjoyed *The Man of the House,*
we would like to recommend the
following books from the Alden Collection
by Isabella Macdonald Alden:

Ester Ried's Awakening
A young woman's spiritual awakening
and its effect on her family

The King's Daughter
A young woman's faith and courage
in the midst of opposition

A New Graft on the Family Tree
Perseverance and a love
for unsaved family members

As in a Mirror
A man's search for truth
and the price he pays to find it

Yesterday Framed in Today
What if Christ had come to
nineteenth-century rural America?

Available at your local Christian
bookstore or from:

Creation House
600 Rinehart Road
Lake Mary, FL 32746
1-800-451-4598